CLOAKED SHADOWS

MELISSA HAWKES

First Paperback Edition February 2021
First Hardback Edition February 2021
First eBook Edition February 2021

ISBN: 978-1-8383260-0-5 (paperback)
ISBN: 978-1-8383260-2-9 (hardback)
ISBN: 978-1-8383260-1-2 (eBook)

To my younger self –
We finally did it.

CLASSES OF MAGIC

SLAYERS

Summon multiple talents.

DESCENDANTS

Control and manipulate objects around them.

SHIFTERS

Shape-shift into different living beings.

ELEMENTALS

Control the elements, including light and dark.

OBJECTORS

Mould and create objects.

TIME WARPERS

See and control aspects of time and reality.

HEALERS

Stabilise and mend wounds.

ONE

I kena rocked side to side in her sleep, allowing the nightmare she was plagued with to consume her peaceless mind. The nightmare that bedevilled her was not the work of fiction, but instead the battered truth that she had suffered five years ago, that being her father's tragic fate. She had been there the day he died and watched as a Sinturi, a damaged magical creature of dark magic whose only means of survival was by consuming the life out of humans leaving nothing but a pile of ash in their place, swooped in and sucked the life out of her father, consuming his very soul. He just about managed the words "run!" and that's exactly what Ikena did. She ran as fast as she could, all the way back home where she cried to her mother about what had happened. Her mother, who was peeling potatoes, sprang into action. She ordered Ikena to grab her younger twin siblings from their cots and hide under the kitchen table.

She whispered to them softly, "Be quiet, my sweets," and covered them underneath the long tablecloth which stretched to the floor on one side so that they couldn't be seen, as she kept watch, peeling knife in hand.

After that day, her mother became frantic and Ikena caught her doing something she now knew to be praying. Who she was praying to, she didn't know, but if it helped her sleep at night then Ikena welcomed it. As the years passed, her mother's panic-stricken self relaxed some, and she entrusted her faith in Ikena, who took it upon herself to keep the family safe. Ikena, however, had a secret. One that was a burden, that she carried with her everywhere she went. She vowed to tell no one.

Back then, Ikena had only briefly heard of the Sinturi, treacherous beings who harvested souls from a living person in search for magic. Yes, that's right. Magic. You see, in the Kingdom of Nevera some folk were deemed more special than others, different even, and were able to do real magic. Ikena heard that it happened spontaneously, as if they woke up one day and could do strange things others couldn't. Some magic folk can see the future, or teleport, or harvest the sun and send it shooting out of their hands.

However, with the great discovery of magic came the great discovery of darkness and the true nature of human beings came about. Some went mad with the power they had and killed, and the more they killed, the darker their magic became until their bodies erupted an unspeakable power. When a magical person used their power for unjustness it triggered something inside them, and it began to harvest away at their own soul until there was nothing, but a dark, in-human force left, ultimately becoming a Sinturi. Once you went that way, there was no coming back. Even the mere mention of a Sinturi was enough to terrify a grown adult, to think that a human became something as terrible as that. It's enough to make anyone scared, even the Cloaks.

The Cloaks are magic folk who run the Kingdom. Well, they did protect it during the Great War, so why shouldn't they? When a Sinturi consumes a human, they obtain power, albeit only for a short-while. If they don't feast, they become frail. If they consume a Cloak however, they gain a vigour that can last for weeks, but only depending on how powerful their victim was.

Years ago, there was a huge war between the Cloaks and the Sinturi. The Sinturi wanted to take over, to create their own world of darkness. Thankfully, the Cloak protectors won, but only just. The Sinturi were not defeated but weakened and they disappeared back into the Caves of Zeridan, where they grew an army ready to attack again. When Ikena was a child, she admired the Cloaks, so much so that she desired to be one, a protector of the world but that changed when her father died. She became 'protector of the house' and she couldn't do that if she was a Cloak.

Ikena woke with a squeal and instantly began to panic, struggling to catch her breath every time she breathed in and out. *It wasn't happening again,* she told herself. *It was just a dream.* Even so, her body began to violently shake as she tried to forget her father's dying face. Her teeth chattered as a chill overcame her and she found herself scratching at the blistered skin at her fingers. She was wheezing. To Ikena's surprise, her mother rushed over to her side and wrapped her ashen hands around her, she had slept by the hearth again, soot covering her worn face.

"Sshhh, it's okay." She rocked her, "You're safe

9

sweetheart. You're safe."

Ikena didn't feel safe. She was scared. Tears streamed down her face, her cheeks wet, her nose stuffy. Her fingers bled because of her intense scratches, but she found comfort in it.

"It was Dad. It was that night," Ikena struggled, blinking back the wetness in her eyes. She found solace in her mother's half-torn cardigan against her face. She missed her father. She missed the way he'd teach her how to set traps for food, or how he'd read her stories or call her his flower.

She suddenly heard a commotion and her two little twin siblings rushed in through the door to her room and excitedly climbed over her making a bit of a fuss.

"She's awake!" little Asher cheered as his twin sister, Aliza, was attempting to braid Ikena's midnight-coloured hair from behind her.

"Yes, I'm awake," she sniffed, trying to hide her teary eyes from her siblings. "Now, get off me!" She couldn't help but smile at being woken with such oomph and allowed a giggle to escape her. At seeing her siblings' faces, she calmed. *It was just a dream*, she told herself once more.

Ikena's mother took the two little ones to be fed bone broth for breakfast whilst Ikena stood up from the sheet covered floor she had made a makeshift bed out of and made her way to the sink to wash herself. After the war, many villages in the Kingdom had been left in severe poverty, they had lost everything, their families, their possessions, and food was scarce. Most of what the villagers had to offer was given to the Cloaks, a small gesture they were *forced* into doing. During the war all work was postponed for fear of the Sinturi invading villages, people were forced to cower in their homes for months on end, their only means of food was by trading valuable furniture or clothing they had, hence why Ikena had only one bed in her house which was strictly reserved for the twins. The Cloak palace seemed to be lavishing in their jewels, riches and technology experiments without offering any help or support for the villages in which they were supposed to protect. Instead, it was, and is still, up to them to find their own food and if you see a Sinturi, well, you better hope you can outrun it. These points added to the reasons why Ikena began to form such an anger towards the King and his magical army. Not all magic folk are bad, but they all worship one King, who was indulged with greed. If it weren't for Ikena's father who had taught her how to set animal traps, and her best friend Sedric who could use a pretty good make-shift wooden spear, then her family wouldn't have survived as long as they had.

Ikena scrubbed her body clean and put on her only pair of overalls which she re-wore daily. They were hand-me-downs from her mother, who had to sew the legs in tighter so that they weren't bulging around her ankles. Luckily, her mother was a whizz with a sewing needle, and even hand-stitched her and her siblings' woolly scarves for the colder months. It was also a way the family earned coin for groceries, she'd stitch scarves, hats, gloves or jumpers out of wool for clients in the village and Ikena would deliver them for her, allowing the family to barter for more food in the traders market, like potatoes or vegetable seeds. She also put on her long black boots and a deer's fur jacket her father had scooped up for himself from trading. Ikena's mother didn't like it, it was too flashy and could give the villagers the wrong impression about their family, but after he died Ikena held on to it, alongside the medallion her father had given her which matched the one he wore. It was a golden circle with the Cloak sigil pressed on it, as a sign that he supported the palace, and she kept hers hanging at her neck at all times. Not that she supported the palace, because she didn't but because it was something that reminded her of her father. After getting dressed she grabbed her sharp hunting knife, straw bag and met her family in the common room of their house.

"Where are my young apprentices?" Ikena playfully questioned, searching for her little siblings who had ran to put on their woolly hats, scarves, and jackets.

"Here!" her siblings exclaimed.

Her siblings were young, both being six years old, but they needed to learn the importance of bringing home the daily bread for the family, so she took them along with her when she went hunting for food.

"Alright then, attention!" she called as the two siblings raised their left hands and put them to their foreheads in a form of a salute. "Let's go."

They rushed out of the door. "Be safe, my darlings," her mother called. She hated when her mother said, 'be safe' and she only started saying it after her father had died. To make it worse, he died in the same forest Ikena hunted in, it was the only forest in Nevrain and lied between their village, Endfell, and the neighbouring village, Lovrin. Ikena had never visited Lovrin, she had never left Endfell for that matter, but she heard it was a quaint little village with welcoming folk and hoped to travel there one day. They reached the overgrown forest and the trees above them swayed in the cold wind that scurried across their cheeks, reddening them. She made sure Asher and Aliza had their scarves tied tightly and secured her own.

First, they checked the traps that they had left overnight and found a squirrel and a dainty mouse inside separate ones. *Hardly enough for dinner*, she pondered as she had the mouse in her claws. Ikena quickly made sure the prey was lifeless, digging her knife into the animal's neck and shoving it into the straw bag she took with her. Her siblings had become accustomed to her knife-wielding ways and had grown used to seeing their older sister kill prey that they would soon cook and proceed to eat for dinner. Ikena hated it, but it's what the family had to rely on for substantial meat and she needed to make sure her siblings understood that it wasn't a choice, but because they needed to survive. She set the traps again, noting that one was broken and tasked her siblings with making a new one. Their small fingers fumbled with the pieces of twig and string and Ikena showed them how to tie it in a certain way so that it made a cage. She had only recently started bringing them along with her, deciding it was time for them to learn how to hunt. Once the line of rope underneath the cage was triggered the cage would fall covering the four-legged victim, which they baited with small pieces of cheese. Asher and Aliza had finished making the trap and Ikena gathered her things when she heard a snap. Her siblings stood instantly and Ikena ushered them behind the safety of herself and wielded the sharp hunting knife out in front of her, brazenly. *Snap.* Another snap again, this time louder than the last one. *Don't be a Sinturi. Oh, please don't be a Sinturi.* She prayed. *Snap.*

The thing was behind the overgrown shrubbery of the forest. Ikena waited. And waited. And waited.

"Come on then!" she yelled, daring the beast to show itself. She hadn't the time to await her death. She expected cold, charred fingers made from skinny bones to appear, the hooded figure of a Sinturi attached to it.

After a tense stand-off, a young deer wandered into the light and stared at the humans, basking in the little patch of sunlight that shone a spotlight on the grass. The deer was a fool, it didn't know what it had just gotten itself into. It had become their dinner. Ikena allowed a slow and quiet breath to escape her mouth as she hushed her siblings, who had grown excited at seeing the deer, making sure they didn't squeal and scare it away. Slowly, she neared closer and outstretched a handful of small berries she had pocketed to have as a mid-morning snack. The deer was the first animal Ikena had seen roam the forest that was larger than a fox and if she could catch it then she wouldn't have to hunt tomorrow, she could finally have a day off. *Just one day*. She had to act quickly.

"Come here," she said softly, prompting the deer to edge itself closer. She felt like a lion had stumbled upon a gazelle and was ready to make the attack.

The deer's head was reaching out, tastebuds longing for those fresh, juicy berries when Ikena leapt at it, forcing her entire weight on the straggling animal, and effortlessly plunged her knife into its side. The deer gave a helpless cry and after a short moment became still and lifeless. *I'm sorry*, Ikena hung her head low and wished things were different. But they weren't. Not in Nevera. Not ever. The deer was heavy, and didn't fit into the straw bag so two of its legs and head were awkwardly hanging out the top. *Murderer*, Ikena thought she heard the poor thing whisper. Ikena checked her siblings over and made sure that they were unharmed. She shoved the deer into the large straw bag, alongside the other animals, and hoisted it over her shoulder.

"That was amazing!" Asher cried, bobbing up and down.

Ikena didn't like seeing him so eager to kill, so uncompassionate, but it was the price to pay for food. If anything, it was exactly what Ikena had taught them. As the evening grew near and traps had been set, they travelled back home, and Ikena noted the envious looks of the local villagers she passed, jealous of her hunting success. Most of the villagers in Endfell were too afraid to head into the disproportionate forest to hunt, not that they'd know how, and meat was too expensive to buy in the market, so vegetarianism was unwillingly common. Ikena had tried to share, but knew she also had to survive, and she had to make sure her family were well-fed too. Besides, it would only make her more of a target for desperate crooks to rob her after her next hunt. Her mother was most pleased when she dumped the heavy straw bag on her kitchen table and together they skinned the thing and de-boned the meat. Her mother made sure to pack two legs worth of meat, seasoned with smoked garlic and grinded pepper, into a nice paper bag and politely asked Ikena to take it to Sedric's house before dinner.

"It'll make his grandma strong," she said.

Sedric was an only child who lived with his disturbingly frail grandma. He rarely spoke of his parents, they died when he was sixteen from a thickening sickness that plagued

Nevrain one year. Ikena had met them a few times and when they died, she tried to be there for him, she knew what it felt like to lose a parent. She insisted on coming to the funeral with him and visited them every day after in the graveyard where they were buried. After a year, Sedric stopped visiting them and asked Ikena not to talk about them anymore. It was as if he had wanted to forget that he ever had a family or else he'd be grieving forever. He became tough and took remarks from others in the village lightly. He was the boy who lived when death loomed in the darkness and survived. Sedric and Ikena would always help each other out when they could and her mother even hand-stitched them woolly hats, scarves and gloves at winter time when thick snow formed.

As Ikena took the bag she became excited to see the look on Sedric's handsome face. He was a tall, broad boy with dirty-blonde hair and a sharp, square face. Ikena had fell for him from the very moment she first met him. He was so cool and handsome and *all* the girls in the village wanted him, it was because of his eyes. He had the most striking, light brown eyes that were warm and reminded Ikena of the comforts of the forest. Sedric had tried to confess his love for her a few times, but every time Ikena shut it down. As much as she loved him, she couldn't be with him for reasons she wasn't ready to share just yet.

Instead, he took to other girls, such as the mayor's daughter, Precious. *What a stupid name for a girl so vile*, Ikena thought, bitterly. Precious was one of those girls who *always* got what she wanted. Her father was the mayor, so they were already the richest in the village. Her clothes were gorgeous and managed to sustain the pastel, worn look that everyone else's clothes had and her hair was a long blonde that was so fine and silky. Meanwhile Ikena's was a black, frizzy mess that could be strikingly compared to a bird's nest. Six months after they met, Sedric joined Ikena's school and their friendship blossomed. They walked to and from school together, partnered up with each other as pairs in classroom activities and shared their lunchtime scraps. Then Precious came along and it all stopped. She flaunted him. And, for some reason, she hated Ikena and, alongside her group of friends, would make rude comments behind her back. Ikena let it slide, because she was above them, and she needn't stoop to their level.

Sedric still came to the forest to hunt with Ikena, but for a while it wasn't what it used to be. One day, Sedric had turned up with a huge smile on his face and his lips were more red than usual. It broke Ikena's heart when he started to ramble on about having his first kiss with Precious and how it felt. It was her red lipstick smeared on his lips. It was only when Sedric left school at sixteen that their friendship began to grow again. Ikena still had two years of school left and it only made her even more of a target to the snide comments Precious threw her way, especially when her and Sedric broke up after he had caught Freddie Bloomer in her bed.

Ikena hurried down the street and over to the market where Sedric's house waited on the corner. His parents sold most of their furniture during the Great War, but the house still had a welcoming demeanour and, subtly, Sedric ensured there were always colourful flowers in the hanging basket outside his front door. A small symbol that Ikena knew reminded him of his parents, who always kept the same. The flowers made the white panes of the front window stand out abruptly. Ikena knocked on the door and to her surprise it was the grandma who answered.

"Oh, Mrs. Plumith. I'm so sorry to disturb," Ikena said and grew worried why a lady as old and frail as she seemed, was standing up. "Is Sedric in?"

"Sedric!" the grandma called through the house. At times, she could be a little… cuckoo. She didn't know where she was half the time and she relied on Sedric to feed her medicine for the constant pain in her blotchy legs.

"That's okay, Mrs. Plumith." Ikena began to apologise when she heard the smirks of Sedric behind her.

"Are you disturbing my grandma again?" he chuckled. "Grandma, why don't you sit down in your chair and listen to the radio?" She slowly nodded and trailed her way back to her seat, humming something about the call of birds as she went. Sedric eyed the paper bag Ikena was carrying and looked suspicious, "What have you got there?"

"Only the *finest* deer meat in all of Nevera," Ikena mocked in a high-pitched and posh voice. Sedric snatched the bag immediately after hearing the word 'deer' and smelt the bloody mess. He reached into his pocket and offered a squirrel in return. "It's the best I've got," he tried but Ikena refused.

"You keep it. It'll make your grandma strong." She reiterated the words of her mother.

The evening drew near and Ikena announced that she best be off. Sedric went to hug her, outstretching his arms wide to bring them around her, but Ikena, stupidly, stuck her hand out forcefully. Sedric gave a quizzical look and, with the very tips

18

of his fingers, took her hand and shook it. Ikena shifted and turned on her heels back into the market she crossed to get home.

Way to make a fool out of yourself, she thought. The market folk were packing their things up and a few greeted Ikena hello as she made her way through. If it weren't for the market then Ikena would never have been able to get warm jackets for her siblings, which they'd soon grow out of, but she had to do something, she couldn't have them freeze to death. She had to trade most of her father's clothes for them, but she kept a few items which she wore herself, not wanting to spare her mother of all her clothing and bade farewell to the more expensive things that she knew she could trade easily without having to barter for what she needed. As she walked closer to the house, she could smell the salty cooked meat and took a deep, blissful breath, allowing the smell to fill her lungs as her stomach growled unusually loud. When she got in, she was terrorised by her siblings who were always so happy to see her.

"You've been gone for ages!" Asher cried. "We've been waiting for you to start!" Aliza shrieked and ran to take her place at the table.

Her mother had a spring in her step as she dished huge pieces of deer meat on to each person's plate and Ikena allowed herself some of the roasted vegetables and bone broth gravy which she had thickened with butter. It was rare to have a meal as good as this. To them, it felt like Winter's Day, a day where they celebrate the year and give gifts and toast to festivities. Oh, how it smelt divine and the tender meat tasted so inconceivably delicious.

"Mother, this is amazing. You've cooked it perfectly," little Aliza exclaimed, suddenly sounding more mature than she was.

Ikena met her mother's eyes and a smile plastered across her face. She had done well for the family today and Ikena felt proud. When Ikena had lost her father it had been hard, especially for her mother who had two toddlers to look after. As a thirteen-year-old Ikena knew she had to become 'protector of the house' and the next day made out to the forest to hunt for food, without the safety of her father next to her.

"The Cloaks will be here tomorrow morning for their assessments. Make sure you're wearing your best," Mother announced.

Oh yes, another day wasted by the Cloaks. Once a month, a group of Cloaks are tasked with visiting each and every village in the Kingdom. They assess every person to see whether they possess magical power or not, and if they do then it's the law that they must train with the Cloaks, leaving their homes forever to become a pawn in their army. It was lucky that Ikena caught that deer otherwise they'd have to starve tomorrow or have bone broth for dinner. She could have maybe traded something in the house for a bag of potatoes but, usually, the entire day was taken when the Cloaks arrived. You must wait in long lines before registering your name and address, just to have your hand held by a random Time Warper, who looks into your past to see whether you possess magic or not. By the time the Cloaks have left, its evening and most go home to have their dinner, or, for some, their first and only meal of the day.

Ikena gulped down the last drippings of the bone broth. "Excuse me." She stood from the table and strode over to her bedroom, if that's what you could call it. There was a broken rail which she attempted to hang clothes on, and the room was filled with other items that didn't belong to her, such as her mother's sewing accessories or pointless trinkets that her mother refused to sell. With a grumble, she changed into her mother's nightgown and spent the rest of the evening reading a book. She had sold most of her books to the market but made sure to keep one or two for light reading of an evening and it sometimes helped with the insomnia she suffered. She made herself a glass of warm goats' milk after a few hours passed and it was still dark outside, before returning to her book.

When sunrise came about Ikena heard her mother in the kitchen and left her bedroom to make sure she had slept well, pouring her mother a glass of freshly squeezed orange juice using fresh oranges from their fruit and vegetable garden. Occasionally, Ikena would see the odd person sneaking around their house, trying to steal a piece of fruit or litter of vegetables, but not before she went out there to give them a stern telling-off about stealing. It was an ongoing battle and, unlike Ikena and Sedric's families, others in the village were dim-witted and did not know how to safely store food or save what was needed for a rainy day.

Ikena poured a glass of orange juice for herself, "What time are the—" As if in answer to her question, she heard a loud horn be blown and the familiar sounds of a Cloak carriage pulling into the village. They were here earlier than expected.

"Quick!" Ikena's mother cried as she rushed to wake the twins up. Ikena didn't bother washing and slipped on the same dress she wore for them every month, the only dress she owned which was long, off-white and embroidered with a floral design. Ikena didn't understand why everyone dressed so nicely when the Cloaks came. Her mother said it was because they wanted to pay their respects but Ikena saw it as more of a lie. Once dressed, Ikena's family headed to the village square where a long line had already formed and swiftly joined the end before more families slotted in behind them.

After an hour had passed, Ikena saw Sedric make his way to the back of the line. A group of village girls giggled and whispered as he walked, and it seemed the entire village of women were in love with him.

"She'll never be good enough for him." She heard one woman say from behind her, one of Precious's friends.

"As if she'd ever be able to make him happy," another with curly brown hair said. They knew what they were doing, speaking oddly loud so that Ikena could hear them, but they didn't need to tell her that she wouldn't be good enough, she already knew it herself. Ikena tried to not let it bother her, but it did. The Cloaks had deemed Sedric's grandma too old and frail to be of any use to them, especially after the last trip she made from her house to the village square where she stumbled over a few stones and broke her hip. Luckily, a Cloak Healer mended the damage, but after that they agreed that she would not be required to participate. After what felt like four hours, Ikena's family had reached the front of the line.

She let her mother take her siblings first and couldn't help but chuckle at her little siblings who shuffled up to the desk which was twice their height. Her mother registered their address before being ushered to a Cloak with long, white hair where half of it was plaited. The Cloak crouched to meet the twin's heights and took their hands. Asher had always found it difficult to stand or sit still, so he played with his feet, using them to draw pictures in the stones below as he did so. The man's face was pale and shiny, and he had striking green eyes with dark, black rims around the irises. He wore a long silver robe which was embroidered with fine stitching and silk trousers underneath, another gift the Cloaks keep for themselves.

Believe it or not, but there are Cloaks who can cast objects before their very eyes, like clothes, utensils and furniture, so magic folk will never know what it's like to live in poverty. The villages also deliver fresh produce to the palace such as eggs or meat, even though it's not like they'd have any trouble hunting for it. There was another Cloak wearing similar attire to the assessor who stood by him and recorded when he said the word 'safe' at mother, Aliza and Asher.

The Cloaks used the word 'safe' when a person did not possess any magic, it was like they were ultimately deemed a dangerous Sinturi if they did have magic and Ikena dreaded the word, 'unsafe'. She had only ever seen one person from Endfell be cursed with magic, it was a farmer's boy, and he was swiftly taken to the palace, surrounded by a personnel of Cloaks like he was a threat to Nevera. It was sickening. When it came to Ikena's turn, the man stood and took her right hand before looking at her intently with a bewildered face. Her reading was taking longer than everyone else's and for a while she became increasingly concerned. *What if I'm magical?* Ikena thought, feeling the sweat clamber in the hand he was holding.

"Safe," he barked after a few moments and Ikena allowed herself to relax.

After their assessment they were allowed to travel back to their home, Ikena noticed Sedric on the way, who seemed to be laughing with Precious in the queue. *They're probably laughing at me,* she thought. Precious caught her looking, and upon locking eyes with Ikena, she kissed him. Sedric looked dazed. *Push her away, please.* But he didn't. His hands crept round her back. Ikena forced herself to look away but she couldn't help the devious twinge of jealousy root in her stomach. She felt sick. On their way home Ikena stayed quiet, something about the way the Cloak looked at her made her feel uneasy. It was like he was unsure about whether she had magic or not, and if she did what did that mean for her? Could she really leave her family like that? They depended on her. It had become her greatest fear to be involved in the Cloak army. She pushed the thought to the back of her mind.

That evening, she ventured into the forest alone for some peace and quiet, bringing with her the hunting gear she carried and a small torch she could use to light her way if it got really dark, but for now she could see without it. She reached a soft spot of ground and laid on her back, staring at the evening sky ahead and listening to the sounds of the trees rustling around her. It was peaceful and slowly her eyes began to get heavier and heavier before she drifted off. She awoke startled at the man who had cosied up beside her, before realising it was Sedric.

"Excuse you," she said laughing as she sat upright, but she couldn't help but feel giddy with how close the pair of them had been.

Sedric sat up himself when he noticed Ikena had a troubled look on her face. She felt ashamed of herself. *How could I let myself fall asleep in the middle of a deserted forest?* Sedric watched her closely as she became flustered and blushed, her cheeks a rosy colour. He wrapped his arms around her and gently rubbed her back, allowing her to snuggle up to him and feel the warmth of his breath on the top of her head.

"I feel like such an idiot," she blurted, picking at her fingernails. "Anyone could be out here, a Sinturi or anything, and I let myself fall asleep?"

Sedric took her hand in his and lightly rubbed it with his thumb, "You're not an idiot. You're only tired."

"How'd your assessment go?" Ikena asked, thoughts of his kiss with Precious flooding back into her mind. Her body stiffened. "I saw you get particularly close with little Miss. Perfect."

Sedric rubbed the back of his neck, "What can I say I'm a lady killer." He forced a laugh. "I felt nothing though. She's kissed me before and each time it's just not been what I want… not who I wanted." He paused for a moment, "How was your assessment?"

Ikena dreaded even the mere thought of her assessment, she was safe, but she didn't like the feeling it had uprooted inside her. Like something was wrong.

"I'm *safe*," she mocked with a disgusted tone that she couldn't help but muster.

Sedric stayed quiet for a while, contemplating what to say. "Ikena… I want you to know that you truly are safe, I promise you. I know you're still a little…" He paused trying to ruminate the appropriate word to use, "Shaken up with what happened to your father. You're probably the only person in Endfell who's actually seen a Sinturi and lived to tell the tale, but I promise you, I won't let anything happen to you. I will *always* be here."

Ikena lingered on every word he said. The truth was, she wasn't only shaken up from what happened to her father all those years ago. She was guilty. She had a secret, one that she had buried since that day. Sedric leaned in closer towards her lips and she felt herself blush. She wanted to kiss him, to give in to the way she felt about Sedric, but she couldn't. She wouldn't. She had to distance herself from him to keep him safe. She was trouble. She pulled away and twiddled her fingers nervously.

"Ikena… I—" Whatever Sedric was about to say, she didn't hear it. Instead, she heard a scream. But not just anyone's scream. It was little Asher's.

"Asher!" she yelled, finding her footing, her head was darting left and right, unable to pinpoint where the voice was coming from. Sedric found his feet, his hunting spear at his side instantly.

"Ikena, this way," Sedric called as he noticed a rustling in the treetops above.

They ran as fast as they could until they saw Asher who had climbed a high tree top and was unable to get down. One fall and he would break his neck.

"Asher. It's me, Ikena. Stay calm, okay?" Ikena lowered her voice and spoke softly, not wanting to startle him.

Sedric leaped into action and began climbing the tree after him, knowing that a boy his age with bones that were still growing, wouldn't survive a fall that high. How had he even got that high in the first place?

"Sedric's coming to get you okay. Just stay still."

"Ikena, I'm scared," Asher cried, and let go of the branch he was holding to wipe his teary eyes, causing him to stumble around on the only thin tree branch which was holding him up.

"Asher be careful!" Ikena screamed, he hung on to the outstretched branch for dear life.

Sedric had almost reached him when the tree began to crack. The branch was loose and, with Asher's weight on top, was barely keeping upright. Sedric was moving faster now, understanding how little time he had left, he had finally reached him and outstretched his hand when the branch came flying down. It had snapped and took Asher along with it. Suddenly, time stood still. Ikena's heart sank as she watched her baby brother fall headfirst through the air.

"NO!" she screamed at the top of her lungs; arms outstretched towards him.

It was almost instinctual but then something peculiar happened. Asher had stopped falling. Was she seeing this correctly? Her thoughts were confirmed by the shock that had plastered itself on Sedric's face, he first stared at Asher, then at Ikena and then back to Asher again. Asher seemed scared and began to cry loudly, not being able to process what was happening to him. He was levitating five feet above the ground, arms and legs outstretched and all. Ikena felt a tight pull inside her and as she relaxed Asher plopped to the ground with a thump. Luckily, he was unhurt and alive.

Sedric began to climb back down the tree as Ikena scrambled towards her little brother, helping the crying boy stand up and checking him over for any damage. He had a bruised arm and a scraped chin but that was all. As Sedric reached the ground he seemed uncertain of whether to move towards Ikena or run, his jaw tightened. Surely, he wasn't afraid of her? After a few moments he relaxed and reprimanded Asher. He didn't mean to yell at the boy, but he was scared and even more so after what had happened. Did Ikena have magic?

"I'm sorry Sedric, I just wanted to hunt again with…with… my sister," he blubbered.

Sedric pulled Asher into his chest and apologised for yelling. He wiped the tears from his wet cheeks and turned his attention to Ikena. She knew exactly what he was going to say but she didn't have the answer. She felt different. The power came from her fingertips and pulled as Asher levitated and her entire body felt energised with a pulse that itched.

"Ikena," Sedric said, looking at her in the most intent way she had ever seen, "What was that?"

Her head swarmed with a thumping headache and her lips were dry and pasty. She was shocked herself and wouldn't dare speak, for fear of confirming the truth.

"I…I don't know." But she had a feeling. If she had really done magic, then that meant that she was a Cloak.

TWO

Ikena spent the night tossing and turning in her make-shift bed, mulling over the day's events. She couldn't shake the fact that *she* had done magic. She felt it rise from inside her until it consumed every piece of her soul. It was like her entire body had knotted at that very moment and only seemed to disappear when she had relaxed. She couldn't control it or even know if she could do it again but one thing for certain was that she couldn't let anyone find out, *especially* not the Cloaks. It wasn't just about leaving her family, but it was also about being so controlled as they were. They weren't allowed to speak to anyone of their own past and they had to follow a strict day-to-day regime, all under the King's selfish command. It wasn't something Ikena had any interest in. Maybe she fantasised about being a protector of the world when she was younger, but now? She didn't want that for herself. She wasn't that kind of person anymore.

At dawn, she heard her mother wake like she did at the same time each day and moved to join her in the kitchen where she poured herself a glass of freshly squeezed orange juice, lightly sipping at it and trying to tarnish the headache that pounded at a constant pace. Her mother carried tired, dark bags under her eyes and hadn't brushed her coarse hair which was a volumized mess atop her head.

"Mother..." She debated telling her what had happened yesterday, about Asher climbing a tree and falling and her saving him using, dare she utter the word, *magic*. After a moment she felt torn, she couldn't do that to her family or put that kind of pressure on them, what if a Cloak came and quizzed her about her daughter, would she lie? She'd be more protected if she never mentioned it again and pushed any thought of confiding in her mother away.

Asher and Aliza came out of their room with tired faces. Aliza yawned loudly whereas Asher stayed unusually quiet.

"Hey there, Captain," Ikena said crouching down to where his sad little innocent face was. "How are you feeling today?" He shrugged his shoulders.

Something was clearly wrong; he had never been this quiet before. Ikena decided to take him to the market with her, maybe it would cheer him up. Ikena's mother handed her a small bag of coin and listed the items she needed from the market. Ikena grabbed her own stash of coin that she had saved, sometimes Sedric gave her a few pieces to help the family out. Aliza cried and protested that she wanted to come along too but after mother had tempted her with the promise of teaching her how to sew, Ikena and Asher were able to slip out the door. She grabbed his hand as they walked, but he made no remark, he walked dully, staring blankly at the floor with each step.

"Asher," Ikena crouched down to his height once again,

"No one is angry with you. What happened yesterday was an accident. We don't have to tell mother, or anyone else, do you understand?" Asher's face looked up at hers with tears forming in his eyes. He must have felt like it was all his fault, like he had cast his family into great doom.

"No one will find out?" he questioned quietly in his soft, high-pitched voice.

"No one will find out. I promise."

With a nod his mood instantly uplifted and he was back to being his childish, loving self. When they reached the market, he begged Ikena for a sweet apple. She had never liked buying them for him but seeing as she wanted to make sure he was cheered up, she obliged, using her own coin. The vendor smiled as he took her coin and asked Asher to choose which apple he liked. Unsurprisingly, he picked the largest one. Asher watched in wonder as the vendor put the apple on a stick and dipped it in a pot of hot, sticky honey. He handed it to Asher who took a big bite, smothering honey all over his face. Her mother would have a fit when she saw the state of him but Ikena didn't mind. Asher had a spring in his step again.

"Make sure you chew it properly," she reminded him as she passed from market stall to market stall and tried to remember what her mother needed. She was low on wool and desperately needed some as she was due to give the mayor his hand-stitched scarf in a few days' time. The mayor was her mother's favourite client and he always made it a custom to tip generously with each woollen clothing item she stitched him. Ikena signalled to the wool lady and purchased one ball of white wool. Then, Ikena met a vendor with fresh eggs and bought a case of twelve. He tried to charge her extra, but Ikena bartered the price down to something more reasonable. They were leaving the market when the daughter of the woman who owned the flower stall, a little girl a year or two younger than Asher, ran up to Asher and handed him a single lavender sprig as a kind gesture. Asher was most pleased.

"Wow, thank you very much!" he exclaimed and smelt the sprig. The little girl giggled and ran back to her mother, it seemed she had grown a crush on him. It reminded Ikena of her and Sedric when they were young, albeit not that young, but Sedric would always find pretty flowers in the forest and give them to Ikena when they went hunting.

When they reached home, Ikena handed her mother the wool and eggs and presented Asher last, his hands covered in sweet honey and his mouth sticky.

"Oh, dear me," her mother chuckled. "Ikena you know I don't like them to have sweet apples."

Aliza felt jealous that she hadn't gotten one and began to cry. "I wanted a sweet apple," she blubbered.

"Aliza, you can come with me to the market tomorrow, how about that?" Ikena said, taking Asher to the bathroom where she cleaned him up. "You are one sticky monster!" She giggled and proceeded to wipe his mouth and hands down with water.

"That was the most yummiest apple I ever had," he exclaimed.

Ikena still had to hunt for the day's food and, when the time was right, snuck out of the house, making sure to bring a scarf with her, wanting some fresh air with her own thoughts for a change. She armed herself with her hunting knife, and straw bag before heading off to the village. On her way she saw the mayor purchasing fresh strawberries from a stall and decided to say hello, she wanted to make sure he had a good impression of their family so that he would continue to be her mother's client.

"Mayor Sedman," she called before greeting him with a friendly handshake. "How are you?"

"Ikena, how nice to see you again. I'm very well, thank you and you?"

Ikena informed him that the scarf her mother was knitting for him was the nicest looking scarf she had ever seen and that it would sure be a treat for him.

"Oh, I don't doubt it! Sweet thing your mother is. Send her my best wishes." And with that he continued on his journey and Ikena continued on hers, passing through the village to the opening of the forest. It was a cold day and Ikena made sure to tighten her scarf. She made off for the first trap and to her dismay there was nothing there. The same result came for the other traps, it seemed tonight's dinner would consist of potatoes and vegetables, which meant she'd have two hungry siblings to keep entertained. Asher would be okay, he'd had a sweet apple and Ikena thought she'd get Aliza one later, not only because she wanted to keep things fair in the household but because it meant she'd be less hungry come dinner time. After relaxing in the forest on the damp grass she headed to the market once more where she purchased another sweet apple from the vendor. She had just caught him and begged him for one as he was closing up for the night. Aliza would be happy with this and Asher seemed to be in higher spirits but Ikena couldn't help but worry for her family and for the first time ever she also worried for herself. She jogged back home and savoured the warmth of the fire her mother had lit which radiated through the house.

"Aliza," Ikena called only to see her excited little sister grab the apple from behind her.

"A sweet apple!" she exclaimed. "Thank you, Ikena." She soon bit into it as ferociously as Asher had.

Ikena's mother greeted her before complaining, "Oh Ikena, not another sweet apple." She peered down at Ikena's open straw bag and noticed it was empty and registered why Ikena had made the effort to get Aliza an apple. "Help me peel the potatoes." Her mother trailed back into her kitchen. Ikena followed, taking off her boots and allowing her bare feet to walk across the dusty wooden floor. She was thankful for their little family; it was more than most people had. "I'm really grateful to have you," her mother began. "After your father's death… I don't know what we would have done without you. You saved our family."

Ikena knew her mother was being kind, but the words left a bad taste in her mouth. Instead of feeling confident, like she should have, she felt scared. It's true what her mother had said. She was a grieving teenager when her father died and the very next day, she ventured out to build traps and catch food for their mourning family, taking on the massive role her father had bore for too long. She met Sedric a year later which helped massively but if she hadn't gone out and gotten used to being in the forest on her own then the family wouldn't have had the access to the meat they had. It all made Ikena even more worried about what her fate was. She was breaking the law by keeping her powers secret from the Cloak army. When a person becomes magical, they are to signal to the army by lighting a flame underneath a large jewel that was placed in the middle of the village centre. They would then know that a magical person has come about and would come to collect them, but that didn't sit well with Ikena. If there was one thing she hated more than most, it was being told what to do by the Cloaks. She wasn't prepared to leave her family and had a month to figure out a plan before the Cloaks came again for the next assessment day.

She embraced her mother who seemed unusually emotional today, was it the anniversary of her father's death? No, that was last month. It seemed she was simply happy to be alive and that thought made Ikena feel a little better. They called the siblings for dinner and, as she suspected, her mother had prepared a meal of potatoes, cabbage, and bone broth.

Asher and Aliza tried to protest at seeing their meatless plates but Ikena quickly scolded them, "Hey!" She raised her voice ever so slightly, "Be thankful for even having this much, and remember you both got sweet apples to compensate for the lack of meat. Now, what do we say?"

"Thank you, mother." Came the replies from the little ones in unison.

Dinner was finished quickly and Ikena dressed in her mother's nightgown before kissing her family goodnight and returning to her room where she read. Funnily enough, Ikena wasn't thinking about the Cloaks, or her magic, or lack of food in Endfell, but was instead drawn to thoughts of Sedric, and of when they first met. She was fourteen years old at the time and was in the forest hunting a rabbit. She was about to cut it with her knife when a sharpened spear made of wood jabbed in its side and narrowly missed Ikena's fingers. A little worried, she looked up at the person holding the spear but when her eyes finished on Sedric's she relaxed. She wasn't afraid of him and had seen him one time in the market, when her mother took her. She had fallen for him then and Sedric insisted she take the rabbit home to her family. They then started to meet regularly in the forest and started a friendship. Ikena felt she could be herself around him and he brought back her laugh that had been lost after the death of her father.

"Your father would always come see my grandma," he'd say. "Wonderful man he was." Hearing him speak so kindly of her father was another reason why she loved him. He was so easy to talk to and he could make anyone around him feel comfortable, even loners like herself. Her thoughts flushed to Precious and their kiss. Sedric was always trailing off after some girl here or there, and perfect Precious had him wrapped around her finger. With that ugly thought she tried to sleep, battling the insomnia that always took hold of her each night. Eventually her eyes closed, and her mind drifted into a deep sleep.

THREE

I kena was plagued with, yet again, another nightmare. Unusually, it wasn't the similar one which relived her father's death but instead that of the Cloak palace. She saw the King of the Cloaks sat on a tall throne made of solid gold and embellished with jewels that glistened. He was younger than Ikena had originally imagined and had a full head of golden-brown hair which was curled at the tips and piercing golden eyes. A tall, golden crown perched on his head and he was dressed in golden robes with embroidered sleeves. Guards stood attentively at either side. A Cloak was allowed in through the doors that stood by the side, where they then spoke directly with the King.

"What is it?" he vocalized sternly.

"My Lord," The Cloak began. "There's been a reading." He then ushered in another Cloak who knelt before the royalty of the King. "My Lord," he began. "I have seen the future of Nevera. It follows the divination that was spoke of long, long ago. There is a girl in Endfell who has had a surge of magic. I saw her, in our Kingdom, victorious after destroying the true enemy."

"Are you sure?" the King spoke again attentively at the news he had heard.

"I am sure, my Lord. We must find her. If she becomes a Sinturi... that would be the end of Nevera... forever."

The King ushered the Cloak away and spoke to the first who came into the room.

"You know what to do."

"Yes, my Lord."

Ikena could feel herself pulling away from the scene before waking, staring at the pale ceiling above her. She couldn't help but feel a little dazed from the dream, her stomach twisting in uncomfortable circles. Was that really the Kingdom she had seen? *It's probably your imagination,* she told herself. She laid in bed for a little longer before getting up for the day and followed the same routine she always had. Get up. Get washed. Get dressed. Go hunting.

She changed into her overalls, jacket and boots and packed her hunting equipment, leaving the house in a hurry. Aliza and Asher begged her to take them with her, but she felt she needed a break from babysitting today. She hadn't seen Sedric yesterday, and after the last time she saw him she felt the urge to make sure he hadn't told anyone of her magic. Not that she ever imagined he would. She wondered how he felt about all this. Was he afraid? Impressed? Worried? It was decided, she'd visit Sedric first before making way to the forest. *It will only be a short detour.* The air was gloomier than usual, and people murmured amongst themselves at the market where Ikena stopped to purchase an apple, whilst there she overheard a group of three people talking, two men and a woman, about the Cloaks.

"They're coming here they are, the mayor told me," one large man with an overhanging gut said. "You remember Nevera's divination from long ago?" That caught Ikena's attention and she remembered the Cloak in her dream had spoken of such a thing. "Well, one of the Cloaks had a vision late last night that the girl's power has finally been released. We could *finally* live in peace, no more Sinturi." This baffled Ikena even further as it appeared to be *exactly* what she had dreamt.

"Oh, imagine it!" the other man clapped. It was impossible to imagine. The Sinturi had been around for decades and Ikena knew that, no matter who came about, the Sinturi would always be around to terrorise village folk.

"What a load of rubbish!" the bewildered woman seemed as doubtful as Ikena felt. Ikena caught herself eavesdropping but wanted to know more of this divination, so she began moving between market stalls to edge herself nearer to where the group spoke. "What's that go to do with Endfell?" the woman questioned; wiping sweat from her brow.

"Well, the Cloaks believe that the girl was born here, in fact they're so afraid that she will become a Sinturi that they're actively looking for her."

Ikena tried to convince herself that she had imagined it. That it was just a coincidence that she had a dream about this exact exchange. What worried her more is that she had done a flurry of magic and if they were actively searching for a girl like her, it meant she would be found out soon enough. Ikena became distracted with her thoughts as the group began to scamper.

The woman barked, "Oh look, here they come now."

Ikena's eyes followed her gaze towards the Cloak carriage that was bolstering up the pathway. The apple dropped from her fingertips. She froze, unsure of what to do. She couldn't be assessed again, and her breath began to fasten. Sedric's house was on the corner and she sprinted for it, banging on the door so loudly that she thought it might cave in. *Come on Sedric. Open the door.* She peered round the corner of the house to where a few Cloaks from the carriage had hopped off and began ordering the villagers into a line, more forcefully than they ever had before. The Time Warpers who pulled the carriages and assessed the villagers were in their usual silk robes, but the others wore their full army uniforms made from tough steel. After a short moment, Sedric opened the door and appeared in his worn-down bottoms and shirtless. Ikena tried not to stare at his bare skin but thought it impossible at the handsome and chiselled sight of him. *Oh, stop it you sleaze.*

"Sedric, they're here. What do I do?" she breathed, suffering from a mild panic attack that left her breathless. Sedric knew what it meant, if they found out about her, she'd be sent off to Nevera's Palace and he'd never see her again. He couldn't let that happen. Ikena felt her arm pull as Sedric tugged her inside the comfort of his house. She hoped she hadn't been seen. Sedric's grandma exclaimed loudly, shocked to see someone else in her house, then she relaxed after remembering who Ikena was and continued to hum away at her radio that was playing an old folk song loudly.

Ikena followed Sedric into the kitchen.

"What's going on? Why are they here again?"

"They're doing another assessment. Look, we haven't got time. We both know what we saw yesterday... I... I can't leave my family."

"But they came yesterday. They wouldn't be here so soon." He formed his answer in more of a statement than a question and Ikena grew a little frustrated that he wasn't attending to the urgent matter at hand.

"Sedric. Now *isn't* the time for explanations. What do I do?"

Sedric lifted the side of a sheer curtain from the window and peered out into the market. It was just like Ikena had said, they were checking people again but seemed to completely ignore the men and only be interested in assessing the women.

"There's your family." He pointed causing alarm to rise again in Ikena's stomach and making it churn. What would they say when her entire family showed up to be checked without her? Would that cause them alarm to specifically seek her out? Her family were taken to the front of the queue by a Cloak in steel armour and the long white-haired man from yesterday took each of their hands, eager to assess them.

"Safe," he barked at each of them.

The family began to walk away when the man called Ikena's mother back, looking angrier. Ikena could already envision his words. "Where's your daughter?".

Sedric let go of the curtain, turned to Ikena and took her by the hand, "Ikena... I think you may need to get out of the

41

village." Before being interrupted by a loud bang on the door. "Get under the table," he ordered and covered her with a long tablecloth, exactly like her mother had done when her father died. Sedric's grandma yelled at him to get the door, seemingly unaware of the situation happening around her. Ikena tried to quieten her rapid breath, listening to the faint conversation as best as she could.

"All women are to report to the checking station immediately," a Cloak spoke with a harsh and deep voice.

"Oh. Right. Yes, of course." Ikena could tell Sedric was nervous. "My grandma is gravely ill and is too old to make her way to the village centre, she's been pardoned from all assessments."

Ikena knew the Cloak wouldn't go away and instead he grew increasingly concerned, seeming unapologetic. He then remembered Sedric's face and said, "Aren't you Ikena Ralliday's friend?" he questioned.

Oh no. Why were they asking for her specifically? Did they have spies in the village? Knowing them, they probably sensed her magic like hounds, scraping for meat. She had to move quickly, if he came into the house then he would see her, he would for sure check under the long tablecloth which was undeniable obvious that something was being concealed behind it. She slowly lifted the fabric from the side and peered out into the quaint room. Sedric had a back door to her left, but there was a huge archway which opened into the kitchen where Ikena was. She could be seen but she had to try. She had to get out of the house immediately. Ever so slowly, she crawled on all fours like a dog. Sedric was using his body to cover the door frame, it was now or never. Ikena took her chance and leapt for the back door, she reached it but in such a rush that she let go of the handle abruptly and heard a smack as it shut behind her. That was sure to bring the Cloak into the house. Around the corner stood a pile of stacked fresh hay that had been left for the farmer to collect. Ikena dived into it, even though bits of hay scratched her, she kept burying herself lower and lower. Sedric's door opened and footsteps edged closer.

Please don't see me. Please. Please. She prayed. The footsteps came dangerously close and the Cloak was standing right beside the hay, watching it for one small movement to make his arrest. Suddenly, the hay on top of her began to move and, as she was about to struggle and protest, Sedric's face stood over hers, his strong arms lifting her out of the prickly pile.

"That was close!" he remarked carrying his wooden spear. "Ikena... I think they're after you. Somehow, they know," he whispered so quietly that Ikena almost didn't hear. Instead, her ears were filled with the pounding of her heart.

"I need to get back to my house."

"Follow me." Sedric took Ikena's hand and led her down an alleyway which was in the opposite direction of her house, from that alleyway was a bridge and after a quick check they both began to run over it and into the nearby forest that lay overhead. This must be how Sedric got into the forest from his end of the village. They edged further in and eventually Ikena recognised certain trees and found her way to the foot of the village, she could see her house opposite but knew she couldn't run over there for fear of being seen.

"We have to go the back way," she said as she took Sedric

round the backs of the houses, being careful not to make too much sound or be seen by any Cloak or villagers who might make a scene and ask why they were acting so suspiciously.

They made their way to the front of the house, ducking low as Ikena fumbled for her key. She had just unlocked the door when it swung open, toppling Ikena over on to the feet of her mother. Sedric followed closely behind. Her mother looked awfully concerned, as did the twins who wondered why the Cloaks were doing another check-up.

"Ikena!" Her mother pulled her to her feet and hugged her. "What's going on?"

"Mum… Something happened yesterday in the forest. I…I did something. Something I couldn't control." She stared intently into her mother's oaken eyes and tried to find comfort.

"You've got magic, haven't you?" she asked, lowering her voice to barely a whisper. Ikena gave one nod, but it was confirmed. "There's a Cloak patrolling the street," Sedric informed and moved away from the front door. Suddenly, her mother sprang into action and began packing a wicker basket with food, string, a scarf, and other essentials.

"What are you doing?" Ikena asked, grabbing her hands, and willing her to stop.

"You can't stay here Ikena. You can't. They will be after you. You *can't* stay here," she said harshly, but in her heart Ikena knew her mother was right.

How could she stay here and risk the Cloaks taking her away? They were after her and there was no way she was going to go willingly. She would have to leave the village and hide from the Cloaks until the hunt for her had quietened, then she'd return home and assess the situation. If it were unsafe, she'd leave again but it beat a lifetime of servitude to the King. Ikena's mother handed her a small pouch and upon inspecting Ikena noticed that it was almost all the entire family savings of coin.

"I can't take this," she spoke but her mother insisted and wrapped her arm around her. Ikena savoured the grassy scent from her mother's clothes. "Mother, you need this."

"No, my sweet. You do." Her mother stuffed the pouch into the bottom of the wicker basket and looped it through Ikena's arm. The twins sobbed to the side and Ikena snuggled them in an embrace. Tears streamed down Asher's face, "I'm sorry. This is all my fault," he sobbed.

Ikena spoke to him directly. "None of this is your fault. I'm different and it's not something anyone could have foreseen or changed. But one thing for certain is that I will *always* love you, all of you." Tears began to build in her own eyes. "I'm sorry I've brought this upon you."

Ikena turned to Sedric with one goal in mind, knowing that if she didn't kiss him now, she never would. With a stride, she was only a few centimetres in front of him, then she felt his hand on the back of her head, bringing her lips to meet his. Sparks bubbled in her stomach and, although time stopped, the flutter intensified. It was as if no one else existed. In that moment it was just her and him. His muscular frame leaned against hers and it felt wrongful, so wrong that it felt right. He pulled away softly and leant his forehead against hers, the corner of his lips pulling up into a smile. She would miss Sedric the most and was eternally grateful for all he had done for her little family. She heard her mother cough behind her, as if to say, 'we're in an emergency so snap out of it'. "Goodbye," Ikena whispered into his ear and walked towards the door when a hand grabbed hers. It was Sedric's. He looked dazed and confused.

"I'm coming with you," he announced and sharpened his spear with her mother's potato peeling knife.

"No... It's too—"

"Dangerous?" he finished, "Look, you set traps, sure, but you're going to need me. You don't know how to use your power yet, or what it even is."

"But what about your grandma?"

"We'll check on her every day and bring her food, Sedric. I promise," Ikena's mother said. "I won't tell a single soul of what I know." Ikena wanted to change his mind. She brought trouble wherever she went. Everything was happening too fast and the walls around her began to close in. She allowed herself to be shook by her mother who had found a wet cloth in the time and put it over her forehead. *Focus*, Ikena told herself and forced her mind back into reality.

"We've got to go," Sedric pleaded, even though she didn't like it, Ikena was grateful to have someone come along with her. She wouldn't admit it, but she was scared.

Ikena took one last longing look at her family, her teary-eyed little siblings who stood clutched to her mother's hands at either side and her mother who, in this terrible time, was smiling at her.

"I love you all." Tears rolled down her cheeks. She turned on her heel and made her way out the front door, knowing that if she stayed a second longer, she'd never muster the courage to leave. She and Sedric ducked behind her mother's orange tree and watched as the Cloak, who was passing up their road, disappeared into another. Nearby, stood a wagon from Lovrin – the trader's village – which was pulled by two horses and had stopped a few doors down to deliver fresh pints of milk to a neighbour.

"Let's hitch a ride," Ikena said, pointing the trader out.

They moved quickly to the man who gave a suspicious look at the two before him, whose eyes were wandering in search of any nearby Cloaks. "We need safe passageway to Lovrin," Sedric began in a hushed tone. "*Safe* passageway… Do you understand?" The trader seemed hesitant at first, yet he clearly knew what they meant. They couldn't be seen.

"I can get you there, but what will I be getting in return?" he spoke, scratching his dirty beard and moustache that gave a foul smell and carried pieces of crumb in it.

"We have gold," Sedric tried.

"I have no interest in gold… but that jacket I should think would suffice. Don't you agree lassie?" he eyed Ikena's fur jacket. Surely not. It was something too special to Ikena's heart. She couldn't just give it up, but what choice did she have?

"Fine," Ikena agreed reluctantly. The trader insisted that they climb on to the back of his wagon and then he buried them under piles of hay. The carriage pulled away and, in the darkness of the hay, Ikena searched for Sedric's hand. His found hers and held tightly. They were on their way and all they could do now is hope. Hope that the trader wouldn't sell them out.

FOUR

I t felt like they had been in the stuffy wagon for at least four hours, and when the trader grabbed them and lifted them out it was confirmed as the day had drawn considerably darker. Neither Ikena nor Sedric had ever ventured past the forest that bordered Endfell, so they looked around eagerly at the picturesque village. Ikena was most excited to see the established windmill that bore long sails which turned delicately in the wind, a statement her mother had told her about. To its left a waterwheel churning up the water around it in unison, near to the bank of the river that ran through the town. Ducks and swans swam gracefully by, satisfied by the peace that surrounded them. And in the far distance to the right of Ikena and Sedric, were yellow cornfields that flurried as far as the eye could see, like small children flying paper kites in the breeze.

"Payment please," the trader demanded and as promised, Ikena handed over the fur jacket to their driver and felt the chill of the cold air on her bare skin. "Pleasure doing business with you," the trader spoke. "There's an inn over there." He pointed to the top of a hill, where a single cobbled path led to a ramshackle house with windowless windows.

Villagers glared at them with strange looks as they walked along the cobbled path, wondering why folk from Endfell were in their village. They didn't belong there.

"We're going to be okay," Sedric spoke with such surety but Ikena doubted the situation. He took off his own fur-lined jacket and slung it around Ikena's shoulders.

They neared the rickety looking inn which bore a sign of a wild boar above the door and entered. Inside, a welcoming fire burned, and warmth gently spread around the room. A tall, beautifully dark-skinned woman with tightly curled hair sat on a stall behind a desk, giving Ikena reason to walk over.

"Excuse me, my friend and I would like a room, please," she said and reached into her basket for the pouch of coin. The inn keeper offered a bed that she had available, which Ikena accepted and paid the coin that was due. She led them up a wooden staircase to the right that creaked with every step and led to the very top of the inn.

The woman pushed open a small door with the number five on. "Here ya'ar." The inn keeper welcomed them inside and made her way back downstairs. The room was strangely rumpled, a dusty bed awaited their arrival, and a warm fireplace was lit giving the room the same cosy demeanour the reception had. Ikena had forgotten what it felt like to sleep in an actual bed and dumped herself on it. Sedric checked the wicker basket and noted that her mother had packed left over deer meat she had saved, along with a whole jar of jam and a pint of goats' milk. It was all she could spare.

Suddenly, Ikena felt guilt build inside her, not only had

she forced her family into probable doom, but she also took the very last scrapings of food they had. *How would they survive?* Sedric took the deer meat and carefully unwrapped it from its papers. Nearby the fire was a poker, which he used to pierce the deer meat and hang over the crackling flames. Ikena sat up and enjoyed watching the meat sizzle, the fatty bits turning crisp at the edges. After it had cooked, Sedric passed Ikena the bigger half and chewed away at his own half, savouring the meat with each and every bite. He grumbled loudly at its savoury delight. "Ikena, this meat is delicious!" he exclaimed.

"I pounced on the thing before it had a chance to run away, came right up to me it did."

The evening drew black and as the fire began to diminish, Ikena and Sedric laid in the cotton sheeted bed. Sedric wrapped a protective arm over Ikena's stomach and drew her close. She could never express how thankful she was to have Sedric with her, and under the comfort of his warmth, she drifted to sleep.

In the morning, she woke to the sound of a rooster nearby and opened her eyes to bright sunlight shining in through the window frame, Sedric was still asleep beside her, his tussled hair covering his beautiful eyes. Carefully, Ikena lifted herself from the bed. She was wary of the Cloaks, but they didn't usually hang around villages and were restricted to the palace most days. As a thank you, she headed to the market with her coin in hand to find breakfast for Sedric. He didn't have to come with her, but he did. He wanted to. She would never forget that. Down the stairs was the inn keeper and a small boy who Ikena guessed was her son.

"Excuse me," Ikena spoke, grasping her attention. "If my friend comes down here can you please let him know that I'll be back soon." The inn keeper nodded with a smile and Ikena ventured into the morning sunlight that created a wave of warmth over her body.

She headed down the hill by the cobbled pathway, eager to get to the traders market quickly and think up a plan with Sedric. The trader's market was a busy bustle of villagers, all of whom were bartering for a day's wage.

"Roll up. Roll up. A dozen of eggs for fifteen coin," one said.

"How about a pint of milk for twelve coin," another said, eager to one-up his marketing opponent.

The man with the eggs didn't like the competition and began to lower his price. "A dozen of eggs for ten coin, going once… going twice..." And then a woman waved at him and he exclaimed, "Sold!".

The man with the milk then came out from behind his stall and stirred up an argument with egg-man but egg-man was twice his height. Ikena kept walking until she found a trader who was willing to give her two large pieces of smoked salmon for ten coin. Ikena paid without trouble, carrying the bag of fish close to her as she worked her way from stall to stall. She came across a bookshop on her way and was utterly perplexed at the stunning books which stared back at her, shining on their shelves, too delicate to touch. *How beautiful*, she thought. The books sparkled in the light and welcomed her. It seemed the village of Lovrin wasn't in poverty, not like Endfell was. Although she'd bet her foot that there were some who struggled for food. In Endfell, market stalls sold sweet apples, or wool, or flowers and the people relied on traders from outside villages to bring them their fish or milk. There was a farmer, but he only sold eggs and manure from crops, and never had enough for the whole village. A glimmer on a children's book cover caught Ikena's eye and as she turned her head, she saw a small pocket book with a striking gold cover that created its own light when the sun reflected on to it. It was beautiful.

"You like that, eh?" the shopkeeper, an old woman with braided long grey hair and white duck feathers tucked in to each segment of braid, stared at Ikena noticing her bemusement.

"Very much so." Ikena picked the book up and ran her fingers over the hard-backed cover which had the Kingdom's name 'Nevera' on it.

"It's the tale of Nevera's divination... a rare thing to get your hands on," the shopkeeper said tutting away at herself, she knew what she was doing, pulling Ikena in so that she'd pay extra for a book such as this and it was working.

"How much?" Ikena asked.

The shopkeeper smiled. "I'll tell you what. If you can muck out my pig pen over there, then I'll give it to you... How's that sound?"

It seemed silly to Ikena, but she felt something come over her like she had a connection to the book. It called her. She simply had to have it. She agreed to tend the lady's pig pen and was given a shovel for tending to the droppings and a hose which she'd fill the troughs up with. The lady left her to it, and she hummed away as she scooped the large droppings into a bag, which the lady could use for manure for crops later. With the hose, she washed out the water trough and re-filled it and filled another one with chopped apples that were left for her on the side, resisting the urge to sneak a piece herself. After half hour, she had finished, and the old lady inspected her work for the day.

"Thank you, dear. As promised, you keep the book. *Mentesen.*" *Good wishes from the Cloaks.* Ikena reluctantly said it back, but she hated uttering the word, which was said as a polite gesture in common talk.

After a satisfied trip, Ikena made her way back to the inn. Sedric was still sleeping, and he looked so innocent and at peace. She lightly seared the salmon using the same technique they had with the deer meat yesterday, using the fireplace poker to pierce the fish and hang it over the top of the flames. Nearby was a wooden chair which Ikena perched atop of and opened the royal-like book she had snagged. With a sniff, she smelt the fresh pages and flicked to the first page which had fascinating hand-drawn images of the Kingdom and Sinturi on. She traced the ink with her fingers.

For too long the Kingdom of Nevera has been plagued
A darkness stirs and threatens to display
But in a small village consumed by forests there will be
A raven-haired woman who at first will flee
To a lake village where an ancient professor waits
He'll teach her to harness her power and create
A world in which the darkness is no more
She is the key to winning the war

Ikena became distracted by the burning smell of the salmon and rushed to put them on a nearby plate, burning her fingers in the process.

"Argh!" she huffed. The fumbling woke Sedric.

"Where'd you get those?" he yawned and sat up on the bed.

"From the market. I got this book too."

"You went *where*?"

"To the market—"

"Ikena, why didn't you wake me?" he grew frustrated and became angry and agitated. "I'm putting *my* life on the line for *you*," he grumbled, tucking into his salmon without even one mutter of the phrase 'thank you'.

"I didn't want to wake you. You seemed pretty tired," a monotone voice came as she spoke. She had enough on her plate, she didn't need Sedric acting like this.

"Well, I don't care. What if... what if you got hurt? Or if a Cloak was there? Or even worse, a *Sinturi*!" His words pained Ikena. She was able to look after herself, she had done for years, why should she stop now? With his agitated tone, Ikena grew angry herself.

"Sedric, it's fine. I got us some salmon for—"

"No, it's not fine!" he yelled. Ikena couldn't work out why he was acting like this.

"Excuse me?" she had snapped. She didn't mean to yell at him, but she did, taking all her frustrations out on him. "If you don't want to be here, then just go!" As she yelled, something inside her felt different. The beating of her heart felt increasingly loud and her veins pulsed with rage, with fear, with relief. Her stomach twisted into knots and her body pulled like something wanted to escape from underneath her skin. A heavy plank of wood fell from the roof, directly on to Sedric's head. With a thump he fell to the floor.

"Sedric!" she yelled as he lay there. The power inside her lessened but it was her who had done this. She didn't mean it, but it was like when she saved Asher. *It just happened.* The inn keeper heard the crash and furiously knocked on the door.

"What's going on in there?"

Reluctantly, Ikena faced her, ready to ask for help and come up with a quick excuse as to why the plank of wood had fallen but it was the inn keeper who apologised.

"Oh my, I'm so sorry!" she exclaimed, running in to check on Sedric, "We've had some heavy winds lately." She grabbed a piece of cloth from the bathroom and ran it under cold water from the tap, placing it gently on Sedric's head.

"He'll be alright. Might have a nasty bruise when he wakes though." The inn keeper chuckled and offered to give back half her coin for their troubled stay. The pair of them placed Sedric back in bed and the inn keeper left them. Sedric looked troubled, even as he lay unconscious. Ikena always forgot that he cared about her, truly, and that she was silly for venturing out into the market without letting him know. What if something had happened at the inn and he couldn't find her?

Ikena couldn't help but think of the man in the book, a professor who would be able to show her how to control her magic. If she met him, she was sure he'd be able to train her without telling the Cloaks. She couldn't hop from village to village without some kind of plan and she couldn't risk hurting anyone else. What if she returned home and it was Asher or Aliza she accidentally harmed or *worse*? She missed them terribly but there was nothing she could do and as much as she hated making her time away from them longer, for their safety, she had to. She couldn't take Sedric along with her, she was too dangerous. She could imagine herself getting angry, or upset, or overjoyed and accidentally killing him. Deep down, she knew she was capable of it and that was what scared her the most. Sedric would be angry at her for leaving, he might even hate her, but she felt it was the right thing to do. Ikena packed her things, leaving a portion of coin for Sedric to make his way safely back to Endfell. She made a swift escape down the wooden stairs and asked the inn keeper for paper and an ink quill.

Dear Sedric,

By the time you read this, I'll already be gone from Lovrin. I am going to find the ancient professor in my book, he might be able to help me control my magic and that means I won't hurt anyone else. I am sorry for the pain I have caused you and I only wish you don't hate me after reading this. Please make it back to Endfell safely and tell my family that I am safe. Sedric, you've been my best friend for as long as I can remember and there will always be a special place for you in my heart. Always.

Love, the little girl you met four years ago, Ikena.

After she had finished writing she gave the paper and quill back to the inn keeper and asked her to give it to her friend when he woke.

"I'm looking for a lake village. Do you happen to know in which direction it might be?" she asked.

The inn keeper took a ragged folded map out from the side of the counter and opened it. She pointed to a village on the other side of a large lake. A village which was, ironically, called Lakeland. It would be a few days journey and safer to make for the nearest villages to stop for rest of a night. The nearest village to Lovrin, other than Endfell, was a coal mining village called Underust, so she sought to head their first. Ikena handed the map back to the inn keeper but she insisted she keep it.

"Where you heading?" she asked.

"Underust is my next stop, do you know of a carriage going that way?"

"There could be a merchant outside who's willing to take you."

Ikena thanked the lady and snuck outside in to the fresh air. She made her way to the market again and asked if there was anyone going that way. She passed houses and stopped in her tracks when she heard the loud sound of a horse in distress. To her right, was a man, dressed in overalls like she was, who was whipping his horse. He laughed to his son, who was beside him as they tortured the poor thing, whacking its head and spitting at it.

The two of them bawled back inside the house and, slowly, Ikena crept closer to the raven horse that had lost the light in its eyes.

"Hey, boy," she whispered, stroking her fingers across his

silky soft fur. "Did they hurt you?" the horse grumbled as if to scream 'yes'. Its eyes were tired, and he had a sad look about him, hanging his head low to the ground. Ikena made the decision then and there to steal it. It was for the best, and she needed a ride. Ikena had never rode a horse before but she loved animals. How hard could it be? To the right of her was a saddle and reins which she used to lace him up in his gear.

"You're not the youngest thing, but you'll take me to where I want to go, don't judge us humans, we're not all like they are." Ikena spoke, and the horse seemed more content in her company.

"Oi!" Ikena heard a clamber from inside the house and, from upstairs, was the son who was staring at Ikena from the top window. "Get away from him!"

"Quick!" Ikena yelled, although not expecting a response from a horse. Using the side of the fence, she hoped on to the horses back and shook the reins. The horse sped off, "Let's go Artax!" she had said instinctively and realised she had given him a familiar name that once belonged to a small, wooden horse she played with as a child, losing it in the forest a year later when out for a hunt with her father. Artax galloped to the front of the village and out beyond Lovrin's border. She was on her way. She had to survive the night and hope that Sedric wouldn't hate her. That was what worried her the most.

FIVE

Ikena had rode all day, across the border and wide stretch of land that stood between her and stopped when she had finally reached her destination, thankful to be done with a day's travel. She was openly welcomed into the soot-ridden village called Underust and slept the night in the stables with her horse who she fed a few spoonfuls of jam from the jam jar her mother had packed. As she slept through the night, a terrible nightmare consumed her peaceful mind. She saw a pack of hooded Sinturis ride into Lovrin on their *Dachrinturi*, dark beasts that resembled horses, but they were anything but. Their bones showed, grey and broken, their shrieks resembled that of a screaming woman and the mist that surrounded them was as dark as darkness could be. They openly rode into the village and attacked the villagers, sucking the life out of each and every human on site, consuming their very souls. She saw Sedric sleeping soundlessly in his bed at the inn and a Sinturi edging its way up to his door, black mist circling the Sinturi's skeletal fingers as it reached for the door handle and in a quick motion the door was open.

Ikena awoke screaming, sweat dripping from her brow. Her breath hurried and something inside her itched. She felt dark, and powerful. There was a little girl, of a similar age to her siblings, screaming across from her, but in Ikena's mind, *she* was the enemy. Her skin faded and she felt a pulsing urge to grab the girl and smother her. Ikena leaned closer. Upon seeing the girls face, tears streaming from her eyes, Ikena relaxed. What was happening? Her old self returned through the cracks of change, and slowly she suppressed that miserable feeling inside her. "I'm sorry," she said. "You startled me." Ikena resisted the urge to bury her head in her hands, but she wanted to. What was happening to her and why did she feel so... angry?

The little girl fiddled with pieces of apple she held. "That's okay, Miss. You looked scary." Scary, is that how others would describe her? "Your horsey was hungry so I fed him some apple."

Ikena calmed down and felt a sudden sense of relief. She was worried that her power might have released as she screamed and thanked the saints that the little girl was unhurt. Then, her mind travelled to the memory of her nightmare. It was as if it were really happening. *It was just a dream,* she thought. *Sedric is fine.* She sat up from the floor on which she slept and scratched her head.

"You did, huh? May I have a slice?" The little girl passed Ikena one apple slice and took one for herself, resting on the back of a beam pole and wiggling her legs excitedly as she ate it.

The little girl reminded her of little Aliza and her hungry

stomach turned guilt-ridden. Once Sedric returned to Endfell, he'd help them with food and the twins knew how to set traps. *They'll be okay.* She took the moment to get out her map and find her next destination, a small village to the west which was called Hylaria and after that was Lakeland.

"What's your name?" the girl asked her. "Mine is Sophia."

Ikena smiled. "Hi Sophia. I'm Ikena." She paused for a moment before beginning again. "I've got an idea. Show me where I can buy fresh fruit and I'll even let you have a piece." Sophia's eyes grew big and she grinned from ear to ear excitedly.

"Maybe we can get something else for horsey too!" She beamed, dragging Ikena from the stables by her hand.

Sophia took her to a nearby market which was set inside a large shack and folk with soot faces spread their goods over cotton blankets on the floor. A few stalls were placed here and there but they were run-down, and pieces of wood stuck out from their poorly made structures. Ikena scanned the room and noticed a boy around the age of twelve selling pears in a corner. She headed over to him and bargained for a bag of five. One for her. One for Sophia. One for Artax, of course, and two for the road. Ikena was ready to leave the market when behind her she heard a loud *crash*. People scrambled around her, children cried, shouts could be heard. Ikena turned to see a handful of villagers gathered around a singular fallen cart and all that could be seen from underneath it were two legs from a child. The cart had devoured her. Ikena dropped the bag of pears and ran towards the group. Men gathered around, trying to lift the heavy object, but it was no use.

"It's too heavy!" one man yelled. The child's mother had noticed that it was in fact her child that was stuck underneath the cart and she began to wail herself, screaming.

"We need to get this thing up!" another yelled in urgency.

Ikena felt torn. She wanted to help, but how could she? Alarm rose inside her. She was about to witness the death of a child. In an instance, she leapt for the stall, trying herself to lift it up, urgency screaming, pounding in her eardrums. The child underneath stopped crying and her legs laid still. *Come on, Ikena. You can do this.* She heaved. Then she felt it. The familiar feeling that pulsed through her veins and called her to release it. Ikena took a deep breath and focussed, still heaving with all her strength. She broke into a sweat and ever so slightly the cart jolted. *Focus, Ikena. Focus.* She kept at it, straining so hard she thought she might collapse. The cart became lighter and she found lifting it easier but, to her surprise, she was the only one lifting. Men stared at her in shock and the shack stilled to a silence. The mother of the child scrambled for her daughter and pulled her free by her legs as Ikena relaxed the power from inside her and dropped the cart with a *smack* on the floor. The little girl who wore a red and black cross-stitched dress woke with a deep breath. The mother wept and crawled to Ikena on all fours, scrambling around her feet. "Thank you!" she cried. "Thank you!"

The villagers gave Ikena blank expressions. Ikena waited. Who would make the first move? "She's a Cloak!" someone called.

"A magical in our village," another said shocked.

It was too late. Ikena felt the crowd close in on her. With long strides she pushed through the people until she felt hands on her, grabbing her. "Please," she tried. "Let me go." She struggled under the firm grips.

"Someone light the jewel!" The mother of the little girl who, not so long ago had almost been crushed, yelled. *Gee, this is the thanks I get for saving your daughter's life.* Ikena pushed back a laugh. Is this really what it had come to in the villages? If someone lit that jewel, a scurry of Cloaks would be in Underust within seconds. "Please stop," she protested again but felt her body being dragged by those who grabbed her. If they didn't know any better, she'd be burned at the stake, what with the way they were acting. The worry took over her, "Stop!" she yelled, arms outstretched. The hands that grabbed her swiftly let go and confused looks rang around the shack. Their bodies felt lighter and ever so slowly their feet began to lift off the floor.

"What's happening?" another spoke as his body began to levitate like everyone else's. "It's her!" a woman shrieked, pointing at Ikena whose feet were firmly on the ground. With a harsh breath Ikena relaxed and let her hands drop to her side causing everyone in the room to fall to the ground in a bundle of *oof's* and *ouches*. She ran. She ran out of the shack as fast as she could and sped towards the stables. Sophia called from behind her, but she kept at a pace, needing to get out of the village as quickly as possible. She was walking out of the stables with Artax when Sophia burst through the doors. "You forgot your pears, Miss," she said, holding the half-torn paper bag out to Ikena.

"Thank you, Sophia," Ikena took the bag and tossed her a

pear. "I must leave the village quickly." Sophia didn't want her to go and her lips turned downwards into a sad frown. "Oh, dear me," Ikena said. "I believe I bought too many pears. Why don't you take another one?" She held the bag open for the little girl who reached in and took the largest with a smile. It had done the trick and Ikena left the stables on horseback without any tears from behind her, she neared the gates of the village when someone from the shack spotted her.

"There she is!" Ikena took a quick look over her left shoulder and saw one of the men, who had tried to help lift the cart off the little girl, talking to a Cloak and pointing in her direction.

"Stop!" the Cloak ordered.

With a whip of the reins Artax sped off. She heard shouts from behind her and hoped she wasn't being followed. It wasn't until half hour passed that she allowed Artax to slow to a walk and drink the water from a nearby river.

"Good boy," she said, stroking the old thing and feeding him pieces of pear. "You should have seen them, Artax. They were like animals." She flipped open the map and decided to head straight for Lakeland, riding past Hylaria. The day was still bright and early, and the Cloaks would expect her to go to Hylaria. It would be the first place they'd look.

On her journey, Ikena re-read the divination book over and over again. *But in a small village consumed by forests there will be.* Thoughts of her family rushed back to her and even though it had been a mere day she had gravely missed them. *A raven-haired woman who at first will flee.* It wasn't the fact that she hadn't seen them in a day, but more so that she knew it would be months, if not years, before she'd be able to see them again. *To a lake village where an ancient professor waits.* Ikena realised she was playing out the divination exactly and wondered if it really was about her as she assumed the Cloaks thought. *Stupid book*, she mused. Why would a divination be about her? She had felt ignorant for even considering it, and then convinced herself that they had got the wrong person. After all, she had done everything for selfish reasons, namely because she wanted to get away from the Cloaks and *didn't* want to be a part of the war between Cloak and Sinturi, it didn't sound like the woman in the book would do that. She never asked for any of this. Ikena slotted the book neatly in her wicker basket and continued to ride. She figured that if she continued to follow the lake then she'd end up in Lakeland – hence its name.

Hours passed and Ikena felt… strange.

There was something about the sunlight that had suddenly disappeared to leave a grey appearance that didn't sit right with her. It suddenly dawned on her that she had been out for far too long and maybe shouldn't have attempted to venture all the way to Lakeland after all. She was too far past Hylaria to turn back which meant she had to ride through the night. Alone. In the dark.

Another hour, and the wind grew cold around her. Her body shook with a chill she couldn't shake. Something was wrong. She felt the darkness scamper towards her. Then, she heard footsteps. At first, they were quiet, and she wondered whether she was only hearing Artax's steps but then the pace quickened, and they grew louder and louder, coming from behind her in the distance. With a quick look over her shoulder, she grabbed Artax's reins, ready to dash off, but it was Sedric, running to her with his spear in hand. "Sedric, what are you—" She didn't need to finish her sentence. From behind him, a pack of Sinturis rode towards her on the same *Dachrinturi* she had seen in her dream. Their black cloaks swayed in the wind and they charged their way forwards.

"Sedric!" she called.

One of the Sinturis sent a spark of dark magic hurrying towards them like a comet of darkness. Artax moved to the right, missing the blow by mere inches, but the blast had spooked him, and he cried, rearing on his hind legs in a flurry. It allowed Sedric enough time to catch up. Ikena hoisted him on to the back of the horse and felt his arms around her stomach, clinging on for dear life.

"Hyah!" she roared, shaking the reins.

Artax cried and sped into a gallop. The Sinturi were closing in on them fast, their *Dachrinturi* longing for the taste of human soul. Another wave of darkness was cast towards them, but a quick dodge to the left ensured they missed, albeit narrowly.

"Come on, boy!" Ikena yelled, willing Artax to run as fast as he could. Their lives depended on it.

They were coming to a drawbridge up ahead. Lakeland. Ikena couldn't risk leading the Sinturi into the village where they'd prey on the defenceless villagers. No, instead she rode into the forest next to it, hoping to lose the pack within the overgrown shrubs.

Sedric made a quick look behind his left shoulder. "They're gaining on us!" he cried.

Ikena willed Artax on, his breath heavy with every heartbeat. "Wait, we've lost them." Sedric announced. "Something has driven them away."

"We need to get into Lakeland now!" Ikena demanded, still riding Artax as fast as she could and with all the might she could muster. "There's another drawbridge up ahead."

She turned Artax to the right and came zooming over the bridge, the village dark and empty.

"Watch out!" Sedric yelled, pointing at an empty stall up ahead which Artax was set on running towards. With a quick pull on the reins, he stopped but hoisted himself on to his back legs in terror.

"It's okay," Ikena told him. "You're safe. You're safe." Eventually he calmed down.

"Do you think the Sinturis will come in here looking for us?" Ikena asked Sedric.

"Yes," he replied sharply. "Lovrin was attacked by a Sinturi pack." He dropped his tone, not that anyone was around to hear, "The inn keeper and her son at Lovrin are dead. I saw it with my own eyes, a Sinturi took their souls, leaving behind a frail pile of ash and bone. It was... horrific, to say the least. I... I barely got out with my life." He was trembling with every spoken word. "I was woken by the inn keeper's screams. I saw through the door window what took hold of her and bolted. I jumped out of the window and well..." He pointed to his arm which was badly bruised, the entire side of it a black and purple colour. "I didn't have time to wrap it up." He seemed horrified at the mangled sight too.

Ikena couldn't stop the tears that began to flow. It was as if all her emotions had compiled into one big outcry. She was scared. Scared of the Sinturis. Scared of the Cloaks and scared of herself. What was happening to her? She had dreamt that the Cloaks were after her and they were. She had also dreamt that the Sinturi would attack Lovrin, and they did. It was as if she was there, but it was worse. It was as if *she* was the darkness. She latched onto Sedric, needing to hug him and wept into the grooves of his neck.

After a few minutes she stifled her tears. "Oh, I'm so sorry. I didn't want to risk hurting you again. I… I didn't know what else to do." She sniffed. "How did you find me?"

Sedric wrapped a protective arm around her and slowly his hand stroked the bridge of her back. "Well, I figured you'd head to the next village, so I hitched a carriage ride to Underust. The village was crawling with Cloaks and everybody was in a frenzy. It seems you left quite the mark."

Ikena snorted, her nose blocked from her crying, "I may or may not have levitated half the village in the air." Sedric's eyebrows raised with a dubious look. "Well, levitated half the merchants. But I did save a child's life."

"I overheard a group of people talking and they spoke of this divination and of how Lakeland was the place to go so that's where I headed. Then, the Sinturi came. I saw a horse and ran for it and there you were," he paused and twiddled with his fingers. "We really need to do something about this magic thing of yours." A soft smile overcame him.

"That's why I came here. There's a professor who might be able to help me. We just need to find… *that*!" Ikena noticed a symbol on the floor that looked oddly familiar and scrambled for the divination book in her wicker basket, flicking through the pages. "Sedric look!" The symbol matched the ones in the book, it resembled a tree and hanging from the tree appeared to be a monkey.

"Ikena, there's another one here." A few feet to the left was another, and then another after that, and another. Together, they traced the symbols to a back alley which had a row of doors lined up on the left, Ikena dragging Artax behind. The first door was covered in the tree symbols and, after tying Artax to a nearby pole, the two pushed their way inside.

Inside the room was the most beautiful garden Ikena had ever seen. Small trees sprouted at every corner, flowers bloomed, a water fountain trickled its soothing sound, and you could hear the faintest sound of birds nesting nearby. To the right, concealed by rugged vines, was a door and the faintest sound of clattering metal could be heard from behind it. Ikena felt the urge of curiosity sneak up on her and together they ventured closer, peeping through the small gap the door offered them.

Inside was an old man who was dressed in long grey robes. He had a bald head with a short, grey beard and was standing, eyes closed, as a Sinturi stood before him. One Sinturi became two, then three, then four. The man was completely surrounded. Ikena tried to push open the door but Sedric stopped her as he saw the magic boom from the old man's hands like lightning bolts. It struck the shadowed face of a Sinturi, causing the beast's mist to lesson into nothingness. Next, he conjured up a whirlwind of water blasting two Sinturis and sending them to the floor, before firing an array of lightening magic prancing around the room towards them in the shape of a wolf. It was nothing like Ikena had ever seen. She couldn't believe her eyes. There was one Sinturi left and the old man took a moment to compose himself. The Sinturi attacked, charging towards the man and the room became even darker than it already was, darkness taking over every last flicker of light. The man put his hands together and then pulled them away from each other, forming a glowing ball in between. He grunted as he flung his hands out wide, causing the ball of light to strike the final Sinturi. The room was left in complete darkness. It was hard not to gawk at the man as he coolly tapped away at a nearby device which flickered the lights on in the room.

"Don't you know that it's rude to stare?" he said with his back turned to the eavesdroppers. "Yes, I am talking to you. Watchers from behind the door." He moved his hand gracefully in the air and the door slid open leaving Ikena and Sedric to fumble to a heap on the floor. "You're the two that brought the Sinturis this way," he remarked, serenely.

"You saw?"

"I helped," the man said, "I happened to be in the forest at the time and drew them away from this village. What is it you want?" He glared, scratching his grey bristly beard.

Ikena ignored his question, "Seeing you fight those Sinturis off was amazing, how did they get in here?"

"They were holograms, my dear." The man touched a remote to his side, not wishing to explain further. Ikena was stunned at the technology she knew *he* created, where had he learnt to do that? Couldn't he make other appliances that could help in the war against the Sinturi? "I'll ask again, what is it you want?"

"Well... I need your help," Ikena began. "I have magic,

70

but I don't know how to use it. I have no control over it, and I've hurt those around me... those I care about. I know you can teach me." She lingered with her words. "I need you to teach me *without* raising alarm to the Cloaks."

"Out of the question." The man's expression didn't change, and he stared glumly. "Now, if you'll excuse me." With a flick of his hand, Ikena and Sedric were pushed back by an imaginary wind that took them out of the room, the door shut sharply ahead of them.

"What just happened?" Sedric was as baffled as Ikena was.

Ikena felt frustrated, she had come all this way and risked her life, risked ever seeing her family again for this man's help. She wasn't leaving until she got what she wanted.

"Now, you listen to me!" She banged on the door and it opened in front of her. "I haven't come all this way just to be turned down like a dog asking for too much food. I understand it's an inconvenience, but I need your help."

"Why should I help you?" Ikena knew there was something he'd want in return, but she didn't have anything to offer. Why should he help her?

"Because my life is in danger. Perhaps from the Sinturi, or maybe the Cloaks, but *definitely* from the unknown. I have magic and I don't know what to do with it. But what I do know is that if I don't learn to control it... I could kill anyone around me." She glanced at Sedric, touching the bruise on his head from the plank of wood and gave a weary smile. She had to protect those around her from herself.

"I understand," the man said, and her answer seemed to trigger something inside him.

71

Ikena wasn't sure why but his brows drew close together and a sombre look disguised his face.

"I will see what I can do to help, but in return you will do jobs for me each day, such as tending to my garden and carrying my groceries back from the market. Do we have an accord?"

Ikena and Sedric exchanged looks in agreement before nodding enthusiastically to the man who introduced himself as Cato. He shook their hands with thrust and Sedric winced at the pain jolting in his arm.

"Right, now that that's settled, do you know where the inn is?" Sedric asked in desperation, clutching his battered arm.

The man grumbled and moved closer to him, assessing the damage. It was badly sprained but thankfully not broken.

"I have a spare room you may stay in," he said. "Boy, come with me."

Sedric followed him, Ikena trailing behind, into a small room with a table and chairs. He gestured for them both to sit and shuffled through a door to the right before returning with a handful of leaves and some kind of oil. He then tended to Sedric's arm, dropping the oil onto the leaves, coating them, and then wrapping them around his arm. Sedric thanked him with a longing sigh. Cato escorted them to the spare room he had said they could stay in. It was an eccentric room which was small but well-made and had an actual bed and wardrobe, alongside a mirror opposite. There were also planks of wood that acted as shelves which were hammered into the wall and delicately perched on top were a few small plants and a silver photo frame, with a black and white photograph encased in it. The photo showed Cato, considerably younger than his

72

present self, and a beautiful, beaming young woman, who smiled at the camera.

It was considerably late and Ikena and Sedric felt their stomachs grumble at the mere thought of food but had to suppress the feeling. Not because they wanted to, but because the villagers from the market would have made away for the day and they'd have to wait till morning to purchase something to eat. They were relaxing, Ikena counting her coins, when Cato appeared by their door. "I hope the room satisfies you."

"Oh yes. It's wonderful. Thank you," said Ikena.

With the door open she smelt the glorious smell of food waft into the room and again heard her stomach rumble, so loud she assumed everyone else heard it to.

"I'm starving," Sedric wept aloud.

"I assumed you were, so I've prepared you a meal. Would you like to follow me?" Cato turned on his heels.

They passed through one room and came to another where three plates were filled with meat, potatoes, vegetables and gravy, all nicely placed on a cream tablecloth. It was glorious and more than Ikena had ever had on Winter's Day. Cato gestured them both to the table and took his seat. Sedric sat next to Ikena on one side of the table and Cato on the other, distancing himself a little more than the closeness between Ikena and Sedric. Before tucking into the meal Cato closed his eyes and began to whisper a few words. Ikena knew what he was doing, praying like her mother once had. It didn't seem like many prayed anymore, maybe they just lost hope after the Great War, but nonetheless she let Cato finish.

She noticed Sedric was already scoffing his way through

the meat piled on to his plate and gave him a kick to the leg underneath the table. He gave her a look of annoyance but immediately put down the knife and fork when Ikena had gestured to Cato. Once Cato had finished praying, he opened his eyes and made a forced smile at the two of them, before beginning his meal. Ikena took that as a sign that she could start and picked up her knife and fork, testing a small piece of the dry meat. It had an unusual taste to it, one that she had never tasted before, but even so she savoured it, especially with hot gravy made from succulent bones.

"Don't you like the food?" Cato caught Ikena in her puzzlement.

"Oh no, I love it. But um... what is it?" Oddly, she stuffed her mouth full of the meat to insist her point.

"It's duck, my dear," Cato said.

"It's delicious!" Sedric spoke with a muffled tone due to the fact that he had since stuffed three potatoes, a pile of meat and a few pieces of cabbage into his mouth. He was struggling to swallow and instead sat there with cheeks the size of a stuffed mouse. Ikena stifled a chuckle.

"You say you have magic, yet you don't want to join the Cloaks. Why is that?" Cato pondered aloud, not exactly talking to them, he was trying to work it out for himself.

"It's not that I don't want to join them. If I had a choice, then I might have considered it—"

"Don't you have a choice?"

"Well..." she thought. "No. Not really. The law states that, if you are a magical, you must contact the Cloak army immediately, where you're then forced to join them no matter what family you have or who you're leaving behind. They don't care. They want you as a pawn. As another body that the King can just throw into countless dangerous situations instead of doing it himself, without even knowing your name. I won't be that person." Cato didn't reject her statement, instead he made nodding approvals as she spoke, seeming to enjoy her distaste for the Cloaks.

"And what of the Sinturi?" he asked.

"What about them?" Ikena asked in return.

"How do you feel about them?"

Ikena didn't quite understand the question. You don't feel anything for the Sinturi but terror. It had suddenly occurred to her that she didn't know who she was dining with. He could be a dark magic fanatic who hadn't yet turned, Ikena wouldn't know and the questions he was asking, why was he so interested? Thoughts flooded back to the day her father was taken from her, as her scared child-like self watched his skin drain from his body, his face a blurry mess as he was consumed. Ikena didn't stay to see the aftermath but her nightmares showed her what became of humans after they had been consumed by a Sinturi. Ash and bone and not much else.

"A Sinturi killed my father right in front of me," she paused but felt anger consume her. "I want them dead."

Cato didn't press further. Instead, he changed the subject from Sinturi to magic. "And you say you have magic. How do you know?"

"I've done a few… tricks." She pondered the word. "I saved my brother when he fell from a tree, he would have died but I screamed and all of a sudden he was levitating above the ground." She paused and took another bite of potato and cabbage. "And… I also got angry and caused a plank of wood to fall down from the roof of an inn we were staying at. It hit Sedric, hence his bruised head." She hung her head in shame.

"I see." Cato spoke and admired her raven hair.

"And…" she continued. "I also lifted a heavy stall from the floor, which had toppled on to a small child." Sedric seemed shocked that she had done so much in the few days they were apart. "And… may have accidentally levitated *half* the village in Underust." *Well, I didn't exactly count. All I saw were half the merchants levitating after they tried to hold me so a Cloak could whisk me away to the palace. And I wasn't having that.*

Cato didn't ask any further questions. They ate the rest of their meal in silence before he excused himself from the table, taking his plate into a separate room before announcing that he was going to bed.

"I have a horse outside, is there a stable nearby?" Ikena asked, remembering that Artax was left tied to the pole outside.

"No stable, girl. If you want my advice, I'd let it run free." Cato said. "We will begin training tomorrow." He shuffled away.

Ikena longed to ask him more about his own past but decided that the time wasn't right and instead sat firmly in her chair and allowed her food to go down. She considered what Cato had said about Artax and, reluctantly, had to agree with him.

"Things will never be the same again," Sedric glumly

said, a morbid depression overcoming the atmosphere in the room.

Ikena didn't have the words to console him. After a short moment she excused herself from the table and left the room to see Artax outside. The darkness was apparent, yet he still bobbed his head up and down in excitement at seeing her.

"Hey, boy," she said, stroking his braided mane. "You've been a real help to me you have, but I'm afraid this is where we depart." She fed him some carrots she had snuck from her dinner plate. "In the morning, I'll try and find you a good home, surely someone in this village will want to buy you, but for now you'll have to stay out here for the night."

He tilted his head in response and flicked his tail before she checked that he was tied tightly to the pole and returned to Sedric who was washing up their dishes in the kitchen. The two of them returned to the guest room Cato had prepared for them and dumped their restless bodies on to the soft bed. It was the most comfortable bed Ikena had ever slept in, and seemed to devour her. Sedric moaned as his back cracked uncontrollably.

"This is nice." He was relieved.

"Let's get some sleep. Goodnight Sed." Ikena blew out the candle next to her and the room was left in darkness.

"Goodnight, Ikena."

Ikena's body slept peacefully but her mind was wide awake.

She was taken to the hollows of a cave where darkness stirred. She had heard rumours of where the Sinturi hid in

77

Riverdosk, in the Caves of Zeridan. From deep below the caves, she saw a Sinturi walk heartlessly into the room dragging something from behind him with a shadowy chain that slivered and hissed like a snapping snake, his other arm cupped over a metallic box. Upon closer inspection, his victim was a Cloak being constricted around the throat. "Dalmask," the Sinturi spoke and another Sinturi, draped in a similar hood that covered his face but with black jewels embedded on his robe, turned from the throne made of charred bones ahead of him. His throne. He was the Sinturi leader. "I have brought you a gift."

He took the box from his follower. "Is this what I think it is?" Dalmask spoke, his voice a whispering slither.

"Yes, master. And here's the Cloak we found with it." He whipped the chain he was holding, causing the Cloak to cower to the ground at the pull of the darkness around his neck.

Dalmask turned his attention to the Cloak and raised his arm towards him. In doing so, dark mist sprung from his hand and lifted the Cloak from the ground. He tried to struggle but it was no use, he was powerless to the dark magic the Sinturi possessed. Dalmask drew nearer to a mere few inches from his face. He sucked in and the being of the Cloak before him began to deteriorate. The leader was consuming him for power. The Cloak screamed in pain, wincing with every last breath he could take before becoming nothing but a pile of dust on the ground. A light pulsed through the Sinturi's veins, the light travelling from mouth to neck to stomach and around him amidst a chorus of cheers and applause. It was the magical core of the Cloak being absorbed. He ravished in his abundance of new power, then once again cowered over the box.

"The end is near!" he roared. "We will be victorious!"

Another holler erupted from the darkness around him and, back in her bed with her white eyes wide open, Ikena felt a deep sense of power root inside her. A kind that made her feel hungry for more. She didn't feel afraid. Only evil.

SIX

A ringing in Ikena's ears woke her up in the early hours
of the morning. She was sweating profusely, and her
breath snagged like it usually did after a nightmare. Sedric
jumped up but, after realising it was Cato, he grumbled loudly
and stuffed his pillow over his head. Cato stood in the
doorway, dressed in a similar grey robe and silky trousers as
the day before, with a gong in hand which he had banged
several times, he was staring at Ikena intently.

"What's wrong, girl?" he asked her.

Ikena had the same feeling when she woke up in the
stables in Underust. She felt powerful, but not the same way
she felt when her magic crept up on her, this was different.
This was *dangerous*.

"Nothing," she managed, barely.

With a concerned look, Cato crossed the room, "Get up
and meet me in the training room in five minutes."

Ikena took a few seconds to relax, her hands shook, and
she felt somewhat disconnected from herself.

She suppressed the feeling and prodded Sedric's back, "That means you too."

Sedric groaned and sat up, inspecting his arm which no longer looked as bruised and battered as it was. "Woah! My arm feels *so* much better." It was as if it were healed by magic. They met Cato in the training room, the room he was in when they first met him. Sedric had come prepared with his wooden spear, although he didn't expect to use it.

"Lesson number one," Cato began. "There is a certain beauty with controlling one's power and from what you have told me it seems your power is that of a Descendant."

A Descendant. When Ikena was a child she had begged her father to tell her everything he ever knew about the Cloaks, and one thing he spoke of were the Descendants. They served as the most powerful of the Cloak army and could control the objects around them, if they wanted to move something with their power they could, say they wanted to crack the earth in half, they could. They held an unspeakable force so powerful that without them the war would have never been won, they served as Generals and Commanders and reported directly to the King himself.

The King of Nevera was a man who was spoken about often, but no person outside of the palace had ever seen him. He was rumoured to be a delicate, handsome man who had learned to control his power when he was an infant. He not only became King of Nevera, commanding the Cloak armies and protecting the Kingdom, but also earned the title of Slayer – what they call people with an unnatural power. A Slayer's magic isn't limited to only one specific talent, instead they can do multiple things. The King was the only known Slayer in the Kingdom, but after seeing Cato use his power yesterday, Ikena wondered if he could be one too.

"As a Descendant you can control objects." Cato filled a cup of water and balanced it on a shelf. "Now, I want you to focus on moving this cup of water to the pedestal over there, without spilling a single drop." He stared at Ikena, expecting her to begin but she didn't know how. Instead, she was foolishly staring intently at the cup. When she did magic before, she had gotten angry or scared, she didn't know how to control it. "Well, I can see you're going to need a little more persuasion." Cato picked up a wooden broom that was balanced against the wall in the corner and moved towards Sedric. With a quick flash, he was in front of him, he struck him in the back of the knees and Sedric crashed to the ground with a *thud*.

Sedric was too gobsmacked to say anything. He jumped to his feet and held the spear out towards Cato daringly. Ikena watched as they fought, unable to do anything to help. Cato came on strong and Sedric had barely any time to think before being struck again, this time behind the neck. He winced in agony. Sedric's skin immediately bared bruises that grew to the surface instantly.

"Stop it!" Ikena urged, but Cato didn't seem to listen. No matter how many times she pleaded he didn't once falter, hitting Sedric again and again with the broom, to the knees, the back, the chest. Sedric cried in agony, pleading for the man to stop, but he wouldn't. He grappled with his spear and took a shot at him, but Cato dodged the attack and wacked him to the floor. Ikena tried to drown out his pleas but with every hit of the broom she felt something rise up inside her.

She could feel it in her feet, her stomach and in her head, before it became a pulse that circulated her body, beating as loud as her heartbeat was.

"I said stop it!" she yelled and suddenly the ground began to shake.

A crack appeared in the middle of the floor and began to spread from corner to corner, splitting the room in half. A bookshelf to the left toppled over under the force, along with the cabinet that the water was resting on and cup of water itself. Cato dropped the broom and Sedric stood from where he was crouched, both staring intently at Ikena. Once Cato had stopped hurting him, Ikena relaxed and felt the power inside her flurry away like a bird, she felt it leave her body and she immediately felt pulled to the floor, breathless. Cato stared at the cracked tiled ground and then his eyes landed fixedly on Ikena. Without saying a word, he outstretched his hands and clapped them together which caused the ground to shake and the crack to slowly disappear, he was repairing the damage Ikena had inflicted. With a flick of his hands the scattered books, bookshelf and cabinet levitated into their rightful position.

"You remember that feeling of the power inside you?" Cato asked.

"Yes." Ikena breathed. A quick glance at Sedric told her that he was unhurt, but a little bruised.

He began pouring the cup of water again, placing it on the cabinet once more. "Summon that power inside you on command. You now know what it feels like. So, you must dig deep, don't think from your head but from your heart. Outstretch your hands if it helps and transport the cup to the pedestal." Cato helped Sedric find his feet and placed his hand over the bruises he had caused. After a second they were gone.

"I'm not sure if I like that." Sedric nervously rubbed the back of his neck and Cato gestured him back to his seat.

Ikena stood tall with her shoulders back and outstretched her left arm, palm upwards in a 'stop' motion, at the cup of water. She closed her eyes. *I can do this.* She thought. *I have to do this.* And then opened her eyes when she realised, she was thinking from her head and not her heart as she was just instructed not to do.

She instead tried a different approach and imagined the power rising up from her toes, and once she felt that pang of reassurance that it was really there, she moved it with all her might up to the tops of her legs, and then her stomach, over her heart and neck before ending at the top of her head, her body circulating the power once more. Now all she had to do was focus. She stared at the cup and saw it sway slightly before sharply raising her hand. At first, it was too forceful, and a little water spilt from the top of the cup as it levitated abruptly but that didn't falter her, and she kept going. She focussed on the power inside her and began to turn and as she turned the cup moved with her. The pedestal was on the other side of the room and slowly, she was levitating the cup towards it. She felt the power lessening and struggled to keep it at bay, with a jolt she placed the cup on top of the pedestal, and it toppled over on its side under her clumsy force, but she had done it. She relaxed and the power inside her flurried away. Sedric beamed with a smile from ear to ear, he couldn't believe his eyes, Cato gave approving nods.

"It was a little messy," he said. "But nothing we can't fix."

Ikena tried again and again until she could move the cup perfectly, and then Cato tasked her with moving other things, from placing fallen books into the bookshelf correctly and in alphabetical order, to using her power to mop the floors afterwards. It seemed like a fine day's work and in the evening, Ikena remembered that she had to take Artax to the village centre. Cato handed her an apple to give to him, which she gracefully took, and she walked outside into the fresh air and peered at the beautiful sunset. Artax tilted his head towards her and eyed the apple, walking towards her like he was about to smother her against the wall if she didn't give it to him then and there.

"Oh, here you go greedy guts."

After Artax finished his apple, Ikena felt a sudden dread as she freed his reins from the pole. She hadn't known Artax for awfully long, but there was something about him that she felt the need to care for. Deep down, she knew that what she was doing was the right thing to do, and with that thought in her mind she walked him to the corner of the back alley.

"Roll up, roll up. I've got one fine stallion who needs a good home," she called to the few people stood around.

Artax moved his head up and down, as if making a bit of a show out of it and Ikena laughed, she couldn't help it. It was like Artax knew what he was doing, and she half expected him to do some odd form of a smile. A few villagers passed when a skinny looking man and a little girl, Ikena sussed to be his daughter, came up to the horse.

"Daddy look!" she cried, jumping up and down in her spot. "Excuse me miss? May I stroke her?" she asked, twiddling her fingers in her hands.

"Of course, you may! Shall we get daddy to lift you up?" Ikena thought to play along and the man behind her lifted her on his shoulders and made his way over to the side of the horse. The little girl stretched her small arms out and patted Artax on the side.

"She sure is a beauty," the man muttered.

"It's a he," Ikena replied. "But yes, he sure is mighty fine. Got me out of a right pickle he did. And he's still got the speed now, even for an old boy."

The little girl began to cry and begged her father for the horse. "I want him," she cried, snot trickling from her dainty nose.

"Now, now sweetheart, we only came over for a look," the man said but his daughter persisted.

"P… P… Please!" she blubbered.

Ikena saw the way the man looked at the horse, he had wanted it but from the state of his clothes and his bony structure, it seemed he wouldn't be able to pay for it.

"I'm sorry," he apologised to Ikena, "We just came to look," he began to walk off, the little girl pulling at his hat but Ikena had sensed he had a good heart. If she wanted Artax to go to anyone, it would be them.

"Wait," she called. "Please." The man and daughter came back and he had a pestered look upon his face, probably thinking she was going to barter a lower price for him to take it, "I can see she really loves the horse and he's useful. He can pull carts and get you to where you need to go without paying for transport or walking. He's also a loyal friend." The man tried to intervene but Ikena held up her hand and stopped him. "If you want the horse, I'd be happy to give him to you. As long as he's going to a good home."

The little girl gasped and immediately began to shout excitedly whereas the father looked more curiously at Ikena, wondering whether he could look after a horse or not. Ikena thought she might have to beg him to take it, but after a short moment, a grateful smile swept across his face and he agreed.

"We'll take care of him as best we can, I promise," the little girl said, and she kissed her father on the cheek, "Thank you daddy!" Ikena handed the reins over to the man, thanked him and then made her way back to Cato's place.

They ate dinner a little awkwardly but were more comfortable in each other's presence. Cato had prepared another truly unforgettable dinner of mashed potato and pork with yesterday's leftover cabbage. Ikena ate every mouthful, including slurping down several glasses of water.

The next morning, she was woken again by Cato and his gong and both her and Sedric made their way over to the training room. Ikena practised moving items around the room for the morning but, come midday, she was ready to target her first holographic Sinturi.

Cato begun his lesson. "The only way you can kill a Sinturi is by striking it with magic. I will show you an example." He tapped away on his remote and one holographic Sinturi stood, draped in their usual long black capes and hood that hid their faceless faces. The room suddenly went dark and the only thing Ikena could focus on was the Sinturi gawking at her. Cato continued, "Every magical person can do something special and unique to them which we call their talent, you can manipulate physical things around you, some can heal others or summon specific elements, but *all* project physical magic in front of them. Imagine that you are doing that, give your magic a form." He demonstrated by building a square-form of magic in front of him, clasped between his hands, it was a bright yellow colour. He then made it form into a ball, moving his hands in such a way before he flung it at the Sinturi who, when hit, disappeared into nothingness. Cato instructed Ikena to give it a try. She found controlling her magic easier but struggled at first to make it into a physical thing. At first it started with a few golden flashes before she managed to form a small golden ball in her hands, which had strings of magic webbing in between, like a ball of glowing string. Cato tapped away at his remote and another holographic Sinturi stood before her. With all her might she released the magic, sending the small ball towards the Sinturi who, like the other one, disappeared when struck.

"That's good. I think we're done for the day." Ikena felt breathless, she hadn't worked this hard at anything ever. "Sedric. You're up," Cato said.

Sedric looked as baffled as Ikena. "What do you mean?" he asked with a nervous smile. Cato tapped a button on his remote and the left wall began to move. A panel in the wall split in two like sliding doors and revealed beautiful steel weapons before them. Not just any weapons, these were from the Cloak army. "Where did you get these?" Sedric questioned as his eyes glided over. They fixated on a silver-headed trident that had a long black and silver shaft. The intricate detail in the delicate handle at the end of the pole, which depicted a bear's head with sharp teeth on show, was bewitching.

"You like that one, don't you? I figured as much." Cato took it down from where it lay gloriously and handed it to Sedric.

The same question plagued Ikena's mind. Who was this man? He was a magical and all of a sudden had an array of Cloak army weapons, Ikena figured he was a Cloak, or used to be, although she laughed at the thought because, as she already knew, no one ever left the Cloak army. He could have stolen them, which seemed most likely, but there were still questions that needed to be answered. She thought of the woman in the photograph on the shelf in their room. Where was she? *Who* was she?

Ikena became distracted from her thoughts as the trident that Cato held began to glow a spectacular blue, so blue it was the colour of a dolphin in an oil-stained sea. "This trident has been charged with power, so although you're not a magical, if it came down to it, you'd be able to defeat a Sinturi." Cato ushered Ikena over and showed her how to charge the trident for Sedric. It involved placing your hand on the shaft of the trident and imagining that you're transferring magic from your body to the weapon. Ikena had to practise a few times but she eventually got the hang of it and found it mystifying how her golden magic suddenly turned blue at the touch of the trident but still glowed its fiery glow. Sedric bubbled where he stood, unable to contain his creeping excitement.

"Now, you can use this trident as you would a spear, but also, with enough force, you can use the magic. For example." Cato jabbed the trident out fast and with the jab came three small blue balls of magic that flew from each point of the trident and smacked into the wall. A gobsmacked Sedric let out a, "Woah!" Cato let Sedric try and he was a natural. The trident was similar to the spear, so he already knew how to hold it and thrust it forward at prey.

After what felt like an hour of watching, Ikena excused herself and left for the market. She had no interest in buying something, but brought the coin nonetheless, and instead felt a desperate need for fresh air. She sipped on the goats' milk her mother had packed as she walked, allowing the cold air to hurry past her face. It was getting late, but there were still a few market stalls out. She had never properly explored the village when they had first arrived but noticed the water that ran through the most part of the village, a long tumbling river to her right that seemed to break off into smaller streams that ran out of the village.

As she walked, Ikena's thoughts were filled with the nightmare she had the other night. She worried that her dreams weren't dreams at all, that instead real scenarios were happening in those moments and if she was correct in assuming that she could tell the future, it meant that the Sinturi had retrieved a box of some kind that could potentially help them destroy the very world she needed. Her family wouldn't be able to survive it and it made her wonder whether she should join the Cloaks after all. She was learning how to control her magic and she didn't want to stand in the way of the Cloaks winning the war, maybe her dreams were valuable and could provide some use? *They meant something.*

As much as she still didn't trust Cato, she had to admit

that he was growing on her. He was an old man, who grumbled most of the time and gave her orders, as well as frequently yelling at her to try harder, but it was working. She was getting a hold on her magical abilities. A thought crossed her mind that, even though she didn't have much to offer him, she could at least make him a nice meal and headed over to the fishmonger who was behind a chilled market stall with fish on display that curled delicately around ice. There were also cooked fish on the side and Ikena brought three large pieces of cooked cod, at a hefty price, she might add. She could add potatoes and corn if Cato had any. After purchasing she made her way back to Cato's place, making sure she was careful about who saw her before quietly slipping down the alleyway and into his humble abode.

Clang. Cling. CLANK. There were loud noises coming from the training room, and grunts along with them. Ikena ran towards the room, regretting leaving Sedric on his own but, to her surprise, he was holding up against Cato who had a long sword in his hand that glowed a bright yellow, the colour of his own magic. Cato lunged at Sedric who swept to his left, narrowly avoiding the sharp blade. Then, Sedric made his move, trident in hand, swinging for Cato who blocked the impact with his weapon. Sedric pushed back, towering over the old man but Cato kicked Sedric's calf and sent him tumbling to the ground, yet he didn't falter. Sedric jumped up immediately and blocked Cato's next move, he grunted in anger and jabbed his trident out forcefully, first to the left, then to the right, sending magic sparks flying towards Cato who used his sword to slash away at them. It was a distraction. Sedric lunged on the attack, but instead of using his trident, he kicked Cato's arm, sending his sword flying high into the air. It smacked the ground hard. There was a tense stand-off and Ikena wasn't quite sure what she had walked into, but then they started to laugh. Sedric was grinning from ear to ear and Cato was genuinely impressed at Sedric's talents. He patted his prodigy on the back, approvingly.

Cato caught Ikena gawking. "He's a fine one he is. I can see why you like him so much." Her face boiled red. Annoyingly, Sedric gave her a flirtatious wink, causing her cheeks to deepen to what could only be described as aubergine. *He can't help himself.*

"What's that smell?" Sedric asked, nose scrunched as he carefully placed the trident back on its stand on the wall.

"Well, I thought I'd cook tonight. If that's okay?" she asked Cato, but it was Sedric who replied.

"You mean we have to suffer from food poisoning?" he teased, winking at her again but pushing his luck. Ikena stuck her tongue out towards him and Sedric gave a chuckle. She missed being silly with him and making him laugh the way she did. One time, when they were younger, Sedric made a joke about the way Lucy Rumple, a busty girl who Ikena went to school with, kissed, and Ikena was so startled that she had clumsily fallen off the side of a rock, she was so angry that she didn't even realise that the rock she had plumped herself on wasn't stable. The two of them were in a fit of laughter and Sedric pulled her close and whispered, "But she's nothing on you."

Cato nodded his approval, exclaiming that he needed to rest his back because Sedric had really done a number on him. Sedric helped Ikena to the kitchen where she unloaded the large pieces of fish on to three separate plates before finding some sweetcorn and boiling it on the stove in front of her. She didn't think Cato would mind if she took control of the kitchen, although she had noticed that he was low on stock, especially potatoes, so stuck to fish and sweetcorn for their evening meal.

"Ikena, this must have cost a fortune," observed Sedric.

He was strangely close and Ikena couldn't help but feel flustered. "They weren't cheap but it's worth it. He's allowing us to stay for free and eat his food. I mean it's the least we can do," she said trying to distract herself.

Sedric crossed towards her and took her hand in his, lightly rubbing the creases of skin that bridged over her knuckles. He wanted to say something, Ikena sensed it. Something was on his mind.

"Ikena, I—"

Shut it down quickly, she thought. "Could you please set the table?" She thrust a few plates in his arms. With a saddened look, Sedric walked away. Ikena had loved Sedric from the moment she met him, but she couldn't protect him. Wherever she went, darkness followed. If she was to confirm what romance she had for him, would he confirm his back? Would he be safe? She pushed those monstrous thoughts away, they would never come to be.

On each plate she served a healthy serving of sweetcorn. Cato had a handful of lemons in a patterned bowl on a shelf in front of her and she thought he wouldn't mind if she used one, so she cut it in to small wedge-sized pieces and placed them delicately over the fish with a sprig of coriander. She had prepared a sauce to go with the fish which was made of mayonnaise, pickle, lemon juice and herbs and it had a refreshing taste to it. She found a small jug which she poured the sauce into before juggling the plates and jug in her arms and taking it to the table where Cato and Sedric were expectantly waiting. Cato seemed tired but she could sense his gratitude at having someone else cook for him.

"This is really lovely, thank you," he remarked and eyed up the sauce she had prepared. "What's that?" Ikena told him the recipe and asked him to taste a small amount, it was something her mother had rooted into her as a kid, that food should not be wasted and you must always be willing to try something new, even if you're sure you don't like it you might be surprised.

Cato placed half a spoonful on to the side of his plate and dipped a small piece of cod into it before gently placing it on his tongue, sceptical. It was almost amusing to see the suspicious look he gave, as if Ikena had created a sauce of poison. His eyes went wide with joy and he reached for the jug, pouring a large helping of the sauce over his fish, smothering it. Sedric did the same and Ikena felt satisfied that she had cooked a scrumptious meal. After finishing, the group disbanded and headed to bed for an early night.

Ikena laid beside Sedric and they stayed up for hours talking about the day's events and reminiscing about when they were children together. When sleeping, she couldn't help but toss and turn in the night as a chill overcame her. Darkness scurried her mind and flash backs of her father's death replayed over and over again, unsettling as it was. She awoke in the early hours panting. Sedric laid next to her asleep. Anger came over Ikena. Fighting holographic Sinturis was great practice, but it wasn't like fighting the real thing. If she faltered, she would be unhurt but if she faltered when battling a real Sinturi she wouldn't live to tell the tale. She relaxed back under the covers and snuggled up to Sedric who held her close, despite still in his sleep. It was decided, in a few days' time, she'd ask Cato if they could venture outside of Lakeland. Not too far, but maybe she'd be able to find a Sinturi lurking in the forest outside of the village. With that thought, she slept and in the morning was woken by the usual sound of Cato's obnoxiously loud gong.

"Wake up! Wake up!" Cato proudly shouted.

"Does he really have to do that?" Sedric grumbled with a ringing in his ears. "*Every* morning."

"Well, at least we're properly awake." Ikena snorted. They plodded to the practice room and trained like they usually did for the remainder of the week.

Cato gave Ikena long drills which practised her magic and Descendant talent powers. She found it easier to call her magic to come to light and to stay hidden. At first it was slow, and she'd take minutes to let the magic flow through her body, but by the end of the week she could do it in seconds. She could also mould her magic into objects such as knives, torches, a hairbrush etc, but she found that whenever someone other than her touched the object it would shock them lightly, Sedric found that out the hard way.

"Only you can possess it's power. It calls to you, and you only." Cato explained.

Ikena found herself trusting Cato increasingly each day, even if she was also tasked with tending to his indoor garden and feeding the birds that nested there. She also went into the market to purchase his groceries which consisted of heavy lumps of bread, eggs, orange juice, vegetables, a sack of potatoes and an assortment of meat. Ikena often wondered how Cato had money readily available to him, so that he could purchase the food he had but thought it rude to ask.

Ikena could feel her muscles grow stronger each day and the same could be said for Sedric, whose muscles were now chiselled and cut in at the edges. Cato hadn't given her any indication that he was working with the Cloaks and it had been an entire week. She decided that, if he were a dark magic fanatic or undercover Cloak, something would have happened by now, but she felt safe. For now.

SEVEN

I kena woke in the early hours of the morning before Cato had even sounded the gong, she woke Sedric who found it easier to rise in the early hours and grabbed his trident which he kept by the side of the bed, and they made their way to the training room. Ikena had noticed that both she, and Sedric, had begun to smell after sleeping in the same clothes and training in them too. She made a note to ask Cato if he had spare garments that they could at least wear whilst she hand-washed their clothing. After the first hour of practising, she voiced her thoughts about challenging a real Sinturi.

"It's swell being able to practise with the holographic technology, but at the same time it's not real. I don't feel like my life is threatened in any way and I need to know how I'll react in that situation."

"It's too dangerous," Cato huffed, not liking her request. "It's not wise to go looking for trouble."

"I'm not looking!" Ikena protested, "I merely want to venture into the forest that lies outside of Lakeland and just... walk. If there's something there then great, I can defeat it, but if not, then at least it'll provide a nice change of scenery."

It was risky and Ikena knew it but it's nothing she hadn't already thought through. They would all go together, and they would have Cato with them. Cato stood tall with his fingers tracing the outline of his beard.

"Fine," he barked, but he seemed stressed. "But we will go at night. There's less of a chance to be seen. For now, let us continue with the lesson."

Ikena readied herself and practised levitating items around the room, making a tea for Cato without spilling a single drop and lifting heavier objects that required more focus, such as cabinets and statues. Ikena was excited for the evening and couldn't wait to explore the forest. Not only did she want to find a Sinturi, but she also wanted to practise using her talent on the elements outside. As Cato explained, Descendants can manipulate the objects around them, so she wanted to practise on something other than cabinets, statues, and tea-making. She wanted to levitate a tree, or a house or practise creating fountains with the lake around them in a secluded place and test how far her power could go. Cato was impressed with Ikena's progress; she was a natural at it. Once she understood how to summon her magic on and off the rest fell into place. Ikena wondered loudly why the Sinturi clearly hadn't entered the village after her and Sedric had first arrived and Cato was the one to answer her.

"I summoned a forcefield to protect Lakeland. No Sinturi or dark magic can penetrate it." That explained it. Ikena thought about whether she should ask Cato what she really wanted to know, who exactly he was. She had assumed he was a Descendant like her, but she had never heard of an ordinary Descendant summoning a forcefield around an entire city before, only the King could do it. He also conjured water from thin air, which only Elementals can do and healed Sedric, a Healers trait. The title, Slayer, danced around in her mind but to confirm that he was a Slayer was a challenge. Only the King was a Slayer. He also sits on his throne through blood, and the only thing stronger than a royal through blood, is a royal through power and if Cato was a Slayer, it meant that he was the King's equal.

"Cato... what exactly are you?" she questioned.

Cato paused for a short second, but it was enough to tell Ikena that he wasn't going to answer the question. "A disappearing ghost." He chuckled, avoiding the question as she had suspected.

They continued practising throughout the day before it was Sedric's turn to train with Cato, Ikena charged his trident, infusing it with her magic and then sat in the corner watching them fight eagerly. Sedric practised with his trident, sending sparks of magic towards the few holographic Sinturis Cato had created. He was also being taught about footing, and Ikena found herself correcting him silently in her head when he made the wrong move. As she sat there watching, her mother's face crept into her thoughts and suddenly she felt sick. Sick with guilt and sick with shame. What if they were starving? What if her family were ill? What if Sedric's grandma was sick? How would they ever know? The questions didn't stop, and they had no answers. It had been over a week since Ikena saw them, and for a family who had lost their hunter, a week is all it would take to send them into starvation.

Pull yourself together, Ikena. She was sure that hadn't happened. Mother would take them out to the forest in the morning to check the traps, and Asher and Aliza would know what to do. They had never killed the animals themselves but now was the time to learn and they would, they understood how important food was in Endfell.

Ikena sauntered to her room and found the royal-like book she had stashed in her wicker basket. Her fingers trembled as she carefully flicked through the thin paper pages and read the familiar rhyme.

For too long the Kingdom of Nevera has been plagued
A darkness stirs and threatens to display
But in a small village consumed by forests there will be
A raven-haired woman who at first will flee
To a lake village where an ancient professor waits
He'll teach her to harness her power and create
A world in which the darkness is no more
She is the key to winning the war

A while later Sedric joined her and asked if she was going to come to dinner but she declined. She couldn't eat when she felt like this, let alone do anything but lay in bed. As the brightness from outside grew considerably darker she was ushered back into the training room by Sedric who informed her that Cato was ready to take them out. He was dressed in different clothing, it looked similar to the Cloak armour, but there was something about it that looked considerably more regal. Delicately laid out in front of him were two sets of armour. One set for Sedric and one set for Ikena.

"This…" Cato said placing a delicate hand over Ikena's armour, "… was my daughters. I don't think she'd mind you trying it on for size." There was a certain glisten to his eyes that told her that his daughter was someone he hadn't seen in a long time and that, by him allowing her to wear it, he was giving up a piece of her to Ikena. She promised to wear it with respect and care and slipped on the burgundy, full body under suit, which was of a stretchy material but looked tough to pierce. On top of that, she slipped on a silver breastplate with golden edges and a burgundy cape that was pinned to the right shoulder and thigh-high silver steel boots.

She caught her reflection in a nearby reflective flower vase and stared. She wore clothes that were not hers to wear. The Cloak armour was so out of place on her body. She looked every bit the soldier, and she hated it. She was not under the command of the King who refused to help poor villages like her own, and yet he took from them whenever he saw it fitting. Sedric's uniform fit him like a glove. He looked undeniably handsome and was wearing a similar-looking silver male breastplate with a black under suit, silver arm cuffs to go on his forearms and a matching pair to go on his thighs with knee-high steel boots. He carried his trident boastfully.

"Are you staring at me?" he said, noticing the quietness of Ikena behind him. "With those heart-filled eyes."

"Of course," she said sarcastically, but her cheeks flushed.

"We look like quite the soldiers, don't we?" Sedric smiled and laughed at Ikena's unimpressed grumble. He may be experiencing   something   tremendous,   but   she   was experiencing the very opposite. The sooner she could get out of Cloak uniform, the better.

The trio gathered in the training room. "Cato," Ikena began, "What does the tree and monkey symbol represent?" she wondered, it was something that was playing on her mind for quite some time.

Cato smiled, "A monkey is nothing without the trees." It didn't seem to explain much, but Ikena thought not to press. They left Cato's, walking to the drawbridge that became an opening to the village. At this time of night, it had been hoisted up, but Cato used his magic to lower it so they could get across. With a swift raise of his right hand, Cato caused the drawbridge to rise once more. They then ventured into the deep forest around them that was overgrown with shrubs, weeds and tall trees stood high above them. The wind was strong and shook the trees which clanged and banged against one another as if they were dancing to the beat of a drum. It was difficult to see and both Cato and Ikena made a form of light using their magic and holding the physical power as if it were a candle. They walked north, climbing through the shrubs until Ikena came to a particularly tall tree in the middle of the forest.

"I want to practise levitating this tree," Ikena announced.

"That would use an abundance of energy, Ikena," Cato intervened but he knew he couldn't stop her.

"If it gets too much I'll stop. I just want to try."

The men stood around her as she focussed, allowing the magic to consume her from her toes to her fingertips before focussing solely on the tree. She outstretched both her hands, palms facing the tree, before moving her arms up simultaneously. She groaned as she felt the magic inside her pull and focussed even harder. Slowly, the tree began to shake. *Come on.* She moved her hands higher with force and suddenly the roots snapped as the tree became loose from the ground and just like that Ikena was levitating a tree. She used as much focus as she could, straining to levitate it higher and higher until she was happy with the distance from ground to tree before slowly releasing the force of the magic and bringing it back down to the ground with a *thump*. Once firmly rooted to the spot, Ikena breathed in deeply. Every part of her body was weak, her arms, her mind and she was overcome with a headache. She sat on the ground catching her breath as Sedric rushed over to her, rubbing the bridge of her back soothingly, comforting her.

Ikena had just recovered when she heard a quiet growl from somewhere behind her. Sedric and Cato had heard it too. Ikena scrambled to her feet, hands out at the ready. Darkness crept towards the spaces where the moonlight hit, and the air became chilled. Ikena's breath was condensed in the air, she knew what that meant. The bushes slowly shook, and the growling became louder and louder. Sedric held his trident out daringly and Cato was staring intently at the bushes, the three of them slowly backing away. From the visible part of the bush, a glaring red eye could be seen, then sharp teeth and then mist that intertwined between the thing and its body. It came into the opening. Ikena's eyes widened.

"What *is* that thing?" Sedric yelled, shocked as much as she was. Before them stood an animal of sorts that had four bulky legs like a bear. Its rib cage could be seen with its black, charred bones. It had a long tail with black spikes that glistened in the light of Ikena's magic and protruding from its boxy snout were two curved tusks. It had small horns jutting from its head and large ears that flopped down to its mouth. *You've got to be kidding me*. Ikena thought. It breathed heavily. Saliva dripped from its mouth. In the candlelight, Ikena realised that it wasn't saliva, it was blood. Thick, sticky crimson from a fresh kill. It was a Sinturi.

"It's a *Berinturi*." Cato said, "A beast formed by the Sinturi. I knew they were experimenting and there were rumours but… it can't be." Cato seemed shocked and for the first time, he looked scared. "You better have been right about this." Cato growled as the beast came charging towards them.

Cato held back and it was Sedric who made the first move, jabbing his trident out towards the creature so that it shot sparks of magic at it. The *Berinturi* was hit, and it staggered around in the dirt, but it wasn't over yet, it regained its composure and Sedric had only made it angrier. It charged once more towards the trio and jabbed its long tail over the top of its body, sending retractable spikes towards the group.

"Get down!" Cato roared as the trio fell to the floor. The beast was still charging towards them and Ikena focussed. She had wanted this, so it was her who had to defeat it.

"Ikena, anytime today please," Sedric urged, causing her to lose focus as the beast crossed the path towards them.

She tried again, building the magic up through her body.

"Ikena, he's really close now," Sedric intervened again, she didn't let his remark allow her to lose focus. The magic had almost consumed her.

"Ikena... Ikena!" Sedric yelled, trident at the ready.

The *Berinturi* was a mere few metres away when she sprang into action, she formed small balls of magic and juggled them in the palms of her hands before shooting them out of each palm like lasers at the beast. Then, she used her Descendant abilities to send a tree toppling on to it, trapping it in its tracks before sending a final ray of magic scurrying its way. The beast roared in pain, a long, piercing growl that lasted until the darkness slowly started to disappear and the animal had perished in sight. *That was close.* A little too close. Ikena felt somewhat disappointed in herself. She had summoned her magic, but she wasn't quick enough.

Sedric gave out a loud, "Phew!" and began hysterically laughing at his near-death experience, but his laughs slowly cowered when the darkness didn't disappear and a Sinturi glared at the three of them, moving out from behind the homely shadows of the shrubs. There was a rustling from behind the group and another Sinturi came out of the shrubs, and then another to their left. The three of them backed into each other. A Sinturi for each of them.

The wind whistled around them and it got colder with every step the Sinturis dared. Ikena didn't know what to think but her breath was heavy, ever so heavy. The Sinturis bore their hoods and flared closer. One gave a chuckle. Not just any kind of chuckle, but a frightening, callous, horrific cackle. Ikena shut her eyes and tried to think of the good she had. She remembered her mother's face, little Asher's laugh, and little Aliza's witty words. She thought of her friendship with Sedric, on her birthday he'd always find the most colourful flower he could find and tie them together with string to create a bouquet. She remembered of how he whispered to her sweet whispers, of how she would always be safe with him. Unknowingly, she was casting her magic at the same time. She felt it rise up inside her, against the darkness that was diminished. She opened her eyes at the daring Sinturi.

"Ikena," the Sinturi whispered with a low, hoarse tone. Ikena drew in a sharp breath. She had never heard a Sinturi speak before, but his breath was heavy like a dog, his skeletal fingers clicked together and made the most irritable of noises. That wasn't what scared her. What scared her was that the Sinturi knew of her name. Ikena did not respond, instead she created darts of magic in her hands and threw them at the Sinturi who dodged them as if it was expected. The Sinturi cast his own fog of darkness and roared as he flung his hands out, sending the fog towering over Ikena. She created a shield made of her magic just in time and knelt on the brown leaf-ridden ground as the darkness tried, and failed, to penetrate it. After it fizzled out, Ikena stood. This time, she shot beams of golden magic out of her palms that danced in the air and attacked the form before her. The being screamed in pain, a piercing scream that pierced Ikena's ears. Before her, the Sinturi began to disintegrate piece by piece. Parts of bone lifted into the evening's air, the dark mist around it slowly becoming less and less. In a flash, it was gone.

She breathed heavily. A quick glance over her left shoulder told her that Cato had defeated his Sinturi. Now all eyes were on Sedric, who was still in the midst of a battle. He dodged left, then right, and jabbed his trident out towards the Sinturi but it wasn't enough. Ikena saw the glimmer of something in the moonlight, something that had reflected in the Sinturi's bone-fingers. Just as she had clocked it, it was too late. The Sinturi plunged a blade made of dark magic in to Sedric's side with one wrong turn.

"No!" Ikena yelled as Sedric moaned, grasping at his side with his right-hand, tumbling to the floor.

Ikena summoned her magic and was ready to blast the Sinturi away from existence when, with the very last of his might, Sedric lunged his trident into the being of darkness, beaming blue light through its body until there was nothing left. Sedric sunk to the floor behind him, crying and clutching at his side. Ikena had never seen him cry before. There didn't appear to be any blood, but something was terribly wrong.

"Help me get him up!" Ikena yelled to Cato.

He grabbed one arm of Sedric's and Ikena grabbed the other, lifting him from the ground and hanging his arms over their shoulders. They swiftly made their way back to the village, dragging him as fast as they could. As they neared closer Cato held out one hand towards the drawbridge which fell to welcome them, and they hurried across it. He didn't bother putting it back up. They made their way back to Cato's place and burst inside, taking Sedric through the garden to the dining room where he was carefully lowered on to the table, flat on his back. He was crying hard tears, his face wet as he clutched his side and a shiver had taken control of him. He focussed solely on Ikena's eyes and seemed to be calling her name.

"It's okay. You're okay." Ikena tried to soothe him but it was no use.

"Get his armour off!" ordered Cato, already lifting

Sedric's breastplate over his head.

Ikena unzipped his black suit underneath, lifting his back to take it down to the waist and gasped aloud when she saw the sight of his bare side. The skin wasn't pierced but, what was prominent was the spread of darkness that had clustered where he had been struck and turned the surrounding veins black. It was spreading.

Cato sunk his head and banged his hand on the table so loud that it shook Ikena and caused the ornaments on the shelves to rattle. "He's been hit with a *Morthrealki* blade. I'm... I'm sorry. It will spread and darkness will consume him." Cato seemed deflated as he placed a damp cloth over Sedric's forehead.

"What are you saying? Help him!" Ikena pleaded through tears that were now streaming down her face.

"I'm saying that, if we don't do something fast, he will become a Sinturi. It's how they built their army in preparation for the Great War. It's how they are building their armies now."

"What do we do?" She hated the sound of desperation that her voice shrieked but she couldn't stop it. She would do anything to save him. *Anything*. Ikena had known Sedric since she was a little girl and she loved him. She loved him with every piece of her she could give. He had to survive. He had to. She whimpered at the sight of him. He looked so scared and his veins pulsated with the infection, the chill causing him to struggle and wince every second.

"Ikena... I know you don't want to hear this," Cato declared with a worrying look on his face, "But there is a man who could save him. I've seen him do it before... to me."

Ikena jumped on the information instantly, "Who?" she practically roared, wiping away tears that trickled down her face.

"The King of the Cloak army."

EIGHT

Ikena didn't know what to think. She was to put Sedric's life in the hands of a man whose greed consumed him and had no regard for non-magicals.

"No," she stated, feeling disgusted at her words but she couldn't stop the word from being spoken.

Cato stared at her, his piercing eyes rooting deep into her soul. He looked broken, like he was experiencing a great trauma from seeing Sedric like he was. His tone was low and quiet when he spoke, and he was nervously sweating. "Ikena, I don't like it either, believe me, but we have to do what's right."

A wet tear dropped from Ikena's eye and rolled down her cheek. She couldn't speak, she was frozen to the spot. She loved Sedric more than anything, but she also loved her family, deeply. If she went to the King, he'd make her stay in the army, she wouldn't see her mother, or Asher and Aliza again. They'd hate her. Asher and Aliza would grow up thinking that she had abandoned them. Could she really do that to them? It was bad enough that she had left them in

Endfell. *What was I thinking?* She thought. She should have brought them with her, at least they'd be together. Cato helped as best he could. He ground some herbs into a paste and infected it with his magic, rubbing the finished product that glistened onto Sedric's side where the infection manifested. After five minutes he excused himself and allowed her time to think.

"I'll be in my room," Cato informed. "If the wound worsens despite my paste, come and find me." He then headed to his room, leaving Ikena to watch over Sedric. It was her decision to make.

She stayed by Sedric's side during the night, desperately clutching his hand and hoping that he'd be okay. He had muttered her name a few times in his sleep, so at least she knew he was alive, for the time being at least. The darkness had spread through him and reached the top of his torso and bottom of his thighs, it didn't seem like it would be too long before... *Don't think it.* But Ikena couldn't help it. He would become a Sinturi. The whole reason why they went on this treacherous journey was because Ikena *didn't* want to join the Cloaks, but if Sedric was in danger what choice did she have? He needed urgent help.

Ikena had made her decision. She left Sedric's side to find Cato in his room, the knock on his door had woken him up.

"What is it?" he asked.

"He's getting worse. I think we have no choice. I don't care about my refusal. We *must* meet with the Cloaks."

Cato nodded approvingly and ushered her to get changed into the armour she had worn earlier, and to bring all her belongings with her, along with Sedric's armour which she stuffed in a straw bag Cato provided and hoisted it over her shoulder to where she wanted it placed. He informed her to dress accordingly, while he set up the transport circle in the space at the back of the dining room. He'll bring Sedric, so she doesn't have to. She changed quickly and made sure to bring her wicker basket with the book, ball of string and the scarf her mother had packed her. She met Cato where he said, Sedric on the mat before him. He had also changed into his armour and carried Sedric's trident by his side. There was something odd about the way he acted. He was nervous and Ikena noticed that sweat had formed on his flustered face. He was also pacing up and down and seemed to have an itch that wouldn't budge.

"Ready?" he questioned and Ikena gave a singular stern nod, "Grab on to me."

She held on to his arm tightly. Cato took a pendent out from underneath his shirt which bared a jewel that looked similar to the ones in each village that call the Cloak army. She placed a hand to her chest where her own pendent sat underneath her under suit and thought of her father. Cato then created a small coin of magic in his hand and pressed it against the jewel which glowed upon being touched with magic and hovered in the air. Cato grabbed Sedric's body and Ikena blinked. She blinked and they were gone. Transported. All three of them were stood outside a magnificent, polished palace. It was a glorious sight to behold. Sedric was still held by Cato, and Ikena decided to relive the old man of the burden, allowing Sedric to put all his weight on her. Before them, five tall towers were connected to the palace by long white walls, and Cloaks with magical bows could be seen peering out from the battlements above them, their bows aimed right at them.

"State your business here or suffer a flurry of arrows!" one of them shouted threateningly, which Ikena took to be their General.

"We have come to speak with His Majesty, the King!" Cato shouted back unfazed, "It is dire that we do so!"

"You may come through," Next, the General looks to all of his archers, "Cease fire and open the gates!"

Before them stood a white gate made of wood, and as it opened with a mechanical grind that surprisingly sounded well oiled, an army of Cloaks welcomed them with disapproving glares, despite how important Ikena thought they felt in all this armour. But for sure they were here. Outside Nevera's Palace. The King's palace. So majestic in fact, that Ikena could not for the life of her hide the scowl that now formed on her face. One of the soldiers leapt forward and pointed a sword at Cato's throat.

"You know better than to return here, Catoeus," the Cloak dared.

"I would not be here unless it were urgent. I request to see King Elion," he demanded, and the Cloaks around him laughed. "I do not see how this is funny." Ikena was surprised at how Cato had kept his serious tone despite all this mockery he was receiving. It made her think even more, that he wasn't a bad person.

"What makes you think he'll see you? Are you forgetting how you betrayed him like you did?"

Betrayed? Ikena stood rooted to the spot, astonished at the news she was hearing. She knew there was something more to Cato, after all he had an array of weapons and Cloak uniforms so he must have tangled with the Cloaks in the past, but to know that he had somehow betrayed the King. It was barbaric. To betray the King was to betray the Cloaks and ultimately, betray the Kingdom of Nevera.

"I never meant to, Osirus. Please!" Cato begged.

As Cato begged the man, Sedric winced in pain, clutching himself like a child with a stomach ache. Ikena noticed that the darkness had spread to his arms and had reached the back of his neck. Osirus noticed Sedric's odd behaviour and moved his sword from Cato, to Sedric.

"What are you doing?" Ikena demanded an answer, angrily.

"Osirus, please. I know how this looks. I know you know what's happening to him, and I know you know how the King can help," Cato alleged and after a tense standoff they were finally allowed to enter.

A troop of Cloaks escorted them to the palace and as they moved aside to flank them in order to watch their every move, a long bridge lit by the equivalent street lights, but silver with magic, could be seen. It led them to the main part of the palace, standing out amidst the evening sky. Ikena and Cato hurried across, carrying Sedric in between them with his arms wrapped around their shoulders and passed a gigantic tumbling waterfall. On either side of the bridge perched large stone statues marking the faces of royal Cloaks that reigned before Elion did, each with a crown upon their heads.

They came to another set of gates which, upon request,

was raised allowing the group to venture inside to where a market awaited them, stalls stood lonely, waiting for their owners to open them when the day became brighter. The Cloaks escorting them pushed the three forward to the other side of the small village where the King's palace stood, daringly. They were welcomed inside by two Cloaks wearing a different uniform to that of those escorting them. The inside of the palace was absolutely breath-taking. Magic was used to light the candles that glowed a flickering light purple, hung above and beside every window of the hall. Ahead of them stood a grand staircase, which was lined with royal blue carpet that welcomed them. The Cloak pushed them forwards, forcing them to advance up the steps.

Ikena noticed the portraits which were hung on either side and displayed the pictures of the Kingdom's capitals and villages in their prime. She caught a quick glance of Endfell. It looked so different to what it did now, but there were features of the market that were still the same. She might have even been able to see her house had she been allowed a more detailed look, making a mental note to view it at a later time if she could. When they reached the top of the stairs, they were guided forwards through rooms that seemed utterly unnecessary, some had barely any furniture and only housed a fireplace and ornaments and there were far too many areas for common space.

People in Endfell are struggling for beds, yet here they have more rooms than they need. Ikena grumbled, reeling of being in such a place. They were then brought into a room which gave Ikena the strangest feeling of déjà vu. Brick walls encased the room and a round, oaken table was placed to the right with velvet cushioned chairs. To the left were large steps that led to a throne. The King's throne. Ikena realised why the room looked so familiar, she had dreamt it the day before she hid from the Cloaks in Endfell. The King of Nevera was sat on the golden throne, draped in the same golden robes she had seen in her dreams, guarded by a personal array of guards below him that stood around the staircase and two guards either side of him. The glistening crown that perched atop his head irritated Ikena. She didn't dare bow.

"Catoeus. I thought I banished you from this palace," the King questioned in a deep voice. He looked even more regal in person; his rolled curls gently styled delicately above his ears and his face was polished. For someone who was the same age as Ikena's mother, he sure looked dashingly young.

"You did, my Lord," Cato spoke, "But you see, my friend here has been struck by a *Morthrealki* blade. He's in desperate need of help... your help."

The King gave a deep chuckle at Cato's request, then threatened him darkly, "How *dare* you come back here after what you did. Asking for *my* help! You will never have that right! Not after you killed the only thing I ever loved!" Cato sunk his head and Ikena saw the guilt-ridden face that overcame him. She knew it all too well and had borne the same face since leaving her family in Endfell.

The King gave a lazy wave of his hand, he hadn't even had the decency to look in their direction, but with that one flick of his hand the Cloaks guarding him moved quickly, grabbing the trio by their arms and attempting to pull them out of the room.

Cato tried to protest, "Elion, please." But the King refused to listen.

A Cloak with a sword butt the hilt on Cato's head, coaxing a grunt of pain upon impact. "That is *King* Elion to the likes of you! Traitor!"

Ikena couldn't let this happen and couldn't believe her eyes. How could the King, a protector of the world, the same King who had fought away the Sinturi during the Great War, so easily pass up a human to the Sinturi just to spite a man he had banished?

She struggled in the hands of the Cloak who grasped her before voicing her opinion, "Would the *true* King of Nevera really do this?"

This warranted a reaction from the King who put his hand out in one swift motion, signalling his men to stop. They let go immediately, even the ones who were holding Sedric who tumbled to the ground, unable to stand on his own.

"I *am* the *true* King. How *dare* you!" The King dared, menace in his voice.

"Then show me," Ikena began, "You don't have to fight with us like this. It's not Cato who's asking for your help, but me. Please! Do this not for Cato, or for me, but for your lost love? Do this for my friend who needs you right now, lest you lose more of what you hold dear to you?"

He mulled over her words for a moment, taking his time in deciding whether he would be the killer of this puny human or not. "Alright," he finally agreed, "What is your name?"

"Ikena Ralliday."

The King stood as soon as he had heard her name and then the armed Cloak guards instinctively closed in on her. The urgency of saving Sedric's life was forgotten, and she found herself surrounded. Ikena saw the scared look upon the King's face. The King, who was supposed to be invincible, the protector of Nevera, frightened by someone as uncouth as her and because of what? A prophecy? Words of consequence that yet hold no cause. *Pathetic*, she thought, and a smile crossed her lips. She could use that to her advantage.

"Get back. Get back!" she roared at the guards, one tried to hit her with a blast of magic, but she retaliated using her own ball of magic to block the blow. Cato had her back and leapt at the guards who were attacking them, using his own magic in the form of a rope, tying up three Cloaks who had challenged him. There were three more that gathered around Ikena, she made the first move, using her magic to levitate them before the King.

"Enough!" The King howled and the candles keeping the room bright, suddenly blew out. He used his magic to cast flames in each candle again. "Let's just all calm down." Ikena released her magic and the three levitating Cloaks fell to the ground. Cato also released his, allowing the magical rope to disappear and the Cloaks engulfed in it to stand. "Has darkness struck you?" the King asked, eyeing her up.

"No. Not me, my friend. I only ask for your help."

"You've been a busy girl, haven't you?" The King tutted and sat back in his throne. "My Cloaks have had a difficult time seeking you out. And now you come here before me. You *attack* my soldiers. I'd consider you a fool if it weren't for your bravery in standing up to me like you did. And for what? A mere *boy*. You have a strong will."

"Then I apologise for how I may have acted. I will gladly

speak with you, but I beg you save my friend first. Could this not be what the prophecy wants? What were to happen if you turned your back on us? What would happen to Nevera?" Ikena was smart, she knew that the King was seeking her out because of the divination and that meant she could barter with it.

"I will make you a deal. I will save your friend's life but, in return, you are to join the army. You must fulfil your duty to Nevera. It is what the divination demands. What were to happen if *you* turned your back on us? Oh yes, what *would* happen to Nevera? What would happen to your friend?" It seemed the King was also smart.

Ikena repulsed him. She repulsed the palace and the army entrusted to keep Nevera safe. Who was she kidding? She had to accept the offer. Sedric's life depended on it. *A life for a life.* "I accept."

"Guards, take Miss. *Ralliday* and the traitor to the dungeons to wait." The King cursed as his Cloaks lingered on his every command, immediately dragging Ikena and Cato out of the room. Ikena shoved them, crying for Sedric. *Please don't leave me now*, she thought.

They were swiftly marched down a long winding corridor and down a long flight of stairs which led to dirty, rat-infested cells. Ikena and Cato were thrown in a singular cell, falling on to mud-soaked floor where rain had gotten in, and chained to each other's ankles. Ikena's belongings were also taken, as well as Sedric's uniform and trident. All they could do now was wait. Ikena noticed Cato, who had been looking glumly at the floor the entire time, had sat up against the wall and after a moment of pondering in the dirt she did the same.

"So, are you going to tell me what that was all about?" she pressed, but to her dismay Cato was silent, not wishing to talk of his wrong doing in the past. "I've left Sedric up there with them, so I highly suggest you tell me if they're a threat or not or—"

"Please stop." Cato cut her off, his voice no louder than a whisper. "Your armour belonged to my daughter who passed away a few years ago... I... I killed her," he spoke and Ikena could feel the heartbreak that shadowed him, "Before the war, my daughter and I were Commanders and lived in this very palace. My daughter and the King were in love with one another and were set to be married in the fall. One night, I was sent on a mission to defeat a group of Sinturi who had formed in the outlaw villages of the castle, but I was struck with a blade just like Sedric. When you're struck with a *Morthrealki* blade, the darkness consumes you from the inside. You become one of them. A Sinturi." He wept as he told his story, reliving that of his past, "I was taken back to the palace, but it was too late, and the darkness had taken over me. My daughter came to my side, intent on knowing that I wouldn't hurt her, but I wasn't me. I took one of the guards' knives and the next thing I knew, she was there on the blade that I used to stab her with. The young King used his magic to suck the darkness out of me, something he spent years practising, but it was already too late. I woke up, like a man who had been trapped under some spell, and what do I see? My daughter's lifeless body before my feet, silent with the knife that I plunged through her heart."

Ikena processed the information but didn't know what to say or how to comfort a man that had so much guilt ridden through him. Instead, she took his hand in his and rested her head on his shoulder. "I never could forget the hateful glare the King gave me. I swallowed in my pity of being banished, stripped of all I knew. You asked me what the symbol meant in Lakeland. I am the monkey, and my daughter is the tree, because I could be nothing without her. But then you arrived. My daughter. You remind me of her," he said, and then went back to being silent. It must have been tough for Cato to come here. Ikena rested her mud-covered face on Cato's shoulder. She prayed for Sedric and hoped, with all her might, that she'd see him again.

NINE

ight peered into the dungeon cell as Ikena and Cato patiently waited for some sign that Sedric was alive and well. The King had promised to attend to him, and if he saved Cato before, he could do it again with Sedric. Since being back in the palace Cato had seemed distant and lost, depressed would be a better word to use. He sat in the mud willingly and Ikena couldn't imagine what he must be thinking right now. She even felt a sense of guilt rise inside her for bringing him back here.

"I'm sorry that we got into this mess, Cato." She consoled him, but it was no use.

There was a clamber from the stairway and two Cloaks appeared with a handful of keys, they unlocked their cell before unlocking the chains at their ankles and piloted them back to the King's chambers. On the way, Ikena noticed the daylight from outside and noted that it had been a considerable amount of time since they had first arrived at the palace. Once in the room, the King huffed and puffed in his royal throne, looking considerably worse for wear. His skin was pale and sunken, and he carried large, black rings under his eyes. Even so he was still regal and perfect. It worried Ikena and she didn't see Sedric in the room. Where was he? She worried that, if he had become a Sinturi, they would have had no choice but to kill him, but she couldn't think like that. She would destroy herself if she did. *Please, Sedric,* she mentally begged. *Be alive.*

"Your friend was quite a handful," the King spoke tiredly, "But, we managed to save him, despite our wasting of time when all of us had attitude boiling up within us. He's a strong soul that one."

Ikena let out her breath that she found herself holding and relaxed with ease.

"Thank you." She struggled to hold back the tears that were already forming in her eyes. "Thank you."

The King waved his hand and two Cloaks disappeared before returning seconds later with a tired-looking Sedric. He carried bags under his eyes, his hair was wet with sweat and he looked sunken but once he saw Ikena, he couldn't stop smiling. Ikena let out a yelp and ran to him, she squealed and jumped into his muscular arms.

"I told you," Sedric whispered gently in her ear, "I'll always be here."

"Now, I trust you will keep your end of the deal." The cleared his throat, distracting Ikena from the joy she was feeling and replacing it with a sudden doom. She had completely forgot that she had agreed to join the army, essentially giving up any chance she ever had of seeing her family again.

"Yes…" A sullen look crossed her face. "But I do have a

few demands, if you please."

The King rolled his eyes and nodded towards her, she took the signal as a prompt to go on speaking, "Well, first of all, I'd like my family to be protected in Endfell. They need two boxes filled with fresh meat, vegetables and food every week." She paused to scan the King's face who nodded again towards her and then clicked his fingers at a nearby Cloak who had an ink quill and parchment paper nearby, scribbling her demands down. "I'd also like to be able to write to them freely."

"We're not savages, Ikena. All Cloaks are allowed to write to their families," the King assured and Ikena continued, she suppressed that information and doubted that it was true.

"Next, I'd like to be given the opportunity to see my family, shall we say once or twice a year?" The King squinted his silvery eyes at her. It was a rule that, from what Ikena had heard, had been so forced.

Not even higher-ranked Cloaks were allowed to see their families, unless they lived in the palace or neighbouring villages. After an intense minute, the King nodded and her demand was written down, "Finally, I'd like to be accompanied on all missions by Sedric and Cato." A loud chuckle came from the King's personnel of guards. She had overstepped the line but if he wanted her, then those were the deals. Cato didn't look best pleased himself and the King noticed it before an evil smile planted across his face.

"Very well." He leaned forward on his chair and made direct eye contact with Cato. "I want you to stay here and be reminded of the mistake you made, *every single day.*"

Cato broke his gaze and lingered with his eyes fixed on the floor. The King demanded that they be taken to their quarters and dismissed them with a wave of his hand. A large group of Cloaks escorted them on their way, Cato in the front and Ikena and Sedric behind him.

"Ikena," Sedric began. "What was that all about?" She knew what he meant. He wanted to know why the King had a certain distaste for Cato, but it wasn't her place to talk about it. It was hard enough for him already.

"It doesn't matter, how are you feeling?"

"It was weird, I remember being carried somewhere and then a bright shining of white light overcame me. It was all I could see. I remember hurting, wanting to cower from the light as if it were dangerous, but then the darkness inside me was gone and I felt like me again. All I wanted was see your face."

The group reached a large common space of the tower which was filled with Cloaks wearing similar clothing, women wore gold and men wore black. They were studying or chatting with others, some looking their way and whispering. When the group were brought into the room there was silence and a hundred eyes were on them, a few laughed at her, noticing that she and Cato were completely covered in mud from the dungeons.

"This is the common grounds," the Cloak who acted as their tour guide spoke, "You'll come here to lounge or study."

The room had plush burgundy seats scattered around large wooden tables and huge panelled windows with a fireplace that glowed bright purple flickering flames up ahead. To the left of the room were two stone staircases that wound their way around a large, golden statue of the King himself, standing over a majestic lion. *Charming.* Ikena snorted at the sight of it.

Then, the group split and Ikena was taken away from Sedric and Cato. She tried to protest, "We come as a package." The tour-guide Cloak shook his head and, although Ikena hated it, there wasn't much point in arguing.

"We'll be fine," Sedric said with a half-smile, at least he was with Cato.

She was taken to the staircase on the right. Ikena allowed herself one last look at Sedric before being coaxed up the stairs by a female Cloak. They climbed the brick staircase, which was narrow and completely made of stone, with no carpet, until they reached a long corridor. She was taken into the first door on the right which showed a room with eight, well-made beds. A few women greeted Ikena as she was taken inside and showed to a bed in the corner of the room but there was one woman with beautiful brown skin, long, braided black hair and a sharp nose, who coldly stared, peeling an apple with a knife, a disgusted look upon her face. Ikena tried to ignore her, slouched forward like that on the bed across the room, bringing the blade to her mouth to tear off each slice she peeled. Ikena's bed had soft lining made of white silk and had golden covers with royal stitching on the edges.

"Now, here are your lounging robes and belongings," the Cloak handed her two pairs of golden silk trousers and a matching top, one to serve as her pyjamas and one to serve as her day clothing, alongside fresh underwear and socks, light-weight slip-on shoes, a toothbrush and a towel. She was allowed to keep her own Cloak army uniform that used to belong to Cato's daughter, which she was instructed to hang on the mannequin at the foot of her bed after cleaning and polishing it. Then, she was given back her wicker basket, most of the contents had been removed, even the gold coin, not that the palace needed it. It added to Ikena's hatred of the King so swallowed by greed. She was allowed to keep her cherished book which Ikena tucked into a side draw and continued to listen to the woman speak.

"Should you need anything else, you need only request it by a senior, which for you is the King's advisor."

"Osirus?" Ikena questioned, remembering his name.

The woman seemed shocked that she had said his name and with a little nod confirmed. "Yes."

The other women in the room gawked between themselves, realising that Ikena must be someone special if she's reporting directly to the Cloak who advises the King and whispers began to increase dramatically.

The woman left the room after giving Ikena a pat on the back and she was left to her own thoughts and in the hands of her new bunk buddies. She couldn't help but notice the stares of the woman by the door who was now tearing into her apple like a horse and decided to change into her fresh garments and slip-on shoes in the bathroom. She couldn't believe her eyes, the bathroom had toilets and sinks and mirrors, but it also had a tumbling waterfall outside connecting to a drainage system, so Ikena could actually bathe. She shut the door behind her and stripped her armour off, before stepping into the cool water. It was beautiful, soothing and her body thanked her as the pain in her back and tension in her shoulder slowly released. She got her hair wet, ringing the muddy water out before washing the thick mud off her armour and burgundy under suit. After towelling herself dry she put on her fresh clothes, they felt soft against her skin, a luxury people in Endfell would never know. She brushed her teeth and after finishing came out of the bathroom where the women stared at her again.

Fresh meat. She thought about herself, but kept to her own, hanging her damp armour and suit on the mannequin above the towel to drip-dry before sitting back on the bed. A tall woman, who was talking in a group to the right of her, moved to sit on the foot of Ikena's bed. She had a skinny face, ginger hair and wore big round glasses that sat poignantly on the tip of her nose.

"I'm Kyra," she spoke and forcefully stuck out her hand in greeting. Ikena shook it, smiled, and introduced herself but it seemed news of the raven-haired girl, the 'chosen one', had spread throughout the Kingdom and she was immediately swamped with questions. "Have you defeated a Sinturi?" Kyra asked, when another girl with strikingly white-blonde hair chirped in.

"Of course, she has. Tell us!" And a buzz swept around the room of excited women wanting to know Ikena's life story.

In all honesty, she didn't really have much to tell, she was born in Endfell with her siblings and mother before she accidentally used her power to save her little brother, before running away and hiding from the Cloak army, only to meet Cato who taught her how to control her magic, before testing it out on a pack of Sinturis where Sedric got hurt, before coming to the palace and begging for the King's help... On the other hand, maybe she did have more to tell than she thought.

Ikena was about to speak when the woman who sat in the corner with braided hair, chucked her apple core into the bedside bin, still staring at her dubiously, and spoke, "Oh, please." She stood slowly and paced over to Ikena causing the women who had gathered around her bed, to move back to their own as if to avoid a fight. All except Kyra. "She'll lead us into doom if she's not strong enough. The Kingdom as we know it will be nothing but a pile of ash and rubble and *everything* we have ever worked hard for will be gone. That is what she will bring us." She stormed out the room, slamming the door behind her and the room was silent.

"Just ignore her," Kyra said. "That's Aella. She adores the palace and is one of its most fierce protectors."

"Well, she clearly doesn't like me very much."

"She'll come around," Kyra promised. "Why don't I take you on a tour through the palace? I've got time."

Ikena wasn't really up for it, but she agreed none the less. The two of them walked back down the staircase to the common grounds and through the corridors and empty rooms. Ikena remembered the large staircase before the door which led out of the main palace and stopped when they were passing it. She jogged down the blue-carpeted steps to the photograph of Endfell she had passed before.

"Your home," Kyra said. Ikena gave her a quizzical look as to how she knew but she answered, "We all know about the chosen one who's from a small forest-hidden village."

Creepy much? Ikena pondered.

She stared at the photograph which showed a large view of her old village. There was the market, which looked in higher spirits than it did now, and a stable full of horses which Ikena couldn't believe. Whoever had those horses must have sold them during the Great War. She spotted Sedric's house, which didn't look much different and far in the back she spotted her own house. In the upstairs window she could see a figure, although it was more of a shadow than a figure but after looking closely, she could see who it was. It was her mother and father, embracing. They looked considerably younger, but she recognised her mother's long blonde hair. It was them. They were smiling and he seemed to have her in an embrace, but it was enough. They were happy.

Ikena looked from photograph to photograph and found wonder in the pictures of the village she had never known. There were The Lost Paths in Serenthia, which was rumoured to house a beautiful creature which held great power and there were also the villages that neighboured the palace, such as Perevya and Teriyell that looked as thriving as they most definitely were now. Not that Ikena had seen them, but as the palace's neighbouring villages they were guaranteed to be in better standards than the villages elsewhere.

Kyra then took her around the palace. There were more pointless rooms and an underground temple for prayer. Ikena liked that room most of all. She had no interest in praying but it was relaxing and quiet, you could hear the trickle of water that ran around the room and ended at a waterfall which protruded from the wall. After two hours, Kyra had to return to her next lesson, and she took Ikena back to the dormitory. Ikena sat in bed in the empty room. Everyone was in their classes and Ikena made the time over by reading from her book again and wondered what Sedric and Cato were doing. As it grew darker, Kyra and the rest of the women returned. Ikena's stomach growled with hunger, she hadn't eaten in two days and when Kyra mentioned dinner, she almost leapt at her. Ikena followed her out of the dorm and back down the steps to the common grounds. Other Cloaks were talking in groups, but all were walking the same way. Ikena peered over heads, trying to search for Sedric or Cato but she couldn't make them out.

"So, are you all on some sort of strict regime?" Ikena wondered aloud but she couldn't hide the distaste reel from her voice.

Kyra chuckled, "Pretty much."

They walked a fair way before reaching two large double doors in the centre of the palace. Inside was a large hall with tall ceilings, floor to ceiling windows and candles on brick walls that glimmered with the same purple flames that danced as if to a bolero. There were long, mahogany tables that stretched the full length of the room and were set in columns. On said tables were huge feasts of food, from different cuts of roasted meat, to jellied fruit, to vegetables, to butter, to cheese, to pasta, it was all there and Ikena heard her stomach growl even louder at the sight of it all. With the pleasant sight of food came the unpleasantries of the King. People in Endfell were dying from starvation and poverty, yet the Kingdom had enough food to feed them all and did nothing to help.

As Ikena stepped into the room there were murmurs from Cloaks around her. She heard whispers of, "It's the chosen one!" and caught Aella's eyes, rolling. She searched for Sedric and Cato again, but they weren't in the room, instead Kyra took her to the corner-part of the furthest table which was a little quieter and they sat down next to each other. She grabbed a plate, handing one to Ikena, and then began to carve chicken for herself from the cooked bird that waited in front of her. Ikena stared.

"Aren't you eating?" Kyra asked.

"It feels, wrong. It's just… People in my village are starving."

"But you're a Cloak now, you need to be well-fed for training which, for us, starts tomorrow."

"For us?" Ikena questioned.

"Yes. I have been to class, but my real training doesn't start until tomorrow. They wait until the first day of a new month to train all new recruits." Kyra chewed on her chicken.

"So, everyone in the class would have joined the army in the last month?"

"That's correct." Kyra proceeded to put thin slices of roast chicken on to Ikena's plate that was lined with silver coated edges and had an intriguing pattern on them. Ikena did appreciate the gesture, and she remembered the deal she had made for her family, that the King would ensure they were well-fed each week too. She'd write a letter to them before bed, letting them know that she was safe and that they could expect weekly deliveries. She allowed herself a few scoops of creamed spinach, as well as roasted potatoes and seasoned vegetables, to pair with her chicken, and a handful of grapes for something sweet afterwards. When she caught a glimpse of Sedric's unkempt blonde hair, she stood immediately and made her way over to him, leaving Kyra at the table.

"Sed," she called and embraced him in a soft hug, his familiar scent filling the insides of her nose. "I was so worried." Cato wasn't too far behind. She took them both to where Kyra was, and they sat opposite.

"Sedric, Cato, meet Kyra. Kyra this is Sedric and Cato." Kyra stood and promptly shook their hands.

"Pleased to meet you!" she beamed. Sedric gave a smile and Cato a welcoming nod, if there ever was such a thing.

"I see you're in uniform," Ikena teased the boys who were dressed in their black lounge wear that matched the other male Cloaks in the room.

"Oh yes, how *generous* of them to help us fit in." Sedric joked and it made Ikena blush.

In that moment she was, surprisingly, happy. Sedric was alive and that's all that mattered, even if she had to bargain her own life and servitude for it. "Kyra, what's the training plan for tomorrow?" Ikena asked but noticed how Cato still looked glumly and picked at a handful of grapes, managing a bite or two before pushing his plate away.

"Well, tomorrow you'll be woken up early to run a daily physical fitness drill, before someone will find you and take you to your first class," she paused to take a mouthful of chicken and Ikena and Sedric exchanged looks. "Then you'll be able to take a break, explore the grounds, meet up with friends, before having another class and then dinner." Ikena made a mental note of the plan and told Cato and Sedric to meet her in the common grounds when they had their breaks.

"How's the boys' dorm?" Ikena asked the boys as she

chewed on a sweet green grape.

"It's alright, I guess," Sedric began. "Cato's a well-known face around here." It didn't surprise Ikena that he was, seeing as he had served as high-ranking Cloak before being banished from the palace. "Everyone seems friendly enough and there's a bit of a joker in our room, Flynn his name is. What about you?"

Ikena took a moment to debate whether she should tell Sedric of Aella or not but decided against it so that he wouldn't worry, besides, she only made a passing comment and Kyra was sure she'd come around.

"Yeah, everyone's nice."

They ate their meal and Kyra filled them in on any recent drama that had happened in the palace. It mostly revolved around her. News of the chosen one had come about and everyone in the palace had to begin study of the divination. They then wondered why she hadn't joined the army yet, some thought she was already on a mission, others thought she was dead. None of them guessed that she had been running from the army, and she thought to leave that delicate detail out. They don't take kindly to deserters. *No one leaves the palace*. Ikena asked about the King but Kyra said he wasn't seen too often around the training or common grounds and ate his food separately with a select few of his personnel.

"Well thank the Saints for that," Ikena grumbled and beside her Kyra gasped.

"You cannot speak about the King in this way." She tore into her final piece of chicken and pushed her glasses up higher on her nose.

"Some King," Ikena muttered under her breath but beside

her Kyra stiffened.

After finishing their food, they retired to their rooms early on a strict curfew. Ikena hated being away from Sedric, especially during the night, but there wasn't much she could do about it. He kissed her cheek and said goodnight, sending flutters down her spine and they parted their separate ways.

Once in the dormitory, she changed into her second pair of lounging garments, brushed her teeth, and allowed her body to sink into the bed she was assigned. Once everyone was in bed, Aella flicked her hand in the air which blew out the red magical flames in the candles, presumably her magic, and the room went quiet. Ikena tried to sleep but she tossed and turned all night, thinking about the day's events and trying to suppress the homesickness that had overcome her, not only was she without her family but, of a night, she was also without Sedric and missed his protective arm around her.

She took an ink quill and piece of parchment paper and shoved them under the covers with her. Then, she made a small ball of golden magic in her left palm, cupping it and using it to serve as a torch. She began to write.

My Dearest Ralliday's,

It is I, chosen one, protector of the great Kingdom of Nevera. I am writing to let you know that I am safe. Truly. Believe it or not but I am actually in Nevera's Palace and have spoken with the King himself. He sends his best wishes and, as a bargain of my profound servitude, he will also be sending you at least two boxes of fresh meat, fruit, vegetables, medicine, and other items you may need each week. Keep the good stuff, Mother. Then, please share with the village, with those you trust. I miss Aliza and Asher every day and will always cherish Asher's ability to always make me laugh and Aliza's wittiness. Dare I say it, she will grow up to be a fine young lady one day. Sedric is with me and I know you're probably wondering about that kiss… there isn't much more to tell right now, but if there ever is I will write to you straight away. Do you remember the little boy who used to find me pretty flowers? My, how he has grown now. How's Sedric's grandma?

I love and miss you all.

Royally signed,

Ikena Ralliday.

Ikena folded the parchment paper and tucked it securely in an envelope before slotting it in the mail bin stationed at the door. It would get to them. They would know that she was safe. She could rest easy tonight. Quietly, she made her way back into bed and drifted off into a deep… dark… sleep.

TEN

I kena's nightmare took her to the dark Caves of Zeridan where the Sinturi slithered and a coldness came over her like it had the last time she saw Dalmask. He held the familiar, metallic box in his fingers before walking away into the darkness and putting it on the floor. Something about the way he moved seemed familiar to Ikena, it reminded her of someone.

He stepped back and outstretched his arms wide and his dark, evil magic protruded from his fingertips, it pained him to do so, to use that much energy. He groaned in agony. It was too much. The darkness consumed the box, warping around it. A smile plastered against his face but then shots of bright white light could be seen, coming out of the box, and fighting with the shadow of magic around it. The darkness attempted to penetrate it, but it could not. The light fought back, beaming into the dark like a lighthouse. The mighty dark leader cowered in the corner for fear of being touched by it. The darkness around the box slowly began to disintegrate underneath the light until there was nothing left but the box. Dalmask took a step forward, unsure of whether it was safe or not. Deemed it was, he picked up the box and brought it into the dim light.

There were symbols on the outside of the box, symbols Ikena had never seen before that, from a blind eye like hers, looked like a bunch of scribbles, but she knew they meant something. Another Sinturi sauntered into the room and wondered why it wouldn't open, but the leader didn't appreciate his tone and dared him to summon all his power at opening it.

"Prove your loyalty to me by doing this, and if you don't use all your energy then I will kill you myself," he whispered like a hissing snake.

The Sinturi did as was commanded from his dark master and summoned his black magic, groaning in agony like Dalmask had before, but instead of conceding, he continued. Bright white light from the box shot out at him and began tearing him apart, disintegrating him limb from limb until he was nothing more but a pile of ash on the floor. Dalmask stood tall and silent.

Ikena was awoken by Kyra who was stood over her, shaking her body. Something inside Ikena snapped, she could feel her veins turn cold and her head pounded.

"Get off me!" Ikena snapped, and the room stood silent.

"I... I was just waking you up." Kyra whispered, she looked at her like she was a monster.

"I'm sorry. I just had a bad dream." Ikena tried, but the damage had already been done.

With a groan, she sat up and had the most piercing of headaches. Others around her were already dressed in the Cloak army black under suits. Ikena hurried to the bathroom, noticing that Aella was missing from the room. Anyhow, she couldn't stop thinking of the nightmare she had, the faceless hood of the Sinturi imprinted into her weak brain. It was time to speak to someone about these nightmares, especially after two of them had seemingly come true and Ikena decided she'd tell Cato and Sedric if she could. For now, she put those thoughts to the back of her mind as she splashed water on her face, towelling dry before putting on her red suit and brushing her teeth. It felt nice wearing it again, although a little unnatural without the strong silver breastplate, cape and leg boots to go on top, and, although a little damp, Ikena had managed to get most of the mud stains out of it.

Even though Ikena had yelled at Kyra, she still stayed behind to wait for her and when she was dressed, she hurried her down the stone stairs to the common grounds and then down the large blue carpeted staircase and outside into the fresh morning air. Ikena saw a large group of Cloaks and noticed Sedric standing with them, next to a smaller-framed man and made a beeline towards him, Kyra following closely behind.

"Hey, where's Cato?" she asked Sedric, who wrapped his arms around her, protectively.

"He was called before the King. I tried to go with him, but they wouldn't let me." And his face resembled how she felt.

She had made a bargain for Cato and Sedric to stay at the palace with her and she knew the King wouldn't betray her trust by banishing or harming him. If anything, he needed her trust most of all. She was sure he'd be fine, but it was still greatly concerning, especially how Sedric was ordered to stay behind.

A Cloak, dressed in full Cloak army uniform that looked similar to the ones Ikena had, barked at the group before him, "Newcomers, I'm Enzo. Oldcomers, you all know how this works," he spoke. "You're each to pair up and run side-by-side with that person, following me. Do you understand?"

The group roared vigorously in unison, "Yes Sir!"

How mechanical. Ikena thought, although she found herself uttering the words along with them.

Kyra was waiting at her side expectantly, but Ikena knew she'd be partnering with Sedric, who still had a protective arm wrapped around her waist. Sedric noticed Kyra's lost look and introduced him to the man beside him.

"Kyra, this is Flynn. Why don't you two pair up?" he pressed, a little too eagerly for Ikena's taste.

Flynn tousled his hair before bowing to Kyra with his hand out. Ikena remembered that Flynn had called him a jokester and she couldn't help but laugh, even to her friend's dismay.

"Looks like we've been paired up, huh?" He winked at her.

Kyra moaned in disgust, but it seemed everyone else was already in pairs, she was stuck with him. "Oh, get beside me. Creep!" she said viciously, and Flynn immediately got in line.

"Meow," he muttered under his breath.

With an approving nod, Enzo began to jog off and group

by group followed closely behind him. Ikena and Sedric filtered in when it was their turn and began to jog their way in unison. It was amazing to see the palace grounds as they jogged, they passed through the main village where villagers were selling traded goods, before jogging on to a mountain side of the palace and climbing up rock steps that lead to the top of the waterfall. The waterfall was beautiful as the water gracefully fell, magical dolphins formed and dived into the deep lake below them causing an excited gasp from Ikena.

She was surprised to see that Enzo had taken them this way as it seemed oddly dangerous, one wrong step could mean falling into the deep lake, many metres below. No one would be able to survive a fall from that height, but nonetheless she kept her mouth shut and encouraged Sedric, who had started to get a little out of breath. Ikena was a natural and had often jogged around the forest at Endfell. Sedric, on the other hand, was naturally muscular and paid no attention to cardio and more on lifting heavy objects.

They jogged down a spiral piece of rock before finding their way to the outside gates where Cato, Ikena and Sedric had first spawned. As they continued, they crossed over the bridge where the statues of King's stood, she wanted to be sure who they were so asked the question back to Kyra and Flynn who were jogging behind them.

"Oh, they're the statues of the Kings who came before King Elion." Kyra said.

So, they are the previous Kings? Ikena scrunched her nose. *Maybe a woman should rule for once,* she thought.

After the bridge they had reached the palace's village once more, jogging through until they ended outside the main

141

palace's doors. Ikena grabbed her knees breathlessly and patted Sedric on the back who had seemed to kneel on the floor, arms rested on top of his head. Kyra and Flynn gathered around them, but they weren't near as out of breath as Ikena and Sedric was.

Enzo dismissed them and Ikena allowed herself some water which was being passed around the group and made Sedric gulp the rest of it down. They were then escorted back to their quarters, Kyra tagging along with Ikena and Sedric and Flynn heading back to their dorm. Ikena fell back on her bed, sweat dripping from her wet face and gulping for air. Aella, who hadn't been in their drill class but was wearing full Cloak army uniform, smirked at her.

"Guess the chosen one couldn't keep up," she laughed rudely.

Ikena opened her mouth and was about to say something when the same Cloak that escorted her to the dorm in the first place came into the room and requested that the group follow her to class. Ikena and Kyra followed closely behind where as Aella, who had also left with them, was talking to the escorting Cloak.

"What is her problem?" she asked Kyra, who shrugged.

"I guess she's threatened by you. She's been known as one of the most powerful in the entire army and she's working on becoming a Commander."

The group were escorted to a small class-sized room where a group of men were waiting, Sedric and Flynn included and Ikena was glad he was here, even though he couldn't partake in the class, it was nice to have someone she fully trusted around her. Aella didn't join the class, instead she went somewhere else and the group seemed to be waiting for someone. After a moment, a familiar face walked through the door wearing his full Cloak uniform. It was Cato. He looked in higher spirits and even had a spring in his step.

"Everyone," he spoke loudly, and the entire class listened. "I will be your new professor."

Wait, what? Ikena wasn't sure how something like this could happen, the King seemed so angry at him so how could he then make him a professor? Sedric and her exchanged looks and a smile formed in the corner of Sedric's mouth.

Cato travelled to the professor's desk and spoke to the class, "Now, each of you know that you can do certain magical skills, for example, Ikena is a Descendant," he announced, and the class stared at her in awe, making her feel slightly embarrassed, she had hoped Cato wouldn't single her out but seeing as he needed all their support she tried to hide her uneasiness, focusing solely on Cato's words. "I'd like you each to demonstrate your talent to the rest of class."

Cato called each pupil up one by one, some teleported to the other side of the room effortlessly, Flynn shape-shifted into a wolf in front of Ikena's very eyes causing others in the class to gasp in excitement, Shifters were rare, even more so than Descendants. When it came to Ikena's turn she focussed on Cato's table and used her power to levitate it before plopping it back down on the floor.

To Ikena's surprise, Cato called Sedric, who at first wasn't sure what to do. He was armed with his trident and showed how he could jab flying sparks of magic out of it, the class cheered him on, encouragingly. Ikena enjoyed seeing him so popular but found her enjoyment fade when a group of girls seemed to be suddenly all-interested in him. He sauntered back to the group and more pupils were called up, one by one. One pupil set fire to Cato's desk and another one used her power to send a wave of water over the flames, extinguishing them. Elementals. They were magic folk who could implement the elements and were the most common type of Cloak. When it was Kyra's turn, she spoke of how she can heal others but wasn't able to demonstrate it as no one was in danger and Cato understood, ushering her back to the group.

After each pupil had done their version of show and tell, Cato informed them of a challenge that would happen in a few days' time, but they'd need to work as a team in order to complete it.

Ikena grew excited, this wasn't what she imagined the army to be like. Although, she didn't like having to adhere to a schedule, she was grateful that they wouldn't be stuck repeating the same magic tasks over and over again and would be able to practise her magic in real-combat situations, which Cato knew was her favourite type of learning. The hour and a half passed, and Cato dismissed them but Ikena and Sedric hung back.

"So… do I have to call you Sir now or?" she joked and was glad to see a smile come across his face, she hadn't seen it since they had arrived at the palace.

"No, not at all," he chuckled. "I bet you're wondering how this all happened." Ikena nodded eagerly and he began his story, "I was in the dorm when a pack of Cloaks came and escorted me to the King's chamber. I had been summoned. I assumed he was going to banish me again but instead he wanted to speak of you." *Me?* Ikena wondered why. "He

144

wants to keep you safe and on the Cloak side of things –"

"What, is he worried I'll become a Sinturi?" she snorted but Cato didn't find her joke funny.

Instead, he nodded, "Yes, actually." And it dawned on her. "So, he's trying to put his hatred aside and made me a professor to give you someone you trust to train with, for now at least." It seemed to explain a lot and Cato seemed happy that he wasn't stuck in the dorms all day. He had been a Cloak for years and was highly skilled, it made sense.

Ikena thought now was the right time to talk about her nightmares, she couldn't keep them to herself anymore, not when it was a matter of life and death. She leaned on the table in front of her and spoke in a whispering tone, "There's something else," she began and both Cato and Sedric moved closer, eager to hear what she had to say. "I've been having these… nightmares, of the Sinturi and the Cloaks. I wouldn't be worried but two of them have actually come true. Back in Endfell, I dreamt that the Cloaks had seen that I had magic, and they did, and then I dreamt of the Sinturi attack in Lovrin. Sedric barely escaped."

Cato studied Ikena closely. "Are you sure?"

"Yes."

"Then I must take you to see the King immediately."

She was a little taken back but felt that it was best to tell the King of the news. She debated whether to tell Cato of the feeling she felt when waking from a nightmare of the Sinturi. When she saw the leader, who looked so familiar, she didn't feel afraid, she felt needed. She felt dark. Evil. Thoughts of Ikena's family flooded back to her, and she stiffened the wetness in her eyes. If the King thought that Ikena was in some way working with the Sinturi, he'd have her executed. She didn't know why she had these powerful feelings after each vision, but she decided it was best kept to herself. They made their way out of the classroom and travelled to the King's chamber where Osirus stood guard and barked that they were not allowed in. Cato pleaded that it was urgent and after a tense stand-off Osirus conceded and allowed them to see Elion. They were escorted into the room and were ushered to bow before him. Cato and Sedric bowed low. Ikena did not.

"I trust this is urgent?" King Elion growled.

"Yes, my Lord," Cato spoke. "Ikena has come to me with some information I believe you'll find useful." And he ushered Ikena forward.

"I've been plagued with nightmares, a few of which have come true." She explained in full before speaking of her most recent nightmare. "Recently, I've been dreaming of the Sinturi. They have hidden in the Caves of Zeridan, but something has come of light, they have found a box. I am unsure of the importance of this box, but the leader is desperate to open it. I feel it is a weapon that could be used against us."

The King leaned forward on his chair and looked between the three of them sceptically, "And you trust what she says is true?" he asked Cato.

"I do."

"But that would make her a Slayer?" the King gawked in his throne.

Ikena had thought it but couldn't bring herself to use the word. The King was the *only* Slayer. Uttering the word itself was a betrayal.

"Yes, my Lord. I am afraid so," Cato spoke and the three of them waited for the next remark.

"I will order my men to study all ancient text we have for any mention of a box, and then be in touch," he spoke, his handsome, olive face glowing in the light that flickered from the magical candles around the room. "Until then, I'd appreciate it if the word Slayer was uttered to no one. Do you understand?"

All three of them nodded in agreement and they were swiftly escorted out of the room by Osirus. Ikena remembered the schedule for the day and noted that she had a long break now before another lesson later in the evening.

"Well, I'm going to explore the palace grounds. Who's coming?" she cheered, a jolt in her step.

"You know I am," said Sedric.

"I think not, I need to prepare for my next lesson." Cato departed.

They walked out of the palace and into the open space where they visited the market, just to window-shop. There were a variety of merchants who were selling fresh fruit, meat and fish to local folk and children playing hopscotch in a group. Once you reach a certain age you are ordered to move out of the palace and into the villages nearby where you can then find a wife, or husband, have children and live with them in your own home. You still have to report to the Cloak army every day and be a part of their missions, unless you're exempt, but once you're a Cloak, you are a Cloak for life. Ikena wanted to go to the villages outside of the palace but she knew it was forbidden. The palace had a border which you could not cross, guarded by Cloaks at every few metres.

People from the market recognised Ikena, the chosen one, and grew in a crowd around her. In a scurry, it was madness. Some called her Queen and saviour and other words Ikena felt distant from. They wanted her to hold their hands, bless them, chant holy words. Ikena did her best to smile and make her way through, but it was torture, and the people were becoming more and more aggressive.

"I am your servant!" one shouted.

"Bless me, your grace!" she heard a cry from another.

Beside her, Sedric had tucked her behind his back for protection.

"Get me out of here, please," she whispered as the crowd grew larger and larger.

"Okay, folks," Sedric began, waving his hands at them and pushing them backwards. "The chosen one needs rest," he looked behind his shoulder and made sure she was unharmed. Then, he grabbed her hand, and they ran, ran as fast as they could, rounded the corner until they were far away from the market. Ahead of them stood a huge plot of bright white roses that had been planted in a field. It spanned as far as the eye could see and was the most beautiful garden Ikena had ever witnessed.

"You're going to have to get used to that," Sedric huffed and wrapped his arm around her.

They made their way to a nearby plaque which was stood at the foot of the roses.

"Each white rose represents the death of a notable Cloak in the Great War. We are thankful for their sacrifice." Ikena read aloud and felt sadness overcome her. All of a sudden, the roses looked different. They did not look as beautiful or as white as they were. In Ikena's eyes, they were stained in blood. She had never known how many Cloaks had lost their lives during the battle. In fact, she had always thought it had been very few. She would never in her wildest imaginations believed it was this many. She envisioned putting a white rose down for Sedric's or Cato's death. Losing them. Mourning them. She wouldn't let that happen, she *couldn't*. She couldn't let the Sinturi take over. She didn't know why, but she was chosen for a reason. She would save the ones she cared about. *She* would save the world.

Sedric grabbed her hand and pulled her close for a moment, moving strands of hair from her face and tucking them slowly behind her ear. Ikena wanted nothing more than to be with him forever, she imagined the two of them getting their own house in the village, with her family who would live next door to them and the grandma who they would take care of. It would be a perfect life and yet, Ikena had a feeling that it would never come to light. There were too many distractions, too many quests, too many rules that would get in the way. For now, she focussed on one day at a time, it was all she *could* do.

There was a nearby bench they sat on and Ikena couldn't help but feel morbid. She wanted to apologise for everything, for bringing Sedric along, for almost getting him killed.

"I'll never forgive myself," she muttered, but Sedric heard.

"What? Why?" he questioned.

She had a stone look on her face and was willing herself

not to cry. She couldn't look at him and instead focussed solely on the white roses.

"Sedric... You almost died because of me. If it weren't for the King I... I don't think you'd be here right now."

Sedric gently took her hand in his and stroked her blistered fingers. "Ikena, that wasn't your fault."

"Yes, it was. It was my fault and I'm sorry. I... I *will* do better," she couldn't stop the tears that strolled down her face and quickly patted them away, not wanting Sedric or any of the Cloaks around to see. "Let's go back in." Sedric sat still, his face focussed on hers. "Please," she practically begged, and he obliged.

They headed back towards the palace and separated at their staircases that led to their own dorms before Ikena and Kyra headed off to the final lesson of the day, studying. They were crowded into a classroom with the same group of men they had seen in their earlier class, Sedric and Flynn with them. The four of them sat together in a group as books were passed down the long tables and Ikena noticed that they were studying the past of Nevera, how it came to be, how the first Cloak came about and, of course, all about the Great War. Ikena found comfort in the silk books that had hand-written passages imprinted in them.

She turned to the first page and read of King Ion, Elion's ancestor, who had supposedly become the first person to ever cast magic. He was a Slayer, like Elion and Ikena, and had multiple talents. Rumour has it he created the Kingdom, forming trees and rivers and houses before people came to immigrate into his world. He offered them freedom and peace and was known as a living God to the people. Then, one by one, folk began to gain magic and, one by one, Ion invited them into his palace, thus beginning the first form of the Cloak army. It was all Ikena could read before the class ended and they were allowed some free time before dinner, which consisted of the same spectacular feast they had witnessed yesterday. Ikena was exhausted from the day and, after eating, retired to her dorm ready for tomorrow's schedule. She was sure it would be eventful.

ELEVEN

I kena slept soundlessly in the night. She was woken in the early hours of the morning by a tireless Kyra and was rushed to wash herself, brush her teeth and get changed into her burgundy under suit before heading outside with Kyra into the chill of the cold air for the morning's drills. Sedric and Flynn met them outside and Enzo barked at them to pair up.

Ikena and Sedric paired up and Flynn and Kyra paired up, without hesitation this time. They jogged the same way as yesterday, circling the palace, heading up the unstable rocky path and passing underneath the tumbling waterfall before coming to the outside gate of the palace, then jogging past the bridge that was suspended over the pit of worrying doom. Sedric struggled but less than yesterday.

Finally, they ended back at the main palace opening and weaved their way back to their dorms to rest before the first lesson. Kyra passed Ikena an apple for breakfast before lounging back on her bed, sweaty from the run as Ikena was.

"So, yesterday you said you could heal people?" Ikena

questioned, wanting to know how Kyra had come to that conclusion.

"Yes, I can. Before I became a Cloak, I lived in Lovrin," Ikena registered that they both lived in Nevrain, "My father... well, he was abusive. He beat my mother until there was nothing left for her to hold on to anymore." Kyra tensed as she spoke. "I used to heal her wounds."

It was difficult for Ikena to remember that all Cloaks had their own lives before the palace. They had their own families and hopes and dreams just like she had.

"I'm sorry." Is all she could offer to console Kyra.

"No, you don't have to. Then the Cloaks came. I tried to hide from them, not wanting to leave my mother in the hands of that monster, but they found me. I was swiftly taken away that same day."

Ikena heard the regret and disgust in her voice. It was something she strongly believed against and it seemed almost barbaric, like a penalisation for a special gift you can't control whether you have or not. Magic was a wonderful, unique gift but sometimes it could also bring burden. It had reached the time for the group to disperse to their lessons and Ikena and Kyra walked towards the dormitory door. Aella, who was lounging in her bed and twiddling with small combat knives that glowed her red-glowing magic, blocked them from leaving. She leaned towards Kyra daringly and whispered, "You're a Cloak now, so if I were you, I'd suggest you keep your precious past to yourself."

Kyra hung her head in shame and Aella let her pass.

"And if I were you, I'd suggest you stay out of our way, instead of interfering in what you don't understand." Ikena

153

couldn't help it, she hated injustice and bullies and that's what she was dealing with. A bully.

The room around them went dangerously quiet as the other women listened. Kyra shook her head at Ikena, but the damage had already been done.

"What did you say to me?" Aella stepped forward, looking down at Ikena's smaller height, but Ikena didn't falter. She held her ground and peered up at the tall, mystic woman.

"You heard me."

"Ikena, let's just go. Please." Kyra tried to pull her away, but she stayed rooted to the spot. The women behind her whispered among themselves at what was happening, but Ikena knew Aella was in the wrong, and she knew that the others knew it too.

"Do you know who you're talking to?" Aella snapped. She shoved Ikena, causing her to stumble backwards.

Ikena let out a gasp. Anger consumed her. If she had any sense, she'd use her magic on her right then and there, but she couldn't risk it. Kyra tried to intervene but Ikena came back, her words a harsh tone, "Quite frankly, no, I do not. But I'm sure you've heard of me. Now, as I said, stay out of our way *or* I'll be forced to inform the King himself of your discourtesy." At her remark the women around her excitedly whispered to their friends, gasping among themselves but smiles came across their faces. Ikena had said a threat and she meant it. She pushed past her, resisting the urge to elbow her in the stomach, and took Kyra away from the situation.

Kyra was stunned. "You didn't have to do that," she giggled.

"Yes, I did! Who does she think she is? Powerful or not, I don't like bullies."

They made their way into the classroom where the men were waiting and stood next to Sedric and Flynn. Sedric noticed the tense look on Ikena's face. "Hey are you okay?" he asked.

She wasn't okay, not really. She had been struggling with her nightmares which, in all honesty, terrified her, they were testing fate as she knew it. Alongside the homesickness that had overcome her and being labelled the sudden *chosen one* and now dealing with bullies.

"I'm okay." But Sedric knew she wasn't.

The rest of the women came into the room, whispering with excitement from the altercation and Cato entered the class shortly after.

The group filtered in a huddle on the side and waited for his words. Yesterday's lesson had consisted of seeing everyone's talent and, from what Ikena had gathered, she, alongside the Elementals and Flynn were the strongest and most skilled. She noted that both Flynn and Kyra's talents were useful in combat and that they would be good allies for the challenge that Cato was planning, she was sure he'd bunch the group together.

"Today, I want you to practise using your magic against the Sinturi." A few people in the class gasped as Cato spoke and Ikena wondered why they had.

She whispered to Kyra, "Have they never fought a Sinturi before?" She would have assumed that all Cloaks would have fought at least one or be sent on missions of some sort.

"None of us have, you only fight the Sinturi if you're a higher rank, like Aella. It's why she's not in the same classes as us. Her group are sent on missions, defeating small packs of Sinturi who get too close to our border." Ikena realised that her and Sedric were officially the most experienced in the room. They hadn't been in the army long, a few days to be exact, and didn't understand the Kingdoms history and she didn't even understand the full extent of her powers, but they had fought the darkness and won.

"We have," she simply said but she noticed Kyra's eyes widen quietly beside her.

"Now, I have invented a device, one in which can portray a holographic Sinturi in front of you. It *cannot* harm you," Cato stressed and the Cloaks in the room gasped. "But the chill that you'll feel in the air is somewhat similar to a real Sinturi." He flicked the button on a remote control next to him and a Sinturi appeared on the other side of the class, causing the purple magic candles in the room to flurry out, leaving only the sunlight to serve as the light source for the class.

Ikena felt a cold rush come over her and the dark, hooded Sinturi neared towards her. The Sinturi seemed almost identical to the ones they had fought in the forest outside Lakeland, it moved around the room instead of standing still like the ones she had originally practised with. Most of the class, including Kyra and Flynn, scampered away from it as it hovered towards them, outstretching its misty, bony hands towards the group, but Ikena and Sedric stood tall, unafraid of the unnatural thing floating above them. *It can't hurt you.* Instinctively, Ikena found herself summoning her magic, she raised her right hand at the Sinturi and swiftly put her hand up at a right angle, shooting golden magic out of her palm and at the Sinturi which upon being touched disintegrated into thin air. The class gawked in silence.

"Well done, Ikena. Great stuff. Who's next?" Cato clapped.

With the click of his remote another Sinturi hovered in the air, portraying another dark being that looked so real, so unnatural, that it was hard to distinguish the fake from the real thing. If Ikena wasn't told, she wouldn't have known. Ikena pulled Kyra from the group, who were still cowering behind one another.

"It can't hurt you," she said quietly. "Summon your power, make it into a physical thing and shoot it at the Sinturi."

Kyra held her breath and focussed. She summoned her pale-yellow magic in the shape of a dagger and with shaking hands she threw it at the Sinturi. The dagger landed in the Sinturi's side and with the touch of magic it disintegrated like the last one had. Kyra beamed and the entire class roared with applause.

Pupil by pupil, they stepped up to defeat their very first life-like Sinturi. The Elemental kids used their talent to shoot water or fire at their Sinturi, before using their magic and Flynn shape-shifted into a wolf, which attacked the Sinturi and ripped into it. His wolf eyes glowed with his orange-coloured magic and his Sinturi disintegrated as had everyone else's. It was amazing to see Flynn morph like he did. Slayers are the rarest type of magical person, but second to that are Shifters. They're also the only magical class who can defeat a Sinturi using their talent, everyone else has to summon physical magic, rather than use their own talents.

Cato seemed impressed by the group and after everyone had practised a few times around, Cato stopped the class to talk about the upcoming challenge which would happen in two days from now, it was something that the King would also watch and, as it was during the free-time period of the day, so would the other students in the palace. It was to be a grand event. He also assigned the class into their teams for the challenge.

Sedric, Kyra, Flynn and a tall, tawny beige-skinned boy called Dax were in Ikena's team, the red team. Dax was an Elemental who could summon and manipulate water and Ikena noted it could be useful. Amongst the group they had a wide range of talents which meant they'd have a better chance at overcoming obstacles, although it didn't guarantee that they would work well together. The other team consisted of four Elementals, including a girl who could beam light out of her and a boy who could turn solid things in to liquid and vice versa. They were the blue team.

"In your teams you will have to retrieve various objects. Each object has a clue leading you to the next, and so forth. Whoever reaches the final destination with their objects assembled correctly will win."

"What do we win?" an Elemental girl from the other team asked loudly.

"The winning team will gain Elite Cloak status," Cato said, and the class excitedly murmured amongst themselves.

Ikena turned to Kyra, "What does that mean?"

"It means that you'd be in the same rank as Aella. Better

yet, you'd be able to go out of the palace on assignments. It's what everyone in the palace strives for."

That means I could find the box. Ikena couldn't stop thinking about her nightmares. If she ranked to Elite and was allowed on assignment, then maybe she could convince the King to assign her the rescue of the box as her first assignment. Ikena felt a deep desire to retrieve this box. It wasn't just because she was deemed the chosen one but also because there was something about her nightmares that scared her. It was like the darkness was calling to her and wielding her in, further and further into the darkness. She felt as if she knew Dalmask, as if he wanted her, needed her and something about that feeling compelled her. She didn't know what it meant, but she had to find out. She had to defeat the darkness and she could only do that by winning the challenge.

"We have to win this, especially if the King is watching," She said to her group. "I say we meet up every free-period and practise. Starting right now."

It didn't take long for the group to agree and she felt relieved that they had desired to win as much as she had. After Cato dismissed the class, she took her group to the training grounds outside of the palace, where all types of Cloak were practising summoning their magic or using their talent. She found a quiet patch of grass and gathered the group around. To her surprise, they were all waiting for her to begin the lesson.

"Why don't we practise summoning our magic quickly? I for one need to work on doing it faster."

She lined the group up one by one next to each other, her at the front of the line, and began practising herself. Upon seeing her practise, the group did as well and all five of them were working on allowing their magic to consume them quicker, focussing solely on the power that ran through their veins. Ikena felt the magic sweep through her body, powering each and every muscle before quickly releasing it. Once she had the feeling of what the magic felt like as it consumed her, she found she could wield it back to that place easier. They then practised forming their magic into physical objects in different shapes and sizes. Ikena went to each one and barked an object and size at them. Kyra was first.

"Dolphin and big," she said to Kyra who struggled, she seemed to be the weakest of the team, although Ikena didn't want to say it, she thought it.

Ikena moved on when she managed to form a dolphin, but she couldn't quite muster enough strength to make it bigger than hand-size. She took a step forward to face Flynn who was next in line.

"Broadsword, small."

Flynn was confident using his magic and easily made a glowing orange broadsword before Ikena's eyes, at first it was the regular size of a broadsword but then he shrunk it to half its size. Ikena was impressed and took another step forward to Dax.

"Fountain, big," she said and with that Dax shot dark blue magic out of his hands and onto the unoccupied patch of grass in front of them. He moved his arms in a dancing motion and started to build an amazing fountain made entirely of blue magic that reflected trickling water. With Ikena's approval he relaxed, and the magic dispersed onto the ground, soaking into the floor as if it were real water. Kyra began to clap and jump up and down, "That was amazing!" she said. Dax smiled at her and Ikena thought she saw them linger at each other a little too long, could Kyra maybe have a crush?

It had gotten late, and the group dispersed to their final lesson which was studying. Ikena picked up where she left off and continued to read about King Elion's ancestors. In the book it read that King Ion was the first magical person, although Ikena highly doubted that. He was probably the first person to openly come forward about it but Ikena was certain there must have been others who were quiet. King Ion was a Slayer and built Nevera. He formed the regions and villages, put forth the water and trees and invited all magical folk into his palace. Eventually, non-magical folk migrated into the Kingdom, but all were ruled under King Ion. She read through the book and made notes before turning to a page that spoke of the Sinturi.

It can't be. The first known Sinturi was King Ion himself. Ikena was sure she had read it wrong, she even checked Sedric's book to make sure, but it was correct. The first known Sinturi was Ion, who wanted to explore how far his magic could go. He was a wicked man who enjoyed killing, royalty had gone to his head and made him mad. He openly killed anyone who questioned his authority and with each kill grew a darkness inside him. It weakened him and he became frail, his skin stretched so tight on his body that he bared black bone. His magic no longer glowed as it once had, instead it darkened to a thick, black mist. He then got a taste for it. Killing. He had to kill in order to grow strong and hated the weak feeling that erupted from inside him when he hadn't killed in a while. Then killing, went to consuming. He realised he could absorb the magic from a magical person or the soul from a non-magical person and it made him stronger than he ever was.

Before he became a Sinturi, he had a son, Irion, who was born a Slayer. Irion couldn't stand to see his father in such darkness and despair and he was worried for his and his mother's safety. After rallying a few Cloaks, he confronted his father. King Ion tried to fight, but eventually the Cloaks had overpowered him, and he was banished from the palace. The book noted that Irion had made a mistake by banishing his father. He should have killed him for if he did then there would be no Sinturi.

After Ion was banished, he travelled to Riverdosk where he hid in the Caves of Zeridan and slowly built an army. He realised that he could make both magical and non-magical folk Sinturis by plunging a dagger infected with darkness into their bodies and village by village he stole folk, swiping lost lovers from their forests and children from their beds. Sinner became the Sinturi. During the Great War, Elion killed King Ion, ashamed of what he had brought to their family name, and thus the Sinturis were deemed leaderless, but Ikena knew that wasn't true. She crossed out the hand-written words in her book that said the words and annotated it to say, 'a new leader has come about by the name of Dalmask'. And made note to annotate it further once she knew exactly who the leader was.

"Hey, the lesson's over," Sedric whispered into Ikena's ear and when she looked up, she noticed that her group was standing and everyone else in the class had already left.

"Oh, sorry. I think I'm going to stay behind. You go on."

Everyone but Sedric left.

"My little bookworm," Sedric teased, nudging Ikena's shoulder.

"It's so interesting! Did you know that King Ion was the first Sinturi and that, if his son, Irion, had killed him instead of banishing him then—"

"Then there would be no Sinturi and we'd be living in a happy, peaceful, thriving Endfell." *Unlikely.*

As it grew darker, Ikena and Sedric travelled to the dining hall where Kyra, Flynn and Dax were huddled around their regular table. Ikena liked Dax, she hadn't gotten to know him properly yet, but she could usually tell when something wasn't quite right about a person, and she didn't have that feeling with him. It seemed the other group stuck together as well and were sat on the opposite table, huddled together and whispering. The three Elementals seemed to be the leaders of their group and sneered at the newcomers as they walked past, hungry bellies rumbling.

"It seems we've got some serious rivalry," Dax spoke, pointing at the other team who he noticed were scowling at them.

Ikena dished herself a slice of chicken pie, and smothered it in gravy, as well as filling her plate with plenty of vegetables which included carrots and broccoli and a few small spoonfuls of buttery smushed potato.

"Well, they're not going to win. Not when we've got this one on our team." Sedric nudged Ikena and winked with a smile, his flirtatiousness always seemed to amaze her.

"Well, I don't know about that," she said modestly but Sedric continued.

"You should have seen her fight off the Sinturi in the forest outside of Lakeland."

"She's fought an actual Sinturi?" Flynn chirped in, but he said it a little too loudly, his voice bounced around the walls and suddenly the entire hall stared their way, specifically at Ikena. "Oops, sorry."

Sedric took Ikena's hand in his and spoke in a hushed tone, "It was amazing, I've never seen anything like it. Although the *Berinturi* did come close, you lose points there," he said with another wink.

"Hey! I was a little rusty!"

"*Very* rusty."

The news seemed to shock the team and suddenly she was bombarded with questions and it reminded her of the day she had first arrived, she quietened the team down and answered their questions tonelessly in yes or no answers, not wanting to entertain for hours. Sedric gave her an apologetic look but she knew he didn't mean to put her in a spotlight position, he was excited about it all.

Ikena smiled deviously and turned the tables on him, "Sedric fought them off too, using his trident." He carried it everywhere with him.

Suddenly, the team were pressed on Sedric and proceeded to bombard him with different questions and Ikena enjoyed the flustered look on his face, and the sneaky feeling of revenge for how he put her in a disadvantageous position. They ate their food and laughed amongst themselves before heading off to bed. Tomorrow was the last day before the challenge where she felt like she had *everything* to prove. She was ready.

TWELVE

Surprisingly, Ikena woke up earlier than those in her dorm and laid awake staring at the blank ceiling. Today was the day before the challenge and she wanted to practise her magic and test her physical fitness as much as possible, she had to be prepared for the group. She sat up in her bed and soundlessly got dressed into her burgundy under suit before making her way down the stairs to the common grounds. There were a few odd students studying early, or leaders preparing for the day's classes but other than that the palace felt empty. She made her way down the royal blue carpeted staircase and out into the fresh morning day air, taking a deep breath and allowing the cold oxygen to fill her lungs. She was stretching when she heard a familiar voice from behind her.

"Ikena?" questioned Flynn, dressed in the familiar black Cloak suit.

"Oh, hey Flynn," she replied, "You're up early too?"

He noticed Ikena stretching and decided to copy her, doing the same on his part, "Well, you know, I thought I'd get in some extra drill practice and do my part," he sighed, wobbling as he attempted to balance on one leg.

"Great minds think alike," Ikena retorted smugly. "Would you like to join?"

"Why not?" he replied with a yawn. "I've got to wake up for today." It allowed Ikena to get to know him better. All she knew so far was that he was a bit of a comical mess and a Shifter. She wondered when he first discovered his powers and thought to ask on the way. Ikena took him the same was as Enzo did, through the back village and up the rocky path which led to the waterfall. Flynn seemed to be immune to the breathlessness that one would come across whilst doing cardio, Ikena on the other hand was focussing on taking deep breaths in and out with every few steps.

"Flynn, I've been wondering something," she breathed.

"What's that?"

"When did you first know you were a Shifter?"

Flynn was quiet and Ikena could sense the awkwardness in the air, she had struck a chord with him and instantly regretted asking.

"Back in my home village, I wasn't very well liked. I was bullied by a group of boys who seemed to single me out. One night, they were beating me, and I felt an immense rush of anger consume me. I felt different, my point of view was lower, and my body felt... deformed. The bullies stopped and stared, slowly backing away before running like the cowards they were. I tried to speak to them, to ask them why they were so afraid but instead of speaking, I roared. I had transformed into a lion."

As Flynn spoke, Ikena felt her mind go to a different place, she suddenly wasn't running anymore but was in a different location entirely. Around her were dark clouded skies and tired-looking faces. She could tell she was in Underust by the coal carts that one man hurried past her. She overheard a conversation from voices nearby and as she explored further, she recognised Flynn. He was talking to another man, who looked to be the same age as him and had soot covering half of his face. They both wore pale, torn clothes that fit the setting perfectly.

"Flynn!" Ikena tried to speak, but she was ignored. She neared closer to him and touch him on the shoulder, but, freakishly, her hand passed right through like she was a ghost.

"Sebastian," Flynn began, "We can't tell anyone about this." He grabbed Sebastian's hand and the two cowered behind an oil tank. He seemed scared, like he was deeply afraid of something and it made Ikena feel uneasy.

"I want us to be together," Sebastian said, grabbing Flynn's face in the cups of his pals,

"We will but you know what the others will say." Flynn slowly leant his forehead on his. Ikena gave quizzical looks. Their lips were almost touching, almost. Until they did. In a flash, Sebastian leant forward and kissed Flynn, a longing, passionate kiss that Ikena had only ever imagined having with Sedric. Ikena could have guessed it, if she tried hard enough, and he looked so happy. Flynn broke away and a smile crossed his face, his eyes became smaller as his entire posture was enlightened. Then, from behind Ikena, another boy, around the age of seventeen, charged through Ikena's body. It gave her a weird sensation, and she felt sick. The boy, of a bigger build, was joined by more men and suddenly they were cornering Flynn and Sebastian.

"He… He kissed me!" Sebastian cried, sweat dripping from his brow. Ikena gasped. He betrayed Flynn. "This *freak* kissed me." Sebastian looked at Flynn in disgust and tears began to form in his eyes.

"Is that so?" The larger boy stepped forward. "Let's beat some sense into him. *Freak*!" Upon his words the entire group began to kick and punch poor Flynn who was crying, cowered into a small bawl.

He pleaded, "Stop! Please stop!" But it was no use, his face became bloodied and bruised and the kicking and punching continued.

Just then Flynn began to change, he roared and before Ikena's very eyes was a lion, roaring dangerously at the group, nearing towards them with drawl falling from his mouth. The boys screamed and ran off and Ikena was brought back to reality.

She was still running but the disorientation she felt caused her to step on the outer edge of the path and the rock underneath her foot gave way, sending her body tumbling. She stumbled and twisted her body to face the path, luckily holding on to the edge with her left-hand. She was dangling. Flynn quickly yelled for her and peered over the edge, noticing how dangerously close she was to losing her grip on the rock.

"Ikena, take my hand!" Flynn roared, lowering to the floor, and laying on his stomach.

He reached both hands down towards her, but she was too far away to grab. Ikena tried to hoist her right hand up but she hadn't managed to catch his hand. Her left hand was beginning to slip.

"Don't you dare let go!"

Ikena tried for a second time and grabbed on to Flynn's hand but barely and their hands slipped from one another.

"Ikena!" He yelped but as he spoke her fingers slipped from the outer edge. She felt herself fall and in an instant time was in slow motion. She closed her eyes and let it be, but instead her body jolted in mid-air. She looked up at Flynn's face, who had reached further and grabbed on to her wrists as she fell. He was barely on the cliff himself and for a second they stayed there, unable to move.

"I've got you!" he winced under the strength he had to muster. Slowly, he began to shuffle his body back from the edge and, once on the path properly, he hoisted Ikena up on to the thin path. Ikena scrambled for the edge and rolled onto her back, her breath hasty.

"Flynn, you... you saved my life," Ikena breathed. "Thank you."

Flynn had kissed the path and moaned as she looked over the edge, dizziness overcoming him. "Let's get off this path." He found his way to his feet and pulled Ikena up on to hers, then took the lead and jogged to the top of the waterfall. Once they had reached the top, and were satisfied that they were safe, Flynn stopped running and instead breathed heavily. "Sedric would have killed me if I dropped you."

"Well, I do hope that wasn't your sole motivation for saving my life." Ikena giggled, *thank the Gods for Sedric*. Her giggling stopped as she remembered what had caused her to fall. "Flynn," she began. "There's something I have to tell you."

"What is it?"

She pondered how to tell him that she may have seen his biggest secret, but she wouldn't tell anyone, not a single person. "Flynn, I... I can see things. It's something new and I'm not entirely sure how it happens. I think... I think I saw your past. I saw you and Sebastian."

The skin on his face went pale and his lips started to dry.

"Ikena," he breathed but she quickly cut him off.

"We don't have to talk about it, and I promise you, Flynn, I won't tell a single soul, not even Sedric. Your secret is *safe* with me."

He stood for a moment and Ikena knew he was unsure of what to do. They had gotten to know each other over the past few days but would Ikena say she completely trusted him yet? No, she wouldn't, and it meant that Flynn didn't trust her either. After a moment he relaxed. "Thank you."

They jogged back to the palace and ended outside where their small drilling group had begun to form. Kyra and Sedric were talking and wondered where they both had gone.

When Sedric saw Ikena he had a troubled look upon his face, he noticed the terrified look on her face and immediately questioned, "Ikena, what's wrong? Where did you go? Are you hurt?" he babbled. He noticed Flynn who had also been missing and had been with Ikena before his expression switched from a troubled look to a jealous one. "You were with Flynn."

"Yes, we went running," Ikena said and noticed that Sedric had stiffened as Flynn drew near. Was Sedric truly *jealous*? The feeling evoked an uncertainty in Ikena, but she liked it. It meant he cared.

"Why didn't you ask me?" he questioned, brows drawn close together.

"It wasn't planned. It was lucky he was there; he saved my life." Sedric bombarded her with questions. "I'm fine, Sed. We ran the drill route, and a part of the rock path broke off beneath me. I almost tumbled into the pit." Sedric's jealousy had suddenly lessoned, knowing that if Flynn wasn't there with her then she wouldn't be talking to him as she was now. She'd be dead.

"Flynn," he called him over.

"Hey, what's up?"

"Is it true? You saved Ikena's life?"

He rubbed the back of his neck. "I guess so, yeah."

Sedric stared at him coldly before patting him on the shoulder and releasing the anger he had built up inside of him. "Thank you." Is all he could manage but the situation had dispersed, and the professor interrupted them. *If only he knew*, Ikena thought. They paired up in their usual pairs and began on their journey.

"Where's Dax?" Ikena wondered loudly, noticing that he wasn't in their morning running group.

"He's not in our dorm, so I assume he has a different morning schedule to us," Sedric replied.

Ikena liked Dax but she didn't know too much about him and she made sure she'd get to know him better. They continued to run, running the same path and the group were careful not to tread too near the edge like Ikena had. They made their way up soundlessly before running back down to the outside gates and across the bridge with the statues. Enzo seemed impressed with the group and he recorded that their time was fifteen seconds quicker than yesterday's run.

The group travelled to Cato's class a little early and waited for the other group to disperse in. After five minutes it seemed everyone had arrived, including Cato who swiftly begun the lesson.

"I want you to get into your groups for the challenge," he said, and Dax had made his way over to the four of them. "Face your opposition." Cato make his way over to the side of the classroom where he wanted them to practise using their magic to block each other's attacks and vice versa. "Sinturi use dark magic just like we would use ours, you need to be ready to block and retaliate quickly." He brought Ikena forward to demonstrate for their team and an Elemental girl from the other team. "Now, Natalia," he spoke to the Elemental. "I want you to cast your magic at Ikena, and Ikena I'd like you to use your own magic to block. Begin!"

Upon the words Natalia began to cast her glowing, green magic and summoned it in her hands, she threw it forward and a web tumbled above Ikena. Reflectively, Ikena cast her own magic into a small shield and held it above her head. The green magic touched Ikena's and dispersed into thin air.

"Well done!" Cato roared and he called Sedric's name and another Elemental, from the opposing team, forward. Sneers could be heard from the other group, thinking Sedric would be a non-magical easy target. They were wrong.

Ikena charged his trident, her magic transforming into his sea-blue colour and he readied himself. Upon being told to begin Sedric leapt forward and swung his trident at the Elemental which she blocked using a ball of magic. He quickly pulled his trident back and jabbed, sending out sparks of his magic which flung from each tip. The Elemental flustered and struggled to keep up with Sedric's pace. Then she used her purple magic to cast a shield in front of her which blocked her from the trident's sparks. She got on one knee and ducked her body behind it and Sedric found he couldn't penetrate it.

The lesson ushered on and everyone was able to use their magic to block each other's blows. Kyra sent magical daggers flying at her opponent who only just managed to block them. Flynn hopped about in a comedic way and dodged magic blows from his opponent and Dax did as well as Ikena had. As it neared the end of the lesson Cato informed the class of the schedule for tomorrow's challenge.

"I hope you are all well prepared for the challenge tomorrow," he began. "You are to wake up as usual for your drills but, instead of participating in them as you usually would, you are to make your way to the very top of the waterfall where you will meet me. You will then be given a riddle to solve, which will lead you to the first clue and so on. Understood?"

"Yes, Sir!" the class chanted.

"Very well. Dismissed."

Ikena's group made their way to the outside training grounds, keen on practising what they had learnt.

"Okay, let's split into two groups and practise casting and blocking each other's magic. Sed, you're with me." The group followed Ikena's every command and readied themselves.

Ikena cast her magic at Kyra who cast back at the same time and they cancelled each other's magic out, then Flynn sent knives of glowing magic flying towards Sedric who jabbed his magically charged trident at them, causing Flynn's knives to disappear, at the same time as this was happening Ikena had to block Dax's magic which was also headed towards Sedric's back. They practised like this until it was time to travel to their studying class.

When it was time, they changed into their lounge wear and met inside the classroom on a long wooden strip of a table. Ikena opened the same book she had been reading, which she had marked, and continued where she left off. King Ion was the first recorded magical folk, who had created the Kingdom, he was also the first Sinturi, his son banished him and he built an army which he used to attack the palace during the Great War.

Ikena really wanted to know how magic came about, there was no mention other than it just appeared, like it did with everyone, but why? Surely, there had to be a root cause or at least something that explained how it came about. From what Ikena knew from hers and her friend's experiences, their magic first appeared when they were suffering something traumatic, and she wondered whether that was the case. That certain people are born with magic and that it only appears when something traumatic or monumental to their life happens. She wrote her thoughts down in the book.

She continued to study and then headed to the dining hall for dinner. The news of the challenge had spread throughout the palace and, as the group walked through the dining hall, people were shouting their names and chanting and one group were even placing bets as to who would win, the red team or the blue team. People bobbed up and down and let them walk through, it seemed the other group were already in the room and were receiving the same treatment from those around them. Ikena and her friends sat in their usual spot and ate their food. Dax was sitting next to Kyra, and they were in a deep conversation, talking about their childhood. Ikena wanted to join in but didn't want to interrupt any moment they may have been having, so instead she picked out a large piece of cod alongside vegetables and fish sauce, similar to what she had made at Cato's place. They giggled between themselves and Flynn was struggling with cutting a large piece of steak, which Sedric had to help him with.

"It's okay, buddy," he said, and Flynn looked at him with sparkles in his eyes.

In the evening Ikena ushered them all to bed for an early night, but she couldn't sleep. She was too nervous about tomorrow and instead went over the tactics she had thought of in her mind and everyone's strengths and weaknesses, including her own. *We got this.* She thought. *We will win.*

THIRTEEN

It was the day of the challenge. Ikena dozed off in the early hours of the morning at around four, before waking up at seven on the dot. It felt like she had slept for mere seconds, but it was really only three hours and that was what she was used to most nights in Endfell where she was overcome with insomnia. Nervousness settled in Ikena's stomach and she rushed to the bathroom where she puked up last night's meal. She wasn't usually a nervous person, so why did this cause so much anxiety within her? She didn't have time to ponder and felt some sort of victory within herself as she woke Kyra up, usually it would be the other way round. Kyra gave a smile and relished having Ikena tell her that there was only half hour left until the start of the challenge.

On the bottom of their beds were bright red under suits, one for Ikena and one for Kyra and she guessed it was because they were the red team. They brushed their teeth, washed, and got dressed before leaving their dorm. To Ikena's surprise, the men were coming down their dormitory stairs at the same time and wearing the same red under suits as they were, and a chorus of applause bellowed at them as student Cloaks were anxiously waiting their arrival. Flynn was excitedly bobbing up and down, lapping up the attention. Ikena remembered that Cato had said that there would be Cloaks watching. *No pressure.* Ikena thought as she gathered her team and moved them out to the fresh air of the palace.

It wasn't a particularly sunny day but not the worst of weathers either and after stretching and gearing each other up, they made their way to the top of the waterfall. To their left, a stone's throw away and surrounded by his personal array of guards, was King Elion, sat on a portable version of his royal throne. In front of them was Cato and to the right was a large group of Cloaks and Commanders who were watching. The group were excitedly whispering to one another and Ikena heard her name get tossed around in the mix. The opposing group joined shortly after, dressed in blue under suits, and Cato began the challenge.

"Welcome to challenge day!" he beckoned to the crowd who cheered in support. Ikena was glad to see Cato in such high spirits.

Cato made the announcement that the winning team would be allowed the chance to rank up to Elite Cloak status and join the Elite army on assignments outside of the palace. Up ahead was a forest which looked similar to the one that lied between Endfell and Lovrin and there were two distinct openings which had seemed to be carved, one on the left and one on the right. Cato lined the teams up, Ikena's team stood outside the left opening and the blue team stood outside the right. Cato then spoke the words to the first riddle which would lead them to the clue.

"Inside, you will find trees and brambles which do not hide, but under the predator's feet bares a passage to the clue where the grey lions stare." He then yelled. "Begin!" Ikena saw the opposing team run into the forest.

She gathered her thoughts before leading her team in at a jog, where she spoke with them upon entering, "Does anyone have something they'd like to say about the clue?" she asked the group.

Kyra pointed at the trees which would represent the forest and recalled the second part of the riddle, "There seems to be a secret passageway beneath the trees and brambles," she said, stating the obvious but Ikena had to figure out where to look first.

"It mentioned a predator… What kind?" The group jogged around the forest looking for anything that resembled a predator but could not see one and they had lost the sounds of the opposing group who had jogged away from them. Then, Ikena had a thought, "I know! Flynn, can you shift into a bird and get a look from above?" The group stood around his expectantly. Excitedly, he jumped up and down on the spot, stretching his arms and legs out in long-strides.

"What are you doing?" Dax asked, as confused as the rest of them.

"I don't want to pull a muscle." Flynn then flailed his arms up and down on the spot, he bobbed his head up and down as if imitating a bird and then slowly his body began to shrink. He grew black feathers and a long beak.

"This is disturbing!" Kyra laughed, it was a bit unnatural to watch.

Flynn then whooshed into the air as a fully formed falcon

and took off, chirping from high above the trees.

"I don't think I'll ever get used to that." Sedric moaned but Ikena thought it amazing.

After a few moments he returned and transformed himself back into his peculiar looking human self.

"Did you see anything?" Dax asked.

"Yes, there is a grey-looking object just ahead, it seems like a statue to me, although I can't be sure. It looks kinda like a lion."

"That's got to be what the riddle meant by predator," Dax blurted.

Flynn led them the way and they jogged further and further into the deep forest. After ten minutes they had reached the tall statue that bared a lion's face.

"Brilliant, well done Flynn!" Ikena beamed and the group took a short moment to catch their breath.

Underneath the predator's feet bears a passage to where the grey lions stare. Maybe underneath the statue. Ikena stared at the heavy-looking object before gesturing to the group to stand back. She closed her eyes and summoned her talent, feeling the power through her hand which she focussed solely on the statue and began to levitate it.

"There's something there!" Sedric called.

Ikena strained and moved the statue to one side revealing a trapped door which could faintly be seen underneath the shrubs that partially covered it. Once moved she relaxed and sent the statue toppling down to the ground with a loud *thwack*. The other team would have heard the thump, so they had to act quickly.

Dax moved towards the trap door and removed the winding shrubs before lifting the hatch to reveal several stairs leading down into the darkness. "They've really thought this through," he remarked with a huff. He created a candle of green magic in his hand and headed down the ladder.

Sedric went next, followed by Kyra, followed by Flynn and Ikena who went last, giving the forest above her a last look before shutting the trap door on them, which made the staircase even darker. Everyone but Sedric, had used their magic to create flickers of flame to light the way. At the bottom, the team waited for Ikena to head first through the open space that awaited them underground and she did so willingly, noticing the candle frames scattered around the walls. She lit them with the flick of her hand. Inside was a large, stone room that had multiple statues of lion's at different angles and it seemed to be some sort of test.

"What is this?" Flynn asked loudly, poking one of them.

Where the grey lions stare, Ikena thought as she recalled the last of the riddle.

"Look at the statues' eyes. Where do they stare?" Ikena asked the group.

"At each other," Sedric spoke. "If we follow their gaze to the lion which isn't staring at another lion then maybe that's where the clue is."

Sedric took lead, hovering from one statue to the next until he ended at the last one whose eyes were fixated on a brick wall to the right of them. The team walked over, and Dax and Flynn began to feel the wall, knocking at certain bricks to listen for any type of difference.

"Let's use magic on it," Kyra suggested after their

knocking hadn't gotten them far.

The group backed away from the wall and allowed Kyra to cast sparks at the wall. With a hit the bricks began to crack and crumble and from the wall fled warps of darkness.

"The Sinturi!" Sedric screamed, his trident at the ready.

From around the room a coldness spread, and a piercing sound could be heard. Half of them covered their ears as three Sinturis were pumped from the dark portal that stirred above them. Dark mist wound around them, and their skeleton fingers could be heard clicking on their bare bones. They moved closer. From the side, Flynn whimpered. Ikena waited for them to attack, she couldn't figure out if they were real or holograms. The Sinturi waited too and one of them outstretched a long, bony encircled in dark mist towards Ikena. It was a trick. In a flash Ikena casted a golden lasso from her fingertips and batted the Sinturi's hand away with it, daringly. It had made contact, and the Sinturi gave off another high-pitched screech as dark flakes slowly peeled off the being. His hood fell to reveal nothingness but ash on the floor as the being had gone.

"Defeat them!" Ikena shouted and the other Sinturis attacked, splurging dark mist from their fingertips as if it was a deck of cards.

The mist above them continued to spit out Sinturis, until each person of the team was battling at least two. Ikena was quick, she used her magic to block blows of darkness that came tumbling at her before shooting golden strands out of her hands and at the beings. She struck one of them who disintegrated but the other had cast his darkness, sending a great mist of death towards her. Luckily, she dodged it and sent magical daggers flying towards the final Sinturi. Upon being defeated she gave a quick look around the room at the others who were holding up, but more and more Sinturi were coming out from the darkness above them.

"Can anyone cover me?" she called over the battle cries.

"I can!" It was Dax who had defeated the Sinturis around him by releasing his magic all around him, chasing after the hooded figures.

He leapt over to Ikena and began to shoot his magic at the Sinturis that were trying to get to her. The snivelled when hit and with all their might tried to hold on to the light. Ikena stared at the mist of darkness above them and raised her hands, palms towards it. With a slow breath she summoned her magic and cast it towards the mist. The power it took from her was immense and she strained. It was too much, but she had to do this. There was something about the darkness that overcame her, the cold that was in the air, it was different and more intense. She had come to the realisation that the Sinturis were most definitely real. Slowly, the mist had lessened, it was working. Her golden magic could be seen fighting with the darkness, a battle of its own. It glowed brightly, so much so that she immediately covered her eyes from being stunned and when she removed her arm, she had found that the dark mist had disappeared. They would not be able to spawn from it anymore. The team finished off the last of the Sinturi and became breathless. Ikena had to kneel, using her knee to hold the weight of her body as she struggled for oxygen.

"Ikena!" Sedric saw and rushed over to her side.

"I'm… I'm fine, just tired." She stood.

"Cato has really stepped up his hologram work." Sedric

helped support her as she stood.

"Let's get out of here," she said, returning to the wall where the bricks had fallen.

On the wall, was one brick which hadn't fallen when Kyra had used her magic. Sedric came over and hit it with his trident which caused it to crack into two, revealing something which could be seen inside. Ikena reached her hand in and took out a small package. Inside, was a strap and base, which looked like it belonged to a watch. There was also a small key attached to the strap and a folded note stuck inside the faceless base. Ikena took the note out and handed the strap and key to Sedric.

"A key to unlock the next clue where water runs at a scenic view. Divide the blue," she read aloud.

As Ikena spoke the lion statues behind her shifted and the last one pointed to the wall on the left, seemingly for the next team to come along and figure it out. The group quickly dispersed the way they came and, once out in the forest again, Ikena put the great lion statue back in its rightful place before the team headed off towards the waterfall. It was the only place where water ran *and* provided a scenic view. They jogged the way back but came face to face with the opposing team running towards them. One of the Elementals cast fire at Ikena which went beaming towards her face. It was inches away when Dax used his Elemental talent to disperse it with water, shooting from his hands like a hose. A rogue spark hit Flynn's leg and the bottom of his under suit caught fire, requiring Dax's assistance once more. Ikena flew daggers of magic towards the opposing group and it became a good enough distraction that her team could slip away.

"We're ahead of them!" Dax called, but Ikena knew it could take only a few seconds to change that.

They jogged out of the forest to an applause that awaited them from the crowd which had grown bigger than it was in the morning. Ikena wasn't sure how much time had passed and, although light outside still, the day had drawn darker. Cato could be seen smiling and he stood next to where the King sat in his throne and watched Ikena intently, a glare of thought crossing his handsome face.

"The key unlocks something here," Kyra spoke, pushing her glasses up higher on the bridge of her nose.

Ikena felt the King's eyes sear into the back of her neck as she consoled her team and remembered the second part of the riddle. *Divide the blue.* Could it mean dividing the water?

"Dax try dividing the water!" she bellowed.

Dax stepped forward and crouched low to the ground. He sunk his hand in the fine water at the tumbling crown of the waterfall whilst the group covered him. He was beginning to part the water when the blue team ran out of the forest and headed straight towards them. The same Elemental who could cast fire, sent a firebomb towards Dax. Dax had his back turned to it and Ikena took in a sharp breath. It almost hit him. Almost. Luckily, Sedric tackled him out of the way just in time, causing the water he had begun to control to splash heavily in one direction then the other. The crowd cheered, wanting blood.

"Protect Dax at all costs!" Ikena roared as she focussed on a large, nearby tree.

With concentration, she raised her hands at it and slowly lifted it from the ground. She strained under the heavy weight that itched her hands. With a groan, she released it, sending the bark tumbling forwards at the other group.

Some had to duck to get out of the way but it delayed them. Dax used his talent again, gaining enough power to begin parting the water but the opposing group were coming on strong. They sent flurries of magic flying towards him. First it was burst of magic, then dagger-shaped magic and then it was flurry upon flurry. Ikena and her team focussed on blocking their attacks with their own shots of magic. Kyra stayed back, making sure she blocked any magic that slipped through the cracks.

From the corner of Ikena's eye, Flynn had begun using his talent to transform himself into a huge grizzly bear. Orange magic shone through his eyes and he roared, saliva dripping from his sharp teeth. With a charge, he sped towards the blue team. Half of them ran back into the forest, scared for their lives, where he continued to chase them but there were two who stayed. These the Elementals. Sedric jabbed his trident out at the two of them, sending sparks of blue magic flying towards them. The Elemental jumped out of the way, but the other used her magic to block Sedric's.

"Something's not right!" Dax called from behind Ikena. She looked behind her shoulder and noticed that the Elemental was tampering with his talent.

"She's an Elemental, she's stopping Dax from parting the water!" Kyra called but Ikena already knew what to do, she ran over to where their advisory stood, her back to her, and kicked her, sending the body flying across the dirt.

The crowd grunted in response before cheering, seeking a vicious battle. Flynn came charging back as the grizzly and scared the other two in the group off before returning to his usual self, just as Dax had parted the water to reveal two chests, one with a red stripe of paint covering the lid and one with blue. Kyra rushed into the muddy dirt and grabbed the red one, before using her hands to dig a hole.

"Kyra, what are you doing?" Dax called as he struggled to hold the water.

"Buying us some time," she replied and Ikena praised her intelligent thinking. She was making a hole big enough to bury the blue team's chest in.

"I can't hold it much longer!" Dax called.

Come on Kyra. Ikena didn't want to see her friend drown before her very eyes or swept off the waterfall with the current. The crowd drew in a tight breath as Kyra grabbed the blue chest and threw it in to the hole, covering it with the dirt she had buried out of it.

"Come on!" Dax called and suddenly the crowd began to call the same thing.

They were on our side, willing Kyra to make it back in time. She threw herself on to the safe, grassy ground as Dax released his talent and the water came together, splashing and crashing at the force, before proceeding to tumble down as if nothing had happened. She breathlessly laid on her back, drawing in the few deep breaths she could muster.

"You're brilliant, Kyra," Dax said lovingly and in awe. He couldn't help himself. Kya blushed.

"Sed, the key," Ikena spoke and Sedric handed the key from the previous clue over.

She unlocked the chest through a tiny keyhole at the front.

Inside were miniscule crabs which scurried out onto the ground as they opened it and Flynn spent the time trying to stomp them in the dirt. They were particularly drawn to him. There was also a small pouch with a scroll attached to it and another key.

Ikena handed Kyra the key and pouch whilst she took the scroll and read, "You're halfway there, I'll give you a hint. White roses lie, find the misprint."

"The memorial." Sedric knew instantly.

Kyra opened the pouch she was holding next to them to display a clock face, but with no handles. She asked for the straps from Sedric and pushed the clock face into the circular base. All that was needed now were the hands. Kyra pocketed it and the group made way for the memorial. They jogged down the hill to the outside gates of the palace, where they crossed the bridge, went through the market, and rounded the corner.

"The misprint could be in the plaque," Ikena said and the group went over to look.

Each whote rose represents the death of a motable Sentimel in the Treat War. We are thancful for their sacrifice.

"This is all wrong." Ikena assessed and picked out the letters that were incorrect, "White should be spelt with an I. notable should be spelt with an N. Treat war should be great war, spelt with a G and thankful is spelt with a K."

"I.N.G.K," Flynn recalled. "What does that mean?"

"It could be an anagram," Kyra mentioned.

"A *what-a-gram*?" Flynn questioned dubiously, causing Kyra to shake her head in disapproval.

Ikena didn't want to seem dim-witted but she too had no idea what an anagram was, so she let Kyra explain.

"An *an-a-gram*," she mocked. "Is a word where the letters have been mixed up. If you re-arrange them, they stand for something else." She stood puzzled for a second, "I.N.G.K. King!".

"She's right!" Dax exclaimed. "It can be re-arranged to spell King!" It meant that the King had the handles, essentially the last test to pass.

"Let's go." Ikena said as she noticed the other team running their way.

They jogged back up the rocky pathway, being careful not to step out towards the edge, and found their way back to the top of the waterfall once again. The crowd roared with applause as they met their faces. Ikena charged Sedric's trident, which was low on juice, and met the King head on. She still refused to bow. The others might not know it, but she was his equal.

"I believe you have something for us," she dared. She wanted her words to sound like a question, but instead it came across as threatening and the crowd around her gasped at the disrespect.

The King didn't seem to mind, he stared into Ikena's eyes. "Do I?" he asked politely, and a chuckle escaped his plump lips, calming the crowd whose voices drew quiet. "It seems you've made it back first, so I will endeavour you. Are you looking for these?" He held out his palm and used his magic which spun like a tiny curtain around his fingers before creating two tiny golden clock hands. His magic was the same colour as Ikena's, only a darker shade.

"Yes, we are," said Ikena.

"Alright, you may have them. But only if... you *kill* Cato." The audience drew gasps as the King's personal guards had surrounded Cato and brought him to his knees.

Cato looked shocked and pleaded with the King, but he was silenced. Ikena was sure it was a test, but she couldn't be one hundred percent certain. She turned to her group and stared at Sedric who had the same shocked expression upon his face.

"You're bluffing," Ikena said, staring down at the King. "Cato hasn't done anything wrong."

"Oh, on the contrary," Elion began. "He has confessed to planning to overthrow me. *Your* King." He stressed the words 'your' and Ikena hated it. The man sitting in front of her was *not* her King.

"Cato... Is this true?" Sedric asked but the old man was silent, continuously staring at the dirt below him.

Ikena was sure it was a test and began to summon her magic. The guards stepped away from Cato, not wanting to be hit by it.

"Ikena, no!" Sedric snapped, grabbing her hand but she reassured him.

"Trust me. Just trust me," she said and continued.

She allowed her magic to consume her before creating it into a ball and flinging it towards Cato. *Please be a test.* She prayed. *Please.* But to her dismay, the magic hit him. He scowled in agony and her eyes went wide. She was sure it was a test; she was sure of it!

"Cato!" she cried, running to his side.

The old man was huddled over in a ball on the ground crying, well that's what the group thought at first, but he wasn't, he was laughing. He stood up from the ground laughing hysterically, completely unhurt. Ikena's team were confused. The other team had made it to the top of the waterfall and stood watching, the crowd still silent.

"Congratulations!" Cato bellowed. It was a test and Ikena had passed. Cato seemed to have somehow reflected Ikena's magic; he wasn't hurt at all. *Slayer*, the word crossed Ikena's thoughts. "The winners!" he bellowed to the crowd who started to cheer, some jumping up and down, hugging their friends and excitedly smiling at the team.

The King raised his hands to quiet them, before handing Ikena her prize. She fixed the hands on to the clock which sealed the object, it was complete, and the watch started to tick away. Sedric lifted Cato up in his arms and the team celebrated amongst themselves before the King cleared his throat and Ikena was suddenly brought to attention.

"As winners, each of you will be now, and forever known, as Elites. Please step forward Ikena." She did so and the King passed her a Cloak army Elite uniform, it was similar to the one she had already, and Ikena realised Cato's daughter must have been an Elite when she died.

It had a burgundy cape which was hung over one shoulder, and a silver breastplate and leg boots, with a burgundy under suit. The silver breastplate and leg boots were slightly different and had gold rims and edges and extra finishing's which gleamed in the light. They were told that someone would collect them from their dormitories in the morning to run through their new day-to-day schedule and that they should be dressed in their full uniforms.

Cato gave Ikena a hug and whispered, "Congratulations."

"Thanks. I see you've upgraded your hologram technology it seems."

"What do you mean?" His brow drew close together. He had no idea what she was talking about.

"When we were in the underground tomb, we broke the wall and a mist of darkness hovered in the air. It spurted Sinturis out at us."

Cato's eyes drew wide and he excused himself before whispering something in the King's ear. Ikena knew they weren't holograms, which meant that the Sinturis may have found a way to form inside the palace walls. Was it not protected?

The crowd dispersed and Cato ushered the groups away. They decided to head back to their dorms to put away their new uniforms and get into their lounging wear before dinner. On the way back, Cloaks cheered as the group passed and when they reached the common grounds inside of the palace they were met by an enthusiastic round of applause. "Well done!" Ikena heard a small girl say, before a man tapped Sedric on the shoulder. "Congratulations!" he said coolly.

Ikena and Kyra were about to head up the stairs to their room when Dax called Ikena's name and stopped her in her tracks.

"We want to say thank you, Ikena. Without you leading us, this wouldn't have happened." Then, to her surprise Dax kneeled on one knee before her. "I will always be at your service." Then Flynn kneeled and said the same and then Kyra. Sedric seemed to hover around at first but succumbed to peer pressure, kneeling also.

"I will always be at your service?" he questioned in a humorous way that made Ikena burst out in laughter.

"Oh, get up you fool," she said before ushering the rest of the group to do so as well. "And I at yours."

She turned on her heel and headed up the stairs swiftly, not wanting them to notice the huge smile beaming across her face from ear to ear. She felt touched by their sweet gesture. In the dorm a few women came up to Kyra and Ikena and congratulated them, excitedly talking among themselves but quietened down when Aella strode over towards them with slow, lingering strides. Ikena thought she might say something horrible again but to her surprise, she didn't. "Congratulations," she managed and prominently stuck her hand out.

Ikena stared at her for a while, unsure whether to take it or not but felt rude without doing so and shook her hand. It seemed they had struck a truce for now. Kyra and Ikena changed and headed to dinner where their group sat at their regular table and ate their food and Ikena even let herself have dessert. Things were starting to look up after all and Ikena couldn't wait to get started on the real business at hand – defeating the Sinturi.

FOURTEEN

Ikena wriggled in her bed at night, her mind in a far, far away distinguishable land of the Sinturi. She was drawn to the box which was encased in a glass pedestal that was infused with dark mist. Then, she searched for the dark leader. He was angry.

"Why won't it open?" He roared, killing a Sinturi who happened to be standing next to him in a fit of anger and rage. A dark vulture perched on his arm and yapped, squawking at his master who stroked him eagerly. His voice was dark and amplified but there was something about it, something about the figure that stood that was recognisable. Ikena didn't know why she felt so… comfortable around this figure, but she did. She felt drawn to him.

"Master Dalmask," a smaller Sinturi cowardly spoke, "It seems we need to find a key."

"A key! What kind of key?" Dalmask hissed and the small Sinturi who had spoken cowered.

"We… We found a book… a book which pictured

this box but spoke of a key."

"And where is this book?" The dark leader growled, losing his patience. Ikena wanted to lift his hood, to see who or what was underneath. To see what about the leader was so compelling.

"We were raided. It was the Cloaks." At the word 'Cloaks' the vulture began to make noises again and so did other Sinturis in the room who distasted the word.

"I want to feast on that army, consuming them one by one!" a larger, more aggressive Sinturi spoke from behind the smaller one.

"Oh, don't worry my pet. You will," said the leader treacherously.

Ikena felt herself slipping away from the scene. She didn't want to leave. She tried to focus but it was no use, her body was brought back from the scene, slipping further and further away until she awoke in the dorm. It was late and the other women in the dorm were sound asleep. Ikena heard the sound of a page being flipped and sat up. Aella was sat upright in her bed, reading from Ikena's divination book, which she had taken.

"Give that back!" Ikena demanded. She stood and lunged for it but Aella was quick and moved it before Ikena could get a hold.

"You know… you talk in your sleep. Something about a box and the Sinturis who had it. It seems… convenient that two days ago my team recovered a book from a Sinturi cave which spoke of such a box. Do tell, *Descendant*. Do tell?" she dared, but Ikena would not.

She was under strict instructions from the King himself not to mention that she was a Slayer.

"I don't know what you're talking about," said Ikena and she made another attempt at lunging towards the book, but alas Aella yanked it away again and Ikena grew annoyed at this cat and mouse game they were playing.

"Oh, I think you do. And mark my words, I *will* find out." She tossed the book at her.

With a scowl, Ikena turned and got back into bed, laying on her side with the book under arm. She knew she wouldn't be able to get back to sleep, but if it meant not talking to Aella then she'd at least pretend. She heard footsteps from across the room and thought Aella was about to cross over to her bed when instead she heard the door open and close. A quick look confirmed she had left the room and Ikena sat upright, thinking over Aella's threat. She had no doubt that she would indeed find out about her, but pushed it to the back of her mind, noting that there were more important things to think about.

Today, she was training as an Elite soldier in the Cloak army and she also wanted to visit the King for an update on this supposed box, especially after Aella confirmed that they had recovered the book she had dreamt about. The Sinturi already had the box and Ikena knew that, whatever the box did, it wasn't good in their hands. They couldn't allow them to get the key, and if it meant that the Cloaks had to track it down first then that's just what they had to do.

Kyra shifted beside her and Ikena whispered her name to check if she was awake. She was. The King had told them that someone would collect them, but he didn't say when so both of them got ready early, dressing in their new under suits and metal armour, careful not to make too much noise. Then, when it was still dawn outside, a female Cloak opened the door to their dormitory and retrieved the two women, taking them down the steps to the common grounds.

They met up with Flynn, Dax and Sedric who were escorted by another Cloak and they all formed a group.

"So, first day as an Elite?" one of the escorts made conversation, "To start, you are to report to Commander Raynik every morning at five, on the dot. We're taking you there now." They stayed in the palace but travelled to the right of it, and Ikena noted that she had never been this way before.

This part of the palace resembled the same interior, in terms of design and general structure, but there was something about it that was different, it looked more regal. They travelled into a room marked with a portrait of King Elion on the door.

Way to feed his ego. Ikena thought as they made their way into the room. Inside, there was a small group of Cloaks which, to Ikena's dismay, included Aella.

"Ahh, here they come," one of the Cloaks spoke and Ikena noted him as the Commander with his purple cape hanging delicately from both shoulders. The group of Elites turned slowly and stared at them, the newcomers yet again, but the moment the Commander spoke to them, they directed their attention back at him. "Your first assignment is to buddy up with one newcomer and show them the ropes. You will pass this assignment only if your buddy passes their induction assessment."

Then, the professor began to call out names followed by a name of one of the newcomers. Sedric was partnered with a man called Jorin. Flynn was with a girl called Teressa and Dax was with a man called Rorin. There were only four Cloaks whose names hadn't yet been called out. Ikena, Kyra, Aella and a man called Burch. *Please not Aella.*

"Aella will be partnered with…"

Please not her, not her.

"… Ikena."

Oh shoot.

Ikena stood there, not wanting to move a muscle and wondered whether she should plead with the professor to let them switch or not. Aella patrolled over to Ikena and stood tall by her side.

"You have one week!" the professor roared, before excited pairs began to talk to each other. Ikena noticed Kyra laughing with her partner, even flirting a little. She looked at him the same we she looked at Dax. Ikena reeled it. Gawking, from the corner of her eye, was Dax, who couldn't hide the jealousy that had plastered on his face.

Ikena awkwardly stood next to Aella and was about to open her mouth when Aella turned abruptly to face her and spoke.

"Listen, I know we've had our past and, to be honest, you're not quite the pick I would have wanted to be the chosen one, but right now all I need to focus on is getting you through your assessment."

Ikena processed the words Aella spoke and couldn't hide

her sullen sadness that was like a dagger to the heart. Hearing that she isn't good enough as the chosen one for some people broke her. She had never asked for any of this, it was forced upon her. A month ago, she had never even known that she was magical, and now look at her. She shook her head and tried to hide her disappointment, if anything at least she had spoken to the King, regularly even. *Aella has probably never spoken to the King.*

"Agreed. I am your student from here on until assessment day. When do we start?"

Aella began by telling Ikena what the assessment was and how every Elite Cloak must pass it before they can leave the palace on assignment.

"The first part of the assessment is an interrogation of sorts. They will quiz you on the past knowledge about the Cloak army, the Sinturi and what some of our rules and regulations are."

Ikena felt bored already. She didn't want to learn about how restricted the Cloaks were, but at the same time she thought it would be fun to count how many rules she had already broken.

"The second part of the assessment is a physical examination with what we call our *Forteys*. They are weapons which only Elite Cloaks are allowed to wield."

"You mean weapons like Sedric's trident?" Ikena questioned, Sedric would clearly pass that part of the assessment as he had been using his trident longer than the rest.

"Precisely," Aella uttered, "Come with me. I'm taking you to the library to check out some study books." She left the room at a fast pace and Ikena chased after her, struggling to keep up with her long strides.

They had left the room, walked down the corridor, and turned right to a door which was straight ahead. Aella pushed the door open, not even bothering to hold it open for Ikena and stepped inside. Ikena looked around at the giant, magnificent floor-to-ceiling bookshelves that stood gracefully before her. There were a few Cloaks dressed all in white who were on elephant ladders that were so tall they made Ikena feel uneasy when she looked up. Ikena heard a whistle and looked back to Aella who had moved to a desk with a prominent looking Cloak behind it dressed in lounging wear and tailed after her.

"We need the full set of Nevera's Heritage volumes one to three, as well as Mastering Elite Status and The Book of Cloak Rules and Regulations, please," Aella said to the librarian.

The librarian clicked her fingers and suddenly those very books started to float from the tall bookshelves around them, some as high as the ceiling, and gathered in a pile on the desk.

"Aren't you going to introduce me to your friend, sweetie?" the librarian spoke to Aella.

"I told you not to speak to me in public," she replied.

"Honey, I'm your mother. I can't *not* speak to you," she had said too much and Aella knew it.

Ikena gave a snort and was nudged in the stomach by Aella.

"Anyhow," the librarian began, "The books are to be

returned in one week and I'll need you to sign for them."

She moved a piece of paper and feathered ink quill forwards and Aella ushered Ikena to sign. She was then given the pile of books to carry, one toppled on to the floor which Aella picked up. Ikena was about to say thank you, for relieving some of the weight from her hands, but to her dismay Aella reached up and rested it delicately on the top of the pile. *Gee thanks.* Ikena followed her as she trailed off, juggling the books in her hands, until they reached a free desk at the common grounds. She dropped the books on to the table with a sigh and rested her back into the nearest chair.

"So, your *mother* is the librarian?" Ikena began, sensing that Aella didn't want to talk about it, but she pressed.

"I'll be having words with her later," she said stiffly. "If you ever tell anyone about this, I swear I'll gut you." She pulled her chair round to the front of the table and sat down opposite Ikena, "First, you'll need to study Nevera's Heritage Volume One." She pointed to the book and flipped the pages to the table of contents at the front. "What do you know about the Kingdom's past so far?"

Ikena tried to remember what she had learnt from her study classes. "I know that King Ion was supposedly the first person with magical power and—"

"Supposedly?" Aella cut her off, a tense tone in her voice. Ikena didn't feel like explaining why she didn't believe King Ion was the first magical person so instead she continued.

"I also know that he built Nevera using his magic, he was a Slayer. Then, he invited all those with magical power to live inside the palace, creating the beginning of the Cloak army." Aella nodded approvingly and she tried to hide her impressed look, but Ikena caught glances of it. "Oh, and he also became the first Sinturi. His son, Irion, banished him from the palace. He should have killed him, but he didn't and then Ion built an army. He was killed by our King, Elion, in the Great War surviving for years and years on end by consuming humans."

Aella nodded, "Move on to Volume Two and I'll quiz you later. You have to memorise this." She got up from her seat, leaving the chair where it was, and walked off.

Ikena grabbed volume two and opened the golden book which spoke of the Great War and how it had come about. It also spoke of how King Elion had led his armies into battle and what the result was. Back then, the Sinturi army had grown immensely to a point where there were more Sinturi then there were humans, and that's when the Cloaks declared war, it was King Elion's decision. The Sinturi came to the Kingdom and charged at the Cloaks, King Elion ordered all troops to the front lines and a battle ensued. There were archers who took high ground, sending arrows of magic flying at the enemy and Elite Cloaks on horseback, wielding their *Forteys*. King Elion rode into battle with them and headed straight for his ancestor, Ion, who was still alive after hundreds of years. They fought. There was a struggle, but the King was victorious, he struck Ion with his magical-infused broadsword and watched as his blood-line relation disintegrated before him.

The Cloaks were winning the war, and they managed to strike down over half of the Sinturi population then and there, but some got away, disappearing into darkness around them. The war was won, but the Sinturi were never defeated. It was an infectious disease that would continue plaguing humans and Cloaks alike until present day, where they have still been in hiding. Ikena had noticed that a significant amount of time had passed and stopped for a brief break, just as well Aella came back to check on her and noticed that she wasn't studying in the moment.

"You have been studying, correct?" she asked pointedly and sat in her chair.

"Yes, Aella, I have. I'm just taking a quick break."

"Nope! No time for breaks. Let's have a little pop quiz." She snatched the book from Ikena's hands and turned it to face her direction, flicking through the pages as she skim read. "What is the King's *Fortey*?"

"A broadsword."

"How did the war come about?"

"The Sinturi army attacked the palace. Enough testing!"

"I'm impressed." Aella turned her lips upwards in a forced smile and Ikena appreciated how Aella was being. "Why don't you take a break? I think I saw Sedric wondering around the front of the palace, he might still be there."

She offered information she knew was valuable to Ikena, causing her to stand immediately. She had longed to see Sedric alone and felt like she had to share him with everyone else who fawned over him. She thanked Aella for her time before swiftly rushing out the doors, through the palace and out into the fresh air of the village square.

Surprisingly, it was sunny outside, even though it was November, and the sun shone into Ikena's eyes. She jogged to the bridge where the statues of Kings laid before them and came to a halt when she saw Sedric walking towards her, trident in hand, across the bridge with a concerned look on his face.

"Ikena, are you okay?" he said, noticing her breath which was wheezing.

"I… I was looking for you," she struggled to say, and it turned out he was looking for her too.

He grabbed her hand and squeezed it as they strolled across the bridge before rounding the corner at the market and coming to a bench that overlooked the white memorial roses.

"This armour is heavy, isn't it?"

"Yes, just a bit." Ikena leaned her head on Sedric's strong shoulder. It wasn't comfortable at all and she found the metal shoulder plates cold under her skin, but she wanted to be close to him. "Sed, I'm sorry about all this."

"Don't apologise. You have done *nothing* wrong and, if I'm being honest, I love it here. I really do. I'm an Elite Cloak and I'm not even magical. In fact, I'm quite sure that I'm the first non-magical person in the army!"

Ikena enjoyed watching him excitedly bob up and down. She loved seeing him so happy and she loved him. There was no doubt that Sedric missed his grandma but for the first time in his life he had a real purpose. Ikena considered this and applied it to her own situation and even though she missed her family terribly, so much so that the thought of them was enough to send her stomach into knots, she still had a *purpose*.

"How's training going?" Ikena asked, with a smile that swept across her face.

"I'm a little worried."

"Don't be silly, you're a natural with your *Fortey.*"

"Yes, I can use my trident pretty well but I'm not magical, Ikena. I must rely on someone else to charge it. Do you really think they'll let a liability like me go on assignments outside of the palace?"

Ikena took his statement seriously and sat up straighter, her brows burying close together. She hadn't even considered that to be a problem and if it were, they wouldn't have agreed to let him into the army in the first place. Besides, as per Ikena's request, Sedric and Cato were both there to protect her. It was what the King agreed to and that included going on assignments with her if she passed.

"Yes, I do. Sed, you're not good with your trident, you're *amazing.*"

Sedric considered her encouraging words but he wasn't convinced. "How's your training going?"

Ikena filled him in on the vast number of books Aella had made her take out from the library. She hadn't been shown the *Fortey* collection yet, but she was most excited for that.

Sedric's mentor had come over to collect him.

"Do you have to go?" Ikena whispered, pining to stay with him for a little longer, but alas duty calls.

Ikena thought it best to head back to the common grounds where she would study again. She did so slowly and met Aella at the desk, she was hunched over her own set of books.

"How's lover boy?" she teased but Ikena declined to answer. She grabbed the book Ikena was previously studying from and flicked to a page which detailed the King's Great

War formations. "You'll be tested on the King's war strategies and formations he used in the Great War."

Ikena was made to study before Aella tested her again five hours later. She wished she had a photographic memory but unfortunately didn't and struggled remembering the numbers, positions and even the titles of the formations. When it drew dark, Ikena dropped the books in her dorm and swiftly headed off to dinner, sitting at her usual bench which was blanketed by the large feast. Ikena dished herself some pasta covered in herbs and pesto alongside a portion of chicken and waited for her friends who arrived shortly after. They each discussed what they had done for the day, what their plans were for tomorrow and if they liked or disliked their mentors.

"My mentor is hopeless!" Flynn sighed dramatically, putting the back of his hand to his forehead.

"Oh, stop being so dramatic," Kyra teased. "Besides, if you're as good as you *think* you are then it shouldn't be a problem now should it?"

Flynn rolled his eyes. "I see none of us have our *Forteys*, well except muscles over there." He gave Sedric a wink unapologetically before giving Ikena a scared look. She wanted to tell him that everything was going to be okay. That even though she saw what she saw there is absolutely no shame in being attracted to someone of the same sex and she would never betray his trust.

"Apparently, we'll all be taken to get our *Forteys* tomorrow at different times." Dax said over a mouthful of broccoli.

"Oh shoot." Ikena had forgotten that she was supposed to

visit the King and ask him for an update on the box. She had been so invested in revising that it completely slipped her mind, and it was too late to head there now. She made a mental note to visit him tomorrow and excused herself from the table, finding her way back to her dorm where she slumped back on her empty bed. Tomorrow was a new day. Kyra came up shortly after and displayed a huge grin on her face. She slumped into bed.

"You look happy," Ikena whispered. She turned her body to face Kyra, who had begun tucking herself under her covers.

"Yes, I am quite." Her cheeks were rosy.

"It wouldn't have anything to do with Dax now, would it?"

"He's a very nice person." She giggled; she couldn't help it. "And yes, actually. My happiness would have something to do with Dax. Ikena, I really like him."

"I think he likes you too."

Her eyes lit up light fireworks. "Really? Do you think so?"

"I see the way he looks at you and he was so jealous when you were gawking at your Elite partner, what's his name again?"

"Burch." Kyra's face deepened. "You don't think he was jealous, do you?"

"Oh, I definitely do!"

The two of them spoke all night and giggled between themselves and Ikena wondered if this was what she had been missing out on for years. She had always had Sedric, but it was nice to have Kyra too.

FIFTEEN

Ikena woke with a jolt. A pillow had been thrown at her, the thrower being Aella, and groaned loudly before being hushed. Everyone else, apart from her, Kyra and Aella, were asleep. As per her new Elite status she had to report to the Commander every morning. She quietened her groans to a silent grumble and hurried to the washroom to get ready for the day, changing into her armour swiftly and carrying her stack of studying books in her arms. Aella hurried them down the stairs, not offering to help. Kyra couldn't hide how tired she was and carried large bags under her eyes that told Ikena she hadn't slept well. On the other hand, Aella looked as radiant as ever. She was used to waking this early and had been doing it for a while. It came naturally to her.

They made their way through the palace with Aella leading the way, and it was just as well because Ikena couldn't remember which way was where. After a few twists and turns she recognised the library and then knew where the room was from there. Aella took them inside where they met with Commander Raynik, a peculiar looking man with a large bald head that gleamed reflections like a mirror.

"Commander, Ikena Ralliday reporting for duty, Sir." Ikena said mechanically, reeling the way she sounded. The Commander nodded towards her with a welcoming smile before turning to Kyra.

"Kyra Stretenov reporting for duty, Sir." The Commander smiled and turned to Aella who reported for duty and the three of them were marked as present.

He waited for the rest of the class to arrive before dismissing them and allowing them to focus on their own projects which, for the mentors, was to have the newcomers pass their induction assessments. Aella tried to take Ikena back to study in the common grounds for the entire day but Ikena couldn't go yet, she urgently had to see the King for an update on the box.

"I must see the King this morning," she told Aella who had a concerned look cross her face. "I'll study afterwards, I promise, but this is important. I'll meet you in the common grounds in ten minutes."

She passed the tower of study books over to Aella who didn't appreciate being told what to do, but if it involved the King then she couldn't raise her voice to complain. Ikena knew King Elion wouldn't be best pleased, especially at being seen so early in the morning but she had to know what was happening. Aella had told her that her team had recovered a book which spoke of the mysterious box that the Sinturi were hoarding. She desperately needed to know what it was and, more importantly, where the key was, so that they could open it. She walked at a quick pace to the King's chambers and pleaded with the guards outside his door,

Cato's old friend, Osirus, being one of them.

"You're not allowed in Ikena. He's in an important council meeting."

"Osirus, *this is* important. I must see him."

Osirus barked no with a stamp of his foot on the ground and Ikena wanted to plaster a slap across his face but restrained. She stood there for a moment, assessing what would happen if she made a move. She would be scolded and de-ranked which, unfortunately, was a risk she wasn't willing to take at the present moment in time. Instead, she made a loud racket, purposely arguing with Osirus loudly so that the King would overhear. After a few minutes, the double wooden doors with golden linings flew open. The King was standing before them with a disapproving look on his face but at the sight of Ikena his expression changed, and he openly welcome her in. She strode in behind him and resisted the urge to stick her tongue out at Osirus.

Ikena walked in and to her right were eight Cloaks sat around the large, oaken round table that she had only briefly noticed. Cato was one of them. The King brought Ikena over to the group but failed to introduce her, so she was left gawking at the high-ranked Cloaks and Commanders. She did recognise the librarian, who happened to be Aella's mother, towering over a book.

"How come the Sinturi were able to get into the palace grounds?" Ikena blurted, speaking her mind. "The day of the challenge, Sinturis spawned in the cave where the second clue was. They weren't holograms."

"It seems that the Sinturi have grown more powerful. With each day they are able to come closer and closer to the palace.

Please do not fret. We have a powerful forcefield around the palace that should prevent any Sinturi from coming close." The King spoke.

Clearly, it's not powerful enough. Ikena thought. "Ikena, I apologise for not bringing you into this conversation sooner, it was a mistake on my part. You have every right to know what's going on." The King spoke before he clicked his fingers and the librarian levitated the book towards her. It was an old book with a ragged red cover that looked as if the stitching was falling apart on it, woven pages hung on, but barely. Ikena went to touch the book but was hissed at by the group.

"Use your talent to move the pages, *do not* touch it," Elion stressed.

Ikena did so, using her Descendant abilities to slowly flick the pages one by one. *There it is.* She couldn't read the text but there was a clear drawn picture of the box she had been dreaming about, the very box which was currently in the hands of the Sinturi.

"I can't read the text," she muttered helplessly and a few around the table gave a chuckled laugh before being scolded by the King.

"Of course, *you* can't," the librarian began, "It's an ancient text, presumably that of King Irion's." She leant over and waved her hand over the book. The words suddenly began to unscramble into words Ikena could recognise.

"Athena's Core," Ikena read aloud.

Athena's Core could only be unlocked by a person with unique magical talents – a Slayer and was powerful enough to wipe out unordinary beings of darkness – the Sinturi. Ikena used her talent to flip the page and continued reading. Athena's Core couldn't just be opened, it needed a special key which would reveal a keylock upon touching the box. The key could not be wielded by any ordinary magical person and, like the box, could only be held by a Slayer.

"The box was formed by my great, great grandfather, King Irion." The King spoke, "He was a powerful Slayer, one of the most powerful that ever lived and he was desperate to find a cure to defeat the darkness once and for all. He had projected his magic into this box, so much so that it killed him in the process." Ikena waited a moment to pay her respects before opening her mouth to speak but she was cut off by Elion who wasn't finished, "Essentially, if we find this box then we can use it to amplify the magic inside of it, causing a nation-wide explosion that would defeat any Sinturi in the world. As the chosen one, you will bare this responsibility. It is as the divination says, *you* are the key to winning the war."

There were protests from around the room. "But she's not a Slayer!" one protested, "It should be you, my Lord!" said another and Ikena relished having that much responsibility put on her, but at the same time, she felt like she needed to be a part of this. She needed to find the key. She didn't know what her connection with the dark master was, but it scared her and if there was any chance that she could defeat him she would take it. That meant finding the key as soon as possible.

"Where is the key?" Ikena asked, and the room quietened at her question.

"We don't know," Cato spoke. "We're working on tracking where it was last seen, but in the meantime please do let us know if you have any more... updates." He was referring to Ikena's nightmares and she understood instantly. There were confused looks from around the room but none of those who knew entertained them.

"I want to be on the mission to find the key."

"Ikena, it's too dangerous." Cato tried to intervene, but he knew better.

"So, the chosen one is not being allowed to fulfil her destiny?" she questioned.

"Well, you may be an Elite, but you're not yet permitted to go out on assignment."

"Not yet, but I have my assessment at the end of the week. If I pass, I *will* be on the mission, and *with* my friends who will accompany me. I trust them more than I do any other Cloak in this retched palace." Ikena spoke well and straightened her back. If they denied her request, then she would find a way to make them change their mind or sneak her way on to the mission somehow. The King annoyingly tapped his fingers on the table, tapping the tune to a song Ikena recognised. She had always had trouble sleeping, especially when she was younger, so her mother would sing her songs to soothe her to sleep. *Our world is bright, merry, and full of light, our world is as bright as can be. Little birds, go to sleep, rest your head, and don't dare peep. Little birds, sleep away, sleep until another day. Sleep until another day.*

"Very well." The King brushed his tousled tumbling locks back, "You may set out to find the key, but only *if* you *and* your friends pass your Elite assessments," he stressed but his words didn't rattle Ikena. She nodded in approval before turning on her heel and strutting out of the room.

Once she was far away from the King's chambers, she let out a deep breath and relaxed her back up against the wall in the common grounds. She didn't want to admit it, but she was struggling with living life as a Cloak *and* the chosen one. She missed her family. She missed her village. She missed her old life. *Stop it Ikena. You're saving the world.* She felt selfish. How could she miss her hungry stomach and makeshift bed? She didn't just feel selfish, she felt ignorant too. If she helped find the key, then it meant she was one step closer to banishing the entire Sinturi population. She wasn't one to label herself, but she had been labelled the chosen one, so it meant that there were people who depended on her. Her family depended on her. All she needed to do was pass the assessment and encourage her friends to pass with her.

She quickly headed back to Aella who was getting impatient and snorted as she hurried into the common grounds.

"You've been gone for far too long!" she huffed, pointing towards the clock where two hours had already passed from when they first woke up. So much for ten minutes.

"I know, I'm sorry. Let's get to work!" She sat in the seat opposite Aella and flipped through her books.

Aella quizzed her on yesterday's reading and Ikena managed to recall the correct answers to all her questions. They moved on to volume three which spoke of the present day. Ikena seemed to know the most about this and managed to get all the questions correct when Aella tested her on them. At lunchtime, she moved on to the Cloak Rules and Regulations manual and noted that, if she were to falter on a topic, it would be this one. There were your obvious rules such as the forbidden practise of dark magic, used to intentionally kill another and also that Cloaks are not permitted to leave the palace unless they are of an Elite or higher status and on assignment, but there was also some not so obvious ones such as common talk with the King was not allowed. Ikena hadn't exactly had common talk with the King but she did have a tendency to bother him a lot. There was also a strict rule on duelling. No magical person is permitted to cause intentional harm to another magical person, unless duelling for training or practise reasons. Ikena couldn't help the snort that came from her as she read the rules and found them to be quite amusing.

There was a long list of how certain people in command should be addressed, for example the King was 'my Lord', Commanders should be addressed by their prefix and professors were to be addressed by their first name.

Time had passed them and Aella allowed Ikena a break, but she refused and kept revising. Aella quizzed her on the formalities and rules in volume three and as afternoon drew near, Aella told her that she was going to take her to choose her *Fortey* and began packing up the books.

"There is a special bond between Elite Cloak and their *Fortey*." She took out a set of steel knives from a holster at her belt. The knives were magnificent. They reflected the sun beautifully and had dips at each side. The handles were made of real silver and at the end of each one was a scorpion's head and tail. "My *Fortey*. Scorpion Knives." Aella allowed the knives to glow a deep red, they were infused with her magic.

Ikena went to touch one of the knives but Aella took it back quickly.

"No. Like I said, there is a special connection between a Cloak and their *Fortey*. It cannot be touched by anyone else but me." Ikena thought of Sedric's trident and wondered if she was connected to it, seeing as she had to charge it, but she thought not. Cato would have mentioned it otherwise.

"Why are there Scorpion's at the end of the handles?" Ikena asked curiously.

"Elite Cloaks have animals attached to their *Forteys* and ultimately attached to them. I didn't choose the Scorpion, it chose me. Do you know what King Elion's animal is?"

Ikena shook her head, eagerly wanting to know.

"The lion. It's why you'll notice statues of the animal around the palace." Ikena did notice a few statues around the palace and in the King's chambers that resembled that of a lion. It also explained why there were lion statues underground as part of the challenge.

They stopped on the way to put the study books back into their dorm. Aella then took Ikena outside of the palace. They travelled a fair way, past the rose memorial and to the very back of the palace where a small tower had been erected from the ground many centuries ago. Ikena had never travelled this far and the scenery was deserted. They neared the tower and Aella pushed Ikena inside. There were steps going up to the top of the tower where an archer would usually be placed, and steps going down which was unusual.

"Down," she eerily ordered from behind Ikena.

On the way down Ikena created a magical candle that glowed golden magic and she allowed the light to consume the passageway. At the bottom of the stairs was a small wooden door with a dainty circular handle. Aella created her own magical candle which glowed red and pushed past Ikena where she opened the door. She had to crouch to fit in and Ikena shuffled through. Through the door was a long passageway that led to another small door. They made their way into the small passage and crawled through the next door.

"Wow!" Ikena fawned at the glorious sight ahead of her.

Inside, it was as if they were in a separate place. The walls were of stone but with royal gold skirting that ran around the ceiling and floor of the room. A magnificent, glass chandelier hung gloriously, elegant glass pearls dangling from it and it was lit with a singular candle. Not a magical flame but the actual fire of a candle. Ikena looked down and saw her reflection in the sparkling floor that welcomed her. The room was seemingly spotless apart from a few odd objects here and there that didn't seem to fit the grandness of the room.

Ikena heard something from behind her and quickly turned, a breathing noise. She neared closer to a brown blanket that was covering something and allowed her fingers to stretch out, to slowly touch the blanket. Ikena shrieked. A small being underneath the blanket screamed and stood immediately. He looked tired and Ikena realised he was sleeping.

"Hey, what's the meaning of all this!" The angry being said. He was a man, there was no doubt about that, but he was small, almost half Ikena's height. She had never seen anything like it. The man noticed her confused looks and gave a long sigh. "You know, it's rude to stare."

"Ahh, Persil. I have Ikena here who needs to choose her *Fortey*," Aella urged from the behind.

The man perked up as soon as he saw Aella. He had a dazed look in his eyes and Ikena realised he was wholeheartedly in love with her. "Oh, Aella. Persil thinks you look beautiful today," he looked at her longingly but Aella wasn't accepting it and instead gave him a cold sneer.

"Stop pestering me and get to it!" she growled rather aggressively.

Persil reached up and grabbed Ikena's hand, taking her to the side wall of the room.

"Why haven't I seen you in the palace?" Ikena asked.

"The King doesn't want Persil to be seen, so this is where Persil stays." Ikena clenched her fists. How could Elion do this? He is so focussed on his image and how he is perceived that he would hide away a person from prying, judgemental eyes. *Why*?

Persil flicked a switch on the side of the wall and the wall shook. Ikena readied herself, there was something about the wall in the challenge, the one that spurred a teleportation of Sinturi, that left Ikena nervous. She had to be prepared at all times for another attack, even if it meant keeping one eye open at night. The wall then suddenly folded away into small panels at the side and displayed an array of steel weapons. It was similar to Cato's wall in Lakeland, but this was far more high-tech. The weapons were stunning. They shined in the light and were propped graciously on their stands. There were some weapons which came in pairs and were small and dainty, others which resembled swords or axes and daggers. Ikena wanted to touch them all but she knew she shouldn't. Only one of them was hers to touch.

"No doubt Aella has already mentioned this," Persil

began, "But there is a special bond between Elite Cloak and *Fortey*. Magical folk can't just choose one they'd like; their magic chooses for them."

Persil asked Ikena to place herself to the right of the wall and she shuffled over whilst Aella stood watch. "Persil would like you to beam magic towards the wall. Please."

Ikena thought it an off request but agreed nonetheless. She raised her hands and let the magic build inside of her. It was screaming to be let out. She allowed it, letting the build-up release from her body. Golden sparks shot at the wall and she watched as they travelled from weapon to weapon. She released the magic from her fingertips. The flakes never settled and, once they reached the last weapon on the wall, fizzled into nothingness. There were confused looks from around the room.

"Oh," said Persil, scratching the top of his hairy head.

"Oh? What is it?" Ikena wasn't sure if she had done something wrong or not. Both Persil and Aella had confused, worried looks on their faces. Ikena went to speak again but she was quickly ushered to give it another go. She let the magic rise inside her and let it build before she released it, she strained until she couldn't anymore and beamed the magic at the wall. It didn't take long for it to quickly disperse. Nothing had changed. The outcome was the same.

"Well, this is peculiar." Persil paced around the room. His long fingernails raked through his lengthy beard.

"What is it?" Ikena asked again.

"What does this mean, Persil?" Aella asked. Ikena didn't like that her left hand was placed firmly on her knife pack at her belt. Was Ikena dangerous? Ikena grew increasingly angry at the little being who refused to answer anyone's questions. Her fists clenched.

"Persil, what's happening?" Ikena said through clenched teeth. As if to anger her even more, Persil grabbed a small stall and placed it next to Aella. With a huff, he climbed on top and stood, he whispered in Aella's ear. Aella was focussed solely on her, her left-hand tightening around her knives. Ikena snapped.

"What is it?" she yelled, and a beam of magic unexpectedly left her body.

Aella stepped in front of Persil and blocked them both using a shield of her own magic that she had created just in time. She took a step towards Ikena, ready to yell at her for doing that but then she became distracted by a persistent glowing from behind them. It was a golden glow that was warm to the eye and came from inside a tall cupboard in the corner of the room. The cupboard was covered in cobwebs and spiders and the wood was chipped. It was one of the items Ikena first noticed and thought it odd and out of place in the grand room.

"It's not possible," Persil whispered; a gasp escaped him.

Carefully, he moved to the cupboard and opened the door. Inside, pinned nicely to white and gold beautiful fabric, were two metal… well… Ikena couldn't quite make out what they were. They looked like fans but had jagged edges and a pointed top bit that resembled that of a bird's wing. The two handles were of pure gold and at the top of each handle stood a carved eagle. Ikena felt a pull. The weapons were glowing with her magic and they called to her. She could hear her name. *Ikena. Ikena. Ikena.* It was being called over and over again, they wanted her. Without thinking, she reached out and picked them up by their handles. Something inside her jolted. She felt *powerful*. Her muscles felt lighter, her being felt *stronger*. She wanted to scream. It was the magic, the magic urged to be released, to be used. Ikena clenched her jaw at the itch that slumped her, she tried to suppress the feeling, but she felt awakened. Distinctly, she heard Persil speak.

"My dear," Percil spoke. "These were made from Nylaria herself." Beside her, Aella gasped. She put her hand to her mouth and Ikena wanted to urge her to close it or she'll catch flies.

"What's Nylaria?" Ikena asked, still reeling from the itch of her magic. The fans in her hands still glowed.

"Not what but who. Girl does not know who Nylaria is?" Persil tutted. "Nylaria is a creature of The Lost Paths. A Goddess."

"These were made by a God?" Ikena released a giggle. She didn't know why it made her laugh, but she found it humorous. First, she'd labelled the chosen one, next she'll be labelled a God. All eyes were on her. "I'm sorry, but it seems fitting. Next you'll all be worshipping me and calling me Saint." She saw a quick smirk from Aella before her smile tensed.

"It was long, long ago. In fact, it was King Elion's father who sought the creature out. He needed medicine for Elion's mother, who was deceitfully sick, poisoned by assassins from Riverdosk. Elion was just a child at the time, no older than six."

The same age as Asher and Aliza, Ikena thought of them as she listened.

"The King met a young peasant boy on the way and, for unknown reasons, agreed that he could join him on his journey. They had made it to Serenthia and travelled East to The Lost Paths. There, in the mist, he heard a cry. It was Nylaria who had been crushed by a fallen tree. The peasant boy, the King and his guards helped lift the tree from the creature and in return she offered The King medicine for his wife and, to the peasant boy, she gave these fans. They were to protect him. They have since been dubbed *Lesenleta em Darrenka.*" *Light over Dark.*

"She'll take them," Aella said from behind, a shocked look upon her face. Ikena knew she didn't mean to show it, but her eyes were wide with wonder.

Persil got straight to work, carefully taking a box from the cupboard which had holsters and leg straps in, ones specifically made for the fans. He handed them to Ikena, and she quickly fastened them to the top of her thighs. He recorded the date and time, as well as Ikena's full name and she had to dip her finger in ink and imprint her fingerprint into a book that held other Cloaks fingerprints from before her.

"You're free to go. *Mentesen.*" Persil stared as they went, a sad look on his face that he tried to hide. He shouldn't be hidden away like he was. Ikena promised herself that she'd visit him often and, if she were the one to find the key, she'd demand the King listen to the changes she'd want to make to the Kingdom. She was the chosen one and, after hearing the story Persil told, she knew that there were some who disapproved of royalty. Ikena being one of them. Although, she wouldn't go so far as to poison them. She wondered if there were groups who wanted to overthrow the Cloaks. There have always been the Sinturi but what of other Cloaks or even non-magicals, how did they *really* feel?

On the way back, Aella was quiet, too quiet and Ikena hoped she wasn't feeling jealous or intimidated by her again. They had become well-acquainted over the last few days and a fallout would only decrease Ikena's chances of passing the Elite induction assessment.

"What's wrong?" Ikena asked as they climbed back up the stairs and out of the tower to the fresh air.

"Nothing," she spat in an aggressive tone before changing her attitude. "It's just… I've worked really hard to get into the position I am in, and to be respected in the palace. But you, you've been here all but three weeks and already you're an Elite. I find it a little unfair."

Ikena understood Aella's frustration, she really did. With her mother as the librarian of the palace and on King Elion's council she must have had certain expectations thrust upon her for her entire life. Ikena was only given special treatment because she was deemed the chosen one and a confirmed Slayer too.

"Aella, I've only been given this opportunity because of a prophecy that's *supposedly* been written about me. There's also the fact that I'm more… unique than most."

"Well, aren't you satisfied with yourself," Aella said bitterly. She began to stride off leaving Ikena to trail behind her.

"No, Aella you don't understand. I'm unique because…"

She paused for a while, to say something would be going against the direct order of the King.

"Because what?" Aella had stopped pacing and turned to look at her.

Ikena stepped closer. "Because I'm a Slayer," she whispered. She had said it.

Aella's eyes grew wide in her face and Ikena grabbed her, as if to calm her down.

"You're a Slayer!" she practically screamed the news. Thankfully, there was nobody around to hear.

"Ssshh!" Ikena urged, "Under the King's order I was not supposed to tell *anyone*."

"Well then you shouldn't have said it." Her expression grew fearful of what the King might say if he found out but Ikena reassured her that he wouldn't know, not unless she told him or anyone else.

"You cannot tell a single soul, do you understand?"

Aella nodded and Ikena didn't feel like she was one to go back on her word. She suddenly felt a lot better about herself and the situation and even Ikena. She began to apologise for how she treated her but Ikena knew she was only apologising because of her Slayer status.

"Please do not apologise or treat me any different than you usually would. How you treated me was wrong, but I'm hoping we've put that aside us."

Aella nodded and had a spring in her step. She took Ikena to the training grounds and ordered her to take out her *Fortey*. Ikena held them in her hands and, with a swift flick of her wrists, flicked the golden weapons open.

"Allow your magic to consume you," she ordered.

Ikena filled her body with the sensations of magic, once again the itch called to her to release it. As she looked down at her fans, she realised they were glowing a bright golden glow like they had before. A crowd of Cloaks began to appear, and mumbles became louder. A few spoke the words, *"Lesenleta em Darrenka."* And Ikena felt a thousand eyes sear like lasers into the back of her head.

"Move it!" Aella roared and the crowd scrambled away from the both of them.

Then, Aella ordered commands to Ikena, fighting moves such as "Jab!", "Sidestep!", "Block!" and at the same time she would quiz Ikena on the contents of her studies, but she didn't fail.

Then, Aella took out her knives which glowed their devious red and threw them one by one at Ikena. She blocked the first using her left fan. Then, she cartwheeled away from the second, the knife flying in between her legs as she did so. Aella threw the third and fourth knives at the same time, in different directions but Ikena noticed. She used her fans to block both of them coming in at her sides, arms outstretched wide. Aella then stepped daringly close and kicked Ikena in the back of the leg, sending her tumbling down to her knees, crashing to the floor.

"Hey!" Ikena tried to protest but Aella did not stop. She was tough on her.

She dared close again and forced her arm out, her fist clenched at the ready. Ikena swiftly jumped to her feet and moved to the left just in time, dodging the blow, she then crouched low and kicked Aella in her knee which sent her tumbling just as she had. If she wanted to search for the key, then she had to be prepared for fights like this. The crowd that had dispersed drew close again but Ikena wasn't focussing on them, she was focussed solely on getting Aella down. Aella flung her knives at Ikena which she successfully dodged by falling on to her back before Aella scrambled on top of her and took a knife out, daringly bringing it down like a dagger to the heart. It was close. Ikena thought she might be struck but, to her surprise, she had instinctively crossed her hands, a fan in each, and blocked her blow. The two of them lay there breathlessly. Ikena didn't know what came over her but she couldn't stop a laugh from escaping her. She laughed until she wept, and it seemed it was infectious. Aella began to laugh as well. It seemed so unnatural to see her smile as she was. The crowd began to clap around them and cheered, they were in awe of the chosen one.

"Come on." Aella laughed. "Let's head to dinner."

The evening had grown close and it was no longer as bright. Ikena retracted her fans and tucked them into her leg holsters securely before walking back to the palace with Aella. They headed to the dining hall and Ikena dispersed the amazed looks that came her way. She saw Cloaks stare at her, then her fans, then back at her and pieced together their thoughts.

"You know, you can sit with us if you want?" Ikena nudged Aella, but she refused.

She pointed towards a small group of men and women who Ikena recognised as the other mentors and nodded in understanding. She had her group of friends and Ikena had hers. They broke from each other and Ikena sat herself down at her usual table where her friends had already gathered and were showing their own *Forteys*.

Sedric had his trident with the silver bear handle which he had leant up against the wall behind them. Flynn showed off his long, straight-edged sword, Kyra had a cool, small crossbow with feathered arrows and Dax had two small, jagged daggers which he could tuck into holsters on his back.

"And what animals accompany your *Forteys*?" Ikena asked aloud to the group.

Ikena's animal was the eagle, Sedric's was the bear, Flynn's was the badger, Kyra's was the fox and Dax's was a shark. Each of their *Forteys* had their animal carved in silver on the handles except for Ikena's whose was carved in gold. The group begged Ikena to show hers. Reluctantly, she took her fans out of the holsters and flicked them open. Gasps drew not only from their table but from around the room.

"You have *Lesenleta em Darrenka*!" Kyra screamed and her glasses fell to the edge of her nose.

"Yes, I know," Ikena rolled her eyes and tucked them back into their holsters, "If any of you start kissing my feet, I think I'll throw this feast at you." She giggled. Sedric looked confused, as did Dax and Flynn. They obviously hadn't done as much reading into the past as Kyra had. With annoyance, she retold the story that Persil had told her. Flynn's eyes grew wide, Dax allowed his mouth to drop and Sedric watched her intently. After speaking, she thought it best to tell them of the key and the mission she wants them to accompany her on. "I have other news," she began. "As per the King's orders, I am to go on an assignment in search for a key—"

"A key to what?" Dax interrupted.

"Jewels? Riches? Oh, I can see it now. King Flynn!" Flynn stood, arms outstretched and looked down at the mere 'common' people.

"No, Flynn, sit down!" Ikena rolled her eyes again. *Always the dramatic*, she thought, but it was rather amusing. "What it leads to right now is of no importance, all I know is that this key is fundamental in defeating the Sinturi."

"Sinturi, furi, puri. I'm sick of those little shi—"

"Anyway," Ikena interrupted Flynn who was beginning to go off on a tangent, "You all are my friends and I trust you more than I trust anyone else in the entire Kingdom... So, I've requested that you come along with me."

"Yes!" Flynn stood, drawing his sword, "I will take them down, one by one. Thank you Ikena, thank you!"

Flynn was such a character that the group seemed to enjoy his quirkiness. Half the time, he seemed like he was drunk, but he wasn't. Ikena would love to see how he'd act when he was though. Kyra whispered something into his ear, and he sat back down, very quietly. Dax didn't seem too pleased by the news and it dawned on Ikena that she was making big plans for the group without even asking if they wanted to do them first.

"I'm sorry. I know I should have asked and if you don't want to join me, you don't have to." She was looking solely at Dax. "Dax, the decision is yours."

Dax had been sitting very still, his brows drawn together, and Ikena couldn't quite grasp his expression.

"I'm in. Let's do it," he said after a moment's pause, but his expression didn't change.

Kyra also agreed to join and Ikena had hoped she would. She was a Healer so Ikena needed her on the team most of all. Sedric looked deep into Ikena's eyes, his soft brown eyes glistening in the candlelight. Ikena knew she wouldn't have to ask him. Flynn had begun talking loudly again but Sedric didn't falter, he very quietly said, "Where you go, I go." And a smile drew across Ikena's lips.

I will always be here. She remembered his words from the forest in Endfell and couldn't help but feel giddy. After dinner, they travelled to their dorms at curfew and Ikena made sure to study in the night before drifting off to sleep. Not a sleep of happy dreams and wonder. No, she was taken to the darkness of the sea.

SIXTEEN

A large blue sea ran underneath her, and she realised she was looking at it from a bird's eye view, as though she were a bird herself, an eagle. She dived underneath the sea, holding her breath. Her being went deeper and soon felt cold, going so far under that she was left in complete darkness. *Where's the key?* She thought and upon that thought a sudden bright, white light shone through the water.

Ahead of her seemed to be a bubble. Her being stepped inside and she found her lungs open to the oxygen she could no longer hold within. She was in some sort of air pocket at the seabed. Before her eyes stood an underwater village and, in a small shack at the back, was a glowing chest. *There it is.* The key was inside the chest but where *exactly* was she? She had never heard of an underwater village which was in the middle of the sea, at no particular point at all. The key would be somewhere specific. She tried to reach out, to touch the chest but as she did so she saw her arm a bony remnant of her true self amidst the shadowy mist that engulfed it. Ice crept through her body and focussed on the warmth of her beating heart. *She* was a Sinturi. She was seeing the key through the eyes of darkness. Another hovered in front of her, it's hooded being a true form of darkness. It was Dalmask. Ikena felt drawn to him, like she was *comfortable* around this being, like she was *connected* to this being. He outstretched a skeletal hand and touched her face. She tried to wriggle away but she was rooted firmly to the spot, looking up at the tall, mystic wrath of dread. Her body felt a pull, she was being consumed. She could feel the magic inside her leave her body and she tried to pull it back.

"No!" She screamed, but it was no use. Her body was draining, and she grew weaker and weaker. "Stop!"

The leader wouldn't stop. Then, a pack of Sinturis came by, grabbing on to her one by one and pulling her this way and that. They wanted to feast on her power and through one eye, which was partially covered by the crowd, she saw Dalmask slowly back away. Slowly and slowly, but there was something she saw. A glimmer of something hanging from the dark master's neck. Something she recognised. *It's not possible.* She thought. It was his, he couldn't have had it. The only other person who had it was…

"No!" Ikena screamed and with her eyes open she found herself sweating and eyes fixated on Aella's face.

"Calm down, you're safe. You're safe," she said soothingly but it felt odd coming from her.

Ikena's head darted in every which direction. They were after her. The Sinturis wanted her. A feeling uprooted in Ikena's stomach, she felt a cloud of mist cover her vision which was replaced by a master of darkness.

"I'll kill you." Ikena heard her voice say, but it wasn't her,

her voice was deep and rattled like the end of a rattlesnake. She had the urge to hurt Aella. Without realising what she was doing, she protruded magic from her fingertips and instead of coming out in bright sparks, it came out in dark flashes. Aella's eyes widened.

"Everyone, get out of the room, now!" She ordered and the girls who Ikena thought were asleep hurried from their beds.

"What's happening?" Kyra wondered, she stood immediately.

As the door clicked shut behind the last girl, Ikena growled in frustration. It was like she had no control over her body, like she was a Sinturi and wanted to kill any Cloak she came across. She built the magic inside her and sent a flurry of darkness towards Aella, who casted a shield of magic to block the blow. Ikena lowered her hands, her breath was rasping.

"Help me!" Ikena managed, as she dropped to the ground. She fought with herself, one part of her was screaming to find the King and kill him and the other was trying to hold on to the light. She needed Sedric. "Sedric." Ikena managed, in shock, her breathing rapid.

"I'll get him." Kyra hurried away.

Ikena couldn't focus on her words, her lips were moving but there was no sound coming out of them. She felt terrified. The Sinturi had got to her and she recognised something that the leader had. *It was a lie. It was just a nightmare, it wasn't real!* A moment later Kyra returned with a half-dressed and deeply concerned looking Sedric. Ikena relaxed at seeing his face and reached out to him. She couldn't breathe, but she felt

232

the darkness begin to flurry away.

"Ikena," he said calmly but rushed to her side, climbing into her bed, and pulling her up in his arms. Him being in the dorm went against one of the Cloak rules, but he cared for Ikena.

Ikena felt herself relax somewhat but continued to take in sharp breaths which felt like a dagger had pierced her heart repeatedly. It ached.

"Ikena, you're in shock," he said and began to run the bridge of her back with one hand, whilst holding her head with the other. "It's okay. Take deep breaths for me." She focussed on his words, and the glimmer of his face in the morning light.

"The Sinturi," Ikena breathed. Her fingers shook and she thought they might stay like that permanently.

"They're not here. You're safe. You're safe."

She leant on him and after a moment felt more relaxed. After she had calmed down, she buried her face in her hands. She was a fool, someone who is supposed to be the chosen one, yet she cowers in the face of the Sinturi. To make things worse, she's asking her friends to accompany her on a dangerous mission when she's seemingly unstable. Ikena forced back the tears that had already started welling in her eyes.

"I'm sorry."

"Ikena, don't ever apologise for being afraid. Never." She didn't realise why Sedric's words hurt her, but they did. She didn't want to be someone who was afraid, she was the chosen one and was supposed to be strong.

"She tried to attack me!" Aella growled from the other side of the room, "Her magic was dark, like a Sinturi! I'm telling the King."

"No!" Sedric and Ikena pleaded in unison. "Aella, I don't know what that was, but you can't tell the King. He'll kill me and I'm the only one who can stop the Sinturi."

Aella paced up the room, twiddling her knives in her fingers. "You're the chosen one," she admitted, "If it happens again, I will not hesitate to go to the King, and kill you if need be." With a nod she stormed out of the room.

"What did she mean? That your magic was dark." Sedric questioned and Kyra watched from beside her, she had seen it.

"What does that matter?" Kyra chirped, saving Ikena from having to admit what had happened, "We must report to the Commander quickly, let's go."

Sedric swiftly left to ready himself properly and Ikena quickly slipped into her uniform.

"Thank you," she said to Kyra, "For not telling Sedric."

Kyra smiled, but Ikena knew she wasn't certain she had made the right decision. The two of them headed to the Commanders room where they checked in before being dismissed to train for their assessments which happening tomorrow. Ikena was nervous, not just for herself but for her friends, who also needed to pass. She found Aella, who looked at her warily, and they headed to the study room where she was quizzed on the past history of the Kingdom, the Cloak rules and the King's army formations and techniques. Their study session was awkward at first, but eventually Ikena felt back to her usual self and begged Aella to train with her fans at the training grounds. Aella was hesitant but eventually she agreed.

Ikena blocked Aella's moves and knives that she swung at her. From the corner of her eye, she saw Dax and Kyra walking side by side with each other and became partially distracted allowing Aella to kick her hard in her jaw. *Dang it!* She thought but managed to sustain the magic she had without releasing it in a fit of rage. She quickly leapt to her feet and allowed her magic to consume her and her fans, swinging them out towards Aella's side who quickly blocked them with her knives.

"I want to show you something," Aella said, stopping the attack. "When you're in the assessment tomorrow, and it's your turn to display your *Fortey* skills, I want you to end with a finishing move." She stood behind Ikena and took her wrists, slowly moving the fans she was holding from the top-left corner to the bottom-right corner of her body. "If you do this motion with your fans, but quickly, it will send magic out towards an enemy. It is an extremely powerful move and if you can master it, you'll get top marks."

Ikena let Aella shoo everyone who was nearby away, not wanting them to accidentally get struck. Ikena stood tall and focussed, allowing the magic to consume her on command, filling her weapons before she raised her fans to the top left of her body at the same height as her head. In one swift motion, she brought the fans down to her bottom-right and stumbled backwards as the magic beamed out of her fans with force. It was the strongest she had ever felt. Aella looked shocked and didn't expect Ikena to do it the first-time round.

The magic that had beamed out of her fans travelled so far that a group of Cloaks had to jump out of the way of it, it continued until it struck a tree at the very back of the training grounds. The tree which had been slashed in half rocked and came toppling down towards them, landing just ahead of Ikena in a heap.

"Wow." Aella couldn't hide her delighted shock. From behind them a Cloak professor, their Commander, furiously stomped over to them.

"Aella! Ikena! What have you done?" Commander Raynik barked.

"Commander, we were training, Sir," Aella spoke with authority.

"I can fix it, Sir," Ikena spoke and gestured to the tree that lay before them. She pointed her hands towards the fallen tree and, using her talent, levitated it. At first, she struggled turning it upwards, but with the move of her fingers she figured it out quick enough. She then carefully placed the tree back on to the roots and used her magic to infuse the two parts together.

The Commander seemed to be satisfied now that the damage had been taken care of and he ushered the two of them into the dining hall to eat their food. Ikena thanked Aella again for the day and returned to her group of friends where they excitedly spoke about tomorrow. They were to wake up early and report to the Commander who would begin the interrogation part of the assessment. Then, they would be taken to an assessment room with walls that could absorb magic where they would be instructed to demonstrate their *Fortey* skills.

After eating they travelled back to their dorms and Ikena tossed and turned in her bed, finding the sheets less welcoming each and every day. She knew what she saw in her nightmare, whether it was real or trickery, she had seen *him*. She couldn't stop thinking about the key and how desperately she had to find it. She was ready for tomorrow's assessment, her life and the lives of the Kingdom depended on it.

SEVENTEEN

T he sun shone through the open window above Kyra's bed and directly into Ikena's eyes. She yawned as her eyes fluttered open. Today was the day of her assessment, she was nervous, but she had to pass. She woke a little too early and used the spare time flicking through her library books, remembering that she had to return them today. Aella woke up shortly after, followed by Kyra and as it drew nearer the time, they scrambled to get ready. Ikena allowed herself to have a cold shower from the tumbling waterfall in the bathroom. The cold water healed her aching bones and prepared her for the day. She had to look her most prim and proper, as knowing how to wear the kit correctly would also contribute towards marks. She got dressed, zipping up her burgundy under suit and layered her Elite Cloak breast plate, burgundy cape, leg boots and fan holsters on top. Aella helped Kyra pin her cape on correctly, to her right-shoulder, and when the time was right the three of them slowly made their way to the Commander's room.

You're going to be simply fine. Ikena tried to reassure

herself, but even as she thought it, she wasn't entirely convinced. In the Commander's office was the Commander and the rest of the Cloaks, Sedric, Flynn and Dax included. Ikena, Aella and Kyra had arrived on time, but they were the last to arrive and Ikena worried that it might affect her score.

"Commander, Ikena Ralliday reporting for duty, Sir," she barked.

After Aella and Kyra had reported themselves present, Commander Raynik separated the pack into two groups, mentor, and newcomer. The newcomers were ordered to line up side-by-side facing their mentors and Ikena quickly found Aella and did as was instructed, standing tall with her hands behind her back. She tried not to fiddle with her fingers.

The Commander inspected each newcomer one by one, jotting notes down on a pad in front of him. He looked impressed with Ikena, Kyra, Sedric and Dax but Flynn was scolded for not fastening his sword's scabbard tight enough to his belt. Then, Commander Raynik worked his way back up the group, quizzing them on the history of the Kingdom, the rules and regulations and the Great War efforts. Ikena's friends were doing well, Sedric stumbled on a few questions but with prompts was able to get the answers correct.

When it came to Ikena's turn, the Commander studied her for a moment before asking her the most difficult ones, which to her didn't seem fair but she knew he was only doing it because she was the chosen one and had to be held to a higher standard, as the Kingdom relied on it.

"What formation did King Elion use during the Great War when the Sinturi reached the foot of the palace?" he barked.

"Formation V, Sir!" Ikena answered. "Cloaks were ordered into a V formation with an Elite slotted in between each one. Archers were also placed at the top of the palace towers and in the centre of the V, Sir!" she elaborated. A quick glance at Aella told her she was doing well.

"What is a Sinturis weakest point?"

"Their chest area. If they are hit in the lower part of their body there is a chance they could survive and attack again, but by hitting the Sinturi with a magical force in the central part of their being it will cause them to disintegrate, thus causing the end of that Sinturis existence, Sir."

"What is the most important Elite Cloak rule?"

"Protect the Kingdom at all costs, Sir."

"Louder!" the Commander barked and Ikena screamed her answer again.

"Protect the Kingdom at all costs, Sir!" she clenched her hands behind her back.

Commander Raynik nodded towards Ikena and gestured to the group to follow him out through the door. They did so in formation, two by two, and followed him through the palace to a back room next to the library. He then ordered the group, apart from Sedric, to follow the steps above and sit in the assigned chairs. They did as was told, but Ikena wondered why Sedric was being held behind. As she reached the top of the stairs, she realised he was to be tested with his *Fortey* first.

They sat in their assigned chairs that were labelled with their names. Mentors were furthest from the stairs in a cluster of chairs and newcomers were to the right of those. In front of them was a see-through floor, Sedric could be seen entering the room with his trident, which Commander Raynik had charged for him as it now glowed its usual blue colour. The Commander came up the stairs and sat in his seat which was in the middle of the mentors and newcomers and lifted a small microphone to his mouth.

"Sedric Plumith, can you hear me? Please look up and respond with a thumbs up." It seemed the microphone was connected to speakers inside of the room below as Sedric responded with a thumbs up as was instructed and readied himself.

The Commander then pushed a button next to him which brought up replica Sinturis in front of Sedric. Ikena recognised them as holograms. They attacked Sedric, but thankfully he was prepared, he blocked a swatch of darkness that had come towards him and swung his trident around to the Sinturi who had cast it, spearing its chest. It disappeared. There were three more left and he dodged their continuous blows before jabbing the trident out towards them, causing magical sparks to fly out of each point in the trident, hitting two of the holograms and causing them to disappear. It was now one-on-one, and this Sinturi drew a sword made of darkness. It came for him. Sedric jumped over the sword as the Sinturi made a swoop with it at the lower part of his legs. He then spent two minutes blocking its blows, trying to come up with a way he could jab at it. Sedric blocked his adversary's darkness that came for him and pushed it back with his trident, where he finished with it through the chest. The final Sinturi disappeared, and his mentor was celebrating in his chair, pumping his fists in the air.

"Yes!" he cheered, and the group clapped as Sedric left the room and jogged up the stairs.

Commander Raynik gestured Sedric to his seat which was beside Ikena and Flynn was next called in. He went through the same routine of confirming he could hear him, then ushered him to begin. With another flick of the button the Sinturis were brought back, this time in different positions. Flynn filled his sword with magic and began to charge at one, who dodged his blow. The darkness then began to gather around him and Ikena felt her hand searching for Sedric's.

As the darkness began to encircle Flynn, he swung his sword in a circle around him, hitting three of the four Sinturis and causing them to disintegrate. The final Sinturi, sent a dagger of darkness flying at him, which caught his armour, but did no damage, it was a hologram after all, but Ikena had seen what that blade would have done. If it had pierced his armour it would have made him into a Sinturi. She worried for Flynn's scoring. Not only was he a Shifter, and one Ikena felt she needed on her team, but he was also her friend. She wanted him by her side when they left to search for the key, if her team was specifically given the assignment to retrieve it. He drove his long sword into the Sinturi which disappeared before him and relaxed against the back of the wall. His mentor wasn't impressed, nor was Commander Raynik and as he walked up the stairs, looking ashamed, Ikena was the first to clap. She clapped and cheered, and the group followed, cheering him on which put a smile on his face.

Kyra was called next. She did just as well as Sedric, her crossbow sending arrows flying towards the pack of Sinturis that gathered. She ducked here and there and managed to defeat her enemies quickly which Commander Raynik would have noted as extra points. Dax went after and did well, although he dropped one of his daggers halfway through and scrambled to pick it up just in time as one of the Sinturi had towered over him. Ikena was called last, to her dismay. She trudged down the steps and into the room, which she noticed was not see-through from looking up, only from looking down. The Commander's words rang around the room, and she held her breath.

"Ikena Ralliday, are you ready?"

She took out her fan blades and opened them with the flick of her wrists before giving a thumbs up towards the ceiling. She focussed as the room went dark, charging her body and fans with her golden-glowing magic. *You can do this, Ikena. Don't falter now.* One by one four holographic Sinturis flickered around, their hooded figures towering over her. She made the first move, attacking one of them with her left fan, causing it to disappear in front of her and she turned quickly to the other three. One shot an arrow of darkness flying towards her and with a quick duck she dodged it, but only just. The three Sinturis were then casting dark magic upon her, attacking her violently, more violently than they had the others. She resisted it, blocking each blow with her blades. It would have been easy to cast a shield for herself but that wasn't the assignment, she had to use her *Fortey* only. She ducked underneath one Sinturi, coolly slicing it with her blades as she did so. Now there were two remaining. Her feet found their way to the floor and she stood glaring at her enemies, their hooded beings aside each other before her. Ikena knew that it was now or never, she had to use her

243

finisher. She shut her eyes momentarily, allowing her body to completely build with the magic that ran through her veins and she felt powerful, more powerful than she had ever felt. With her right fan she took it to the top-left of her body and in one swift motion sliced it down to her bottom-right. She felt the magic burst from the fan and caused her to stumble backwards but she was able to regain her composure quickly. The magic sliced through the monsters in front of her and they disappeared into nothingness.

After they had all been defeated, she tucked her fans back into her leg holsters and strolled back up the steps to where the group sat. She had hoped she looked strong but in reality, she felt drained. Aella had a big smirk on her face and upon being seen, the entire group roared with applause, stunned to see the chosen one use such a defying move as she had. She sat back in her seat and Sedric put a loving arm around her shoulder.

"You did great," he whispered and couldn't help but kiss her on her rosy cheeks.

Commander Raynik spent a few minutes writing on his pad before he stood and turned towards the group. "You've all done extremely well, and I can now confirm your results." He called out Sedric's name and Ikena felt Sedric's hand squeeze hers tightly as he held his breath. "Pass!" the Commander barked and Sedric celebrated, his muscular arms flying around as he punched the air, pleased with himself. Next was Flynn and the entire group fell silent, out of everyone he was by far the worst but Ikena saw that he wasn't terrible. There was some hope for him. "Pass!" The entire class applauded him as he stood and took boastful bows. Both

Kyra and Dax had passed and Ikena found herself holding her breath as she waited for Commander Raynik's verdict.

"Ikena Ralliday," the Commander spoke. "Pass! And with *full* marks." She let out a big breath and felt Aella clapping in the other group.

Ikena was gobsmacked. She couldn't hide the smile that displayed on her face, her rosy cheeks beaming in joy. She was now, officially, an Elite Cloak, a protector of her family, her friends, and the Kingdom.

"Your new statuses will be posted around the common areas and the King will be notified swiftly. Dismissed!" Commander Raynik roared with a skip in his step.

Ikena heard mention of the King and felt it best to go to him immediately, to inform him of the nightmare she had last night. Aella had waited back for her. "Thank you so much, Aella." She offered a hand and Aella seemed to take it, willingly.

Ikena wanted to bring her friends before the King, after all they would be the ones accompanying her on the assignment, so they had to be updated too.

"Hey everyone, I must see the King and I'd like you all to come with me. You're a part of this assignment to find the key just as much as I am, and I think it's only fair that you're there with me." The group agreed and nervous looks came across Kyra, Dax, and Flynn's faces. They had never seen the King before, let alone spoke to him. Sedric grabbed Ikena's waist as they walked and stared at her in awe. After a short walk, Ikena led them to the King's chambers where Osirus stood guard and, as usual, barked that they were not allowed in.

"Now, now, Osirus," Ikena mocked. "The King requested that I inform him of any suspicious dreams that I may have had."

"And what about this lot?" Osirus questioned, eyeing up Sedric and Dax in particular, as though he didn't like them at all.

"They relate to the matter," Ikena said and Osirus finally allowed them inside.

Ikena took her friends in to the room and around the corner where the King sat in his suspended, royal golden chair that towered above them. Behind her, her friends bowed. She still did not.

"Ikena," he gracefully welcomed. "What do I owe this pleasure?"

"I've had another nightmare and now know the whereabouts of the key."

"And where is this key?" the King asked, his handsome face glistening in the candlelight.

"I don't know exactly. I saw it in an underwater village in the middle of the sea, which seems to be enchanted."

"Enchanted how?" Dax asked from beside her.

"And who might you be?" The King asked eyeing each extra person from head to toe.

"These are the courageous Cloaks who will be accompanying me on this assignment." Ikena said firmly. King Elion gave a chuckle, but he agreed, but only if they had passed their assignments.

"They have." Ikena said, "As I was saying, the village lies underneath the water in an oxygen pocket, so we'll be able to

246

breath. I must request that we are sent on this mission immediately. I see it as a matter of urgency."

"And yet. I have not officially given you this assignment. You assume too quickly."

"It is dire that I go!" Ikena shouted, causing a tension to rise in the chamber.

The King sat still for a moment or two, scratching his chin and wondering, before he gracefully spoke, "Well it just so happens that I know which waters and village you speak of." He clicked his fingers and one of his personal guards who Ikena had never seen before, walked in from behind a column with a map. He placed it on the council table and gestured the group over as the King continued, "Long ago, there was a village called Aquarin, the village upon the sea. It was where the Kingdom received its main supply of fish." The guard pointed to a blank space on a map, circling it. "One night, a storm brewed, and the waves became particularly harsh, they crept over the village until the sandy ground began to sink like quicksand. The village was gone, sunk to the bottom of Atlantia's Ocean."

"So, we have a place to start. When can we go?" Ikena hurried.

"You are adamant, aren't you?" The King was silent but after a moment he agreed. "Very well." He paused. "Who do you intend to bring along as a symbol of authority?"

"I would like Cato to join us." Ikena suggested quickly.

"I see. Very well. Tomorrow at dawn, you will be taken by carriage to the docking station at the end of the waterfall. From there, you will be able to meet your crew and sail *Ememfray* to your destination."

Ikena couldn't believe her ears, not only was she permitted to find the key which she was destined for, but she was to take the King's royal boat to do so. *Ememfray.* Ikena and her friends were swiftly dismissed and taken out of his chambers where they were allowed to relax until dinner, which was an hour away.

"Ikena, you need to fill us in on everything right now," Dax said sternly. They travelled outside of the palace and near to the rose memorial where they sat on the fresh green grass.

"I'm sorry. I've been secretive about things that I shouldn't have been secretive about and if you're to come on this journey with me then you deserve to know the truth." She took a deep breath, "Where to begin... I am a Slayer."

"*What?*" Was the general response, apart from Sedric and Flynn, who was drinking water and upon hearing the news began to choke. "Oh my," Flynn said with a breath after his panicked choking had subsided. "That makes sense now!" he barked, and all eyes were on him. Ikena remembered how she had seen his past, she was surprised Flynn hadn't guessed at it, "Never mind," he swiftly passed comment with a nervous smile.

"Yes. Yes, I know. I'm a Slayer. I am a Descendant, and it seems I can also see the past and future." She allowed the information to sink in before continuing. "I've been having nightmares of the Sinturi which... well... the dreams are real. They have found a box called Athena's Core which has enough power inside it that, if released by a Slayer, could destroy the Sinturi entirely."

"And I assume this key we've been sent to find opens the

box," Kyra spoke softly, always quick to work out the intellectual problem.

"Precisely. I'm not going to pretend like this assignment is going to be easy. It's not. There may be Sinturis seeking the key, so it'll take a battle to kill them. But…" She paused and the smile on Kyra and Sedric's faces told her they understood. "I can't protect you out there."

Sedric leaned over and grabbed Ikena's hand, squeezing it tightly. "I'll go *anywhere* with you." he whispered softly in Ikena's ear and it sent a warm chill down her spine.

"Ikena, we're with you on this." Kyra expressed and she reached out for Dax's hand. "Yeah, we are," Dax agreed followed by Flynn who reached for Ikena's other hand. It was agreed. They would find the key and save the Kingdom. They were ready.

EIGHTEEN

I kena woke just before dawn and lay, tossing and turning in her bed. There was a wrath of nervousness and worry in the pit of her stomach which she constantly willed to inexistence whenever it crept upon her. How could she not be nervous? She was risking everyone's lives. Hers. Her friends. Sedric's. Cato's. Hadn't she caused them enough trouble already?

When it neared dawn, she hopped out of bed and woke Kyra up, the two of them got changed and packed their things. Ikena remembered to pack her book, she wanted it with her wherever she went. To Ikena's surprise, Aella was not in her bed, but she assumed it was because she was at her daily meeting with the Commander. She folded their lounge wear and pyjama sets in her wicker basket.

Once the both of them had their armour on and items packed, they began to leave the dormitory and Ikena took one last look over her shoulder at the empty bed, which lay there coldly. The boys were already waiting for them in the common grounds and the group set for the waterfall where a carriage would be waiting for them. Sedric found Ikena's hand and the two of them took a slow walk behind the group, parting some distance between their friends who were listening to Flynn's ramblings.

"Ikena," Sedric spoke and stopped her in her tracks. His face was more serious than she had ever seen it, and even with his concerned look Ikena couldn't help but think of how handsome he was. His soft, tumbling blonde locks hanged elegantly on his forehead, his perfect complexion, and that jawline. "I will do my very best to protect you, I promise." He seemed to feel a need to make sure Ikena felt safe. Ikena noticed the seriousness in his tone and smiled, drawing closer to his chiselled body.

"I know. And I you." His lips drew close to hers and she wanted them to. Then flashbacks appeared of her father's death, of how *she* had caused it. She couldn't let Sedric in, she couldn't. His lips were a few centimetres away, but she turned her head. She would not bring that upon him. Sedric's brows drew close together, was she giving him mixed signals? She didn't mean to, but she was so confused, she wanted to give up every part of her to him, but darkness cannot consume him, he cannot be taken from he and she was trouble. In the distance she could hear whistling coming from Flynn. The group had stopped before the rocky steps and were watching the two of them, Kyra with a huge smile from ear to ear, her white teeth showing, Flynn, who was whistling and cheering, making a clamorous noise and Dax who stared at the two of them. Ikena felt a burn in her cheeks, what were they expecting?

Once they had reached the top of the waterfall there

was a large, white carriage with golden lining and red velvet cushioning inside with golden pillows that had embroidered pictures of the Great War. The carriage was pulled by two white horses with one coachman sat at the top of the carriage. The group was escorted inside by four Cloaks who guarded the carriage around them. *Must be extra protection after the Sinturi spawned inside the palace.* The thought made Ikena feel queasy again. After a half hour journey, they arrived at the dock with *Ememfray* waiting ahead of them.

Ikena could hear voices being yelled from the deck above them, and orders being given by a familiar sounding voice. Once they departed the carriage, they were ushered to climb the rigging that led to the deck of the ship. Once up, Ikena's thoughts were confirmed. The voice she heard barking orders was Aella's, who stood a few feet ahead of her ordering commands to the few Elite Cloaks who served as the crew, and to the right of her stood Cato.

Ikena rushed over to him. He looked younger and fuller of life since Ikena first met him. He no longer had such a frail face and was able to walk without his usual hobble. She remembered that the Sinturi consumed the souls out of humans and magic folk to stay powerful and wondered if magic folk stayed powerful when they used their powers. He helped the rest of the group onboard and paid extra attention to Flynn who got his foot caught in the net on his way up.

"Aella," Ikena called, grabbing her attention. She turned instantly, wiping her long black braided ponytail in Ikena face. "Ouch," Ikena sarcastically said before returning to her question. "You're accompanying us?"

"So it seems. Commander Raynik has given *me* my

first role as a Commander in training. The crew are under *my* command and *I* am to get you to Aquarin waters safely." Ikena couldn't help but force a smile at Aella's wittiness.

"How long is the journey?"

"If we keep at a steady pace, around five days." *Five days. A lot could happen in five days.* Ikena tried to hide her disdain at it not being a shorter journey. Once all were aboard safely, Aella barked orders at the crew, "Hoist the sails! Raise the anchor! All hands on deck!" It was amusing to see her bark the way she did and Ikena was thankful because she knew nothing about boats, actually this was the first boat she had ever been on.

"Cato, what do I do?" she asked him, hoping he'd have a little more advice.

"Let me show you to your quarters," he chuckled and gathered the group.

They made their way through a small door that had stairs leading down to another, which led to a long hallway along the ship. From that hallway were different doors that led to other rooms and in other directions. Cato stopped at the door on the left and slowly pushed it open showing a cramped room with multiple bunk beds inside. "For the crew," he said. He then pushed a door opposite open to display a well-made bed with a wardrobe, cabinets, and bathroom as well as one circular window. "Aella's room." They were swiftly ushered on. Further along was a door to the left which was Cato's cabin and opposite that was Dax's. Dax was ushered inside to rest until he was called. Along from their cabins were another set of doors. To the left was Kyra's room and to the right was Flynn's. Her friends' rooms bared the same grand layout as the first, with similar furnishings and bedding. There was a door straight ahead which Cato took Ikena and Sedric through. Inside was a grand room with a mahogany table that shined in the sunlight and purple velvet plush chairs situated around it.

"The council room. We'll talk here shortly." Cato said and took them further to the back of the boat through another set of doors and another small corridor. After the short walk they reached grand double doors that had carvings of trees on the mahogany wood.

Cato pushed the doors open and before Ikena's eyes laid a large King-sized bed with velvet blue sheets and a soft, woollen blanket on top. Opposite the bed was a small mahogany table and next to that were the wooden wardrobes and cabinets which looked equally as grand. On the opposite side, in the corner, was a stool with a velvet blue top that matched the covers of the bed and a desk with lots of little drawers and on top of it sat a grand mirror. Cato gestured to a door on the right, and Ikena opened it. There was a toilet and sink but also a beautiful bath. Ikena almost rejoiced then and there. The bath was made of ceramic carvings that welcomed her. She had never seen a bath so grand before and, back in Endfell, her family had to use pieces of ragged cloth that they could spare to wash with from the sink. How had the King had so much wealth, to be blessed with a bath, and yet not shared with the regions he ruled over? The King was lavishing in his grand robes of silk, hearty feasts and freshly washed skin and yet shunned the folk who struggled for meat on a daily basis and re-wore their clothes for months on end.

"Well, I hope you *two* find the room settling and I'll

call for you in a few hours." Cato left the room and Sedric allowed himself to plop on the bed that sprang underneath him, outstretching his arms.

"I guess we're bunking together, at last," he snorted with a wink which still made Ikena blush the deepest red.

She didn't know what to say but she knew that she was doing what was right and that meant more to her than anything. They spent the next few hours unpacking what little they had brought and exploring the room. As it drew darker, a small knock happened upon the door and Kyra and Flynn peered in through a small gap.

"We're not kissing, you can come in," Ikena said as if she were talking to little children. *Why do they have to make it so awkward?*

"Thank goodness for that!" Flynn bolstered through the door. "This room is perfect!"

"It seems we've been given the King's room," Sedric said boastfully as Flynn glanced over to him and gave him a look Ikena could only describe as idiotic. "Yes, it's *our* room."

"I'd like to see the sea from the deck, who's coming?" Ikena said with a skip in her stomach, needing to change the weird atmosphere as soon as possible. On the way, the group grabbed Dax from his room and headed for the main deck where Aella sat by the helm and Cato stood near with a long spyglass. Ikena looked around and noticed that they were in the middle of the sea with no pier or tree or village in sight. She had never seen the sea before, she had seen pictures and drawings but never the *real* thing. It was breath-taking. The sea slumbered in its blue cloak and greeted Ikena with crashes against the side of the boat, welcoming the chosen one to its lands. Up above, seagulls squawked and hopped on and off the boat. Ikena gloried in the sight but her stomach felt queasy.

"I trust you've settled in well?" Cato strode over, eyeing up Flynn who hadn't quite masked his sea sickness and was currently spewing in a bucket. He crouched down to the floor and tried to grab hold of the floorboards as if one jolt would throw him off the boat. "I don't think I can do this," he said with a barf.

Cato handed him a cloth to wipe his mouth. "Why don't we go to the council room to talk." He called for Aella who passed the wheel to an Elite Cloak with big, boulder-like muscles, before following them to the council room.

The group made their way back through the corridors of the boat and into the grand council room with the overly large mahogany table which stood waist high in the middle. They took their seats on the plush chairs around it and Cato outspread an old map of the kingdom. It labelled where each and every village was and looked like a large, older version of the one Ikena had, which she had never taken the time to look at properly. There was Riverdosk to the bottom right which held villages such as Ranja and Teraska. It also held the Caves of Zeridan where the Sinturis formed. Above Riverdosk, in the top right-hand corner, was Serenthia. Ikena remembered Persil's story of Nylaria, who spawned in The Lost Paths. Serenthia also housed villages Ikena had never heard of before, such as Retaska and Olavia. On the left side of the map, in the bottom right-hand corner, was her home. Endfell. The little village was marked inside the Nevrain region with Lovrin and finally, above Nevrain was Carcoona where Lakeland sat amongst other villages. Ocean Atlantia could be seen and from it swarmed lakes that ran through villages such as Lovrin and Lakeland. Aquarin could be seen labelled in the middle of the sea, surrounded by nothingness.

"Now, who has sailed on a boat before?" Cato asked the group.

Aella raised her hand and, to the groups surprise, so did Dax. "Before I became a Cloak, I lived in Retaska, my family constantly sailed for fish," he said. The rest of the group kept their hands firmly rooted at the sides and it seemed Cato expected just as much.

"Right, well there are a few things you should know. On land, we worry about the Sinturi… but in the water there is something else. Something much, *much* worse. It is a devilish creature which rules the sea, the Okratica."

Beside him, Dax gasped, and it was enough for Ikena to question whether she made the right decision leaving the safety of the palace or not.

"Fisherman have been known to go out to sea and never come back and old tales put it down to the Okratica, a sea creature which matches the description of a shark, an octopus and a snake all rolled into one." Dax said in barely a whisper.

"How likely is it that we will come across this creature?" Ikena asked sternly.

"Recent sightings have placed it in the very south of the sea. We will be in the middle, so there isn't necessarily a high chance, but it *could* happen." Cato said and he opened another book next to him to a drawing of this supposed creature, it was terrifying.

It had a long snake-like scaled body, but with six slimy tentacles at the front of it that had tiny suction cups like an octopus. The head of the beast resembled that of a shark with rows upon rows of razor-sharp teeth. Ikena had a bad feeling, and, although she knew she was just being suspicious, it was a feeling she couldn't seem to shake.

"My men have been trained to defeat this beast should we ever happen upon it," Aella scoffed, she plunged one of her knives into the book, which pierced the drawing of the creature.

"Are there any other creatures we should know about?" Sedric asked.

"There are the usual sharks, jellyfish, piranhas, but they're no match for this boat. Just don't fall into the water," Cato stressed, and he stared at each one of us with piercing eyes. Ikena felt her back straighten. It had drawn incredibly dark and her stomach grumbled. It was as if Cato had heard because he chuckled loudly and said, "I imagine you all must be hungry by now. Let's eat."

Cato whistled and multiple cooks began to pour in from every door with an array of seafood from cod to oysters, to roasted pig with potatoes and an array of vegetables, alongside champagne which Flynn almost grappled from the woman holding it. Ikena didn't like the taste of champagne, it always seemed out of place in her family but each year, on Winter's Day, her mother had always insisted on drinking a bottle and toasting to their father. *May he rest in peace*, Ikena thought as she gulped a sip down, the bubbles popping down her throat as she swallowed. She allowed herself a helping of the roasted pork, rejected the cooked duck the chefs offered her, alongside a few roast potatoes which were the perfect golden brown and drizzled in oil, creamed vegetables, and pork gravy. It was the most food she had put on her plate in a long time but eating might quench the upset stomach she had from the boat that jolted on the water, bobbing up and down contently. Ikena was distracted from her thoughts by Kyra and Dax. Dax seemed to have whispered something in Kyra's ear which made her burst out laughing and she couldn't help but smile. She wanted to join in, to ask what was so funny, but she knew the two were falling for each other and didn't want to interrupt. She thought of Sedric, of how he's always been there to help her.

"Thank you for protecting me," Ikena whispered closely in his ear. He didn't immediately reply but she was sure she heard him mutter, 'Always' under his breath.

Cato and Aella were in the midst of talk about the boat's functions. Dax was casually eating a large piece of carrot which had been smothered in gravy and Ikena thought to start a conversation.

"So, Dax. You're from Retaska?"

"Yes," he replied after chewing. "My family owned a small shack and I was part of the fisherman's regime alongside my father."

"And what did that entail?" Ikena pressed, she loved to hear about other villages in the kingdom and had always dreamt of travelling one day.

"Well, a group of us would board a small boat and head out into the sea in search of fish, my father was always with me and he'd know the best spots for the rarest fish. It would take us the entire day, and once back each fisherman would take a fish from the caught load, bringing it home to cook with their families." Dax smiled. "Sometimes my father would take two, just to feed my oddly large family."

Ikena enjoyed seeing him so happy and wondered aloud at how many siblings he had.

"Guess." Dax played along.

"Five." Ikena guessed.

"Six." Sedric guessed.

"Seven." Kyra guessed.

Flynn didn't just guess. He stood and roared that he knew the answer, he was swaying from side to side, a little drunk and slurred his words, "I... I know how many. Twelve!" He banged his glass of champagne on the table sending the full champagne glass to splash on to the wooden mahogany. Cato and Aella gave a disapproving look, they were too caught up in their own conversation to play along, but the rest of the group laughed. Ikena laughed so hard that tears began to fall from her eyes.

"Alright, tell us," she said, stiffening a sniffle.

"You won't believe it." Dax said with a grin from ear to ear. "But Flynn got it right. I have twelve siblings." Flynn stood, his arms wide and gracefully accepted the applause we gave him, bowing and tipping even more wine onto the table, and half over Kyra for that matter. Ikena couldn't help but laugh again and found her hand reaching for Sedric's. She was glad to have him with her, she was glad to have them all with her.

It was when Dax asked Ikena about her own family that her smile lessened and she became suddenly extremely homesick again. She excused herself from the table and paced back to bed, a pit of guilt in her stomach. She didn't want to think about her family, about not seeing how much Asher and Aliza had grown without her or how bad her mother was coping. Sedric joined shortly after and, as she was drifting off to sleep, she felt the nudges of his body behind her, his arm slung over her stomach, his warm breath warming the back of her neck. She pressed herself into him like a cocoon and slept peacefully to the aches and creaks of the boat. It was Sedric's whisper she fell asleep to. *Always.*

NINETEEN

I kena woke to Sedric's snores from behind her and she had to give him a little kick to stifle them as it had become too loud at one point and she thought he might wake up the entire corridor of their sleeping friends. Deciding that she couldn't go back to sleep, she got up and went to the bathroom to have an early morning bath. Her body ached and a nice relaxing moment to herself is just what she needed, so she ran the bath, leaning over to turn the hot knob on and in doing so she accidentally knocked a bar of soap in, noticing that it created bubbles in the water, so she spent the most part crumbling the soap into the water to coat a thick foam of bubbles on top. She slipped her silk golden pyjamas off, leaving the door slightly ajar in case of an emergency, and sunk in. Oh, how her body thanked her for it. The warm water relieved her muscles from the stress they had carried and willed her to relax. Ikena floated, allowing her head to rest on the edge of the bath with her eyes closed. She was woken ten minutes later by a smirking Sedric.

"Excuse you!" she cried, sitting upright, and jerking more

bubbles over her body, which was already covered by a thick coat. "Can I help you?" she said at his gawking face.

"That remains to be seen," he said with a harmless wink. Sedric had a way about him that made everyone feel comfortable and flirting just came naturally to him, but it was something foreign to Ikena, her flirting went as far as a hold of a hand and even that caused her to blush. *How pathetic*, she thought about herself.

"Well, I'm not going to invite you in," she chuckled, relieving the room from awkwardness. "But we can talk if you want to bring in a chair."

To Ikena's surprise, a red blush could be seen on Sedric's cheeks and he nodded before swiftly disappearing and returning with the plush stall that was by the mirror in the room. He placed it a few feet away from the bath and sat, tussling his flowing locks which had tumbled into his face.

"How do you feel?" Ikena asked him.

"I feel fine."

"Just fine?"

"Yes."

"You don't have to pretend with me, Sed. We've been friends for forever," she said and raised her right-leg, looking at her toes which had crinkles over him, before realising how provocative it must have looked and quickly dipped it back in, taking note of the red tomato that was now Sedric's face. "Oops," she nervously chortled. "Anyway. What's the matter Sed?"

"If I'm being honest, I'm a little worried about my grandma."

"Homesick?" Ikena had felt it since they had first left and she was so wrapped up in doing what was right for the kingdom that she hadn't even thought of how Sedric might be feeling about everything. At least her mother and siblings were young, for all they knew, Sedric's grandma could have had an accident or old age could have taken her.

"Oh, Sedric, I'm so sorry. I'm sorry to have brought you along." Ikena offered but in her heart, she knew sorry wasn't enough.

"Ikena, what have I told you about apologising?" he said with a half-smile. He had told her a few times to stop apologising but she couldn't help it. It seemed wherever she went, darkness followed. A terrible thought appeared across Ikena's mind. So terrible, she immediately felt sick. If she was correct in knowing who the Sinturi leader was then it meant he would know how to hurt her and that meant targeting her family or Sedric. She had hoped she wasn't right, that the darkness wasn't so recognisable, but she wasn't sure.

"What's wrong?" Sedric asked, noticing the worried look on Ikena's face.

She debated whether to tell him or not, of what she saw in her nightmare but pushed it to the back of her mind. It was ridiculous. "Nothing, I was just thinking about Endfell," she lied, "What do you think it's like now? The old folks don't even know what's going on."

"No. I bet the news of the chosen one from Endfell has sent them into a rally. You know what the mayor is like, this would be enough to send him into a frenzy. I bet he's hosting a village party, in your honour, tonight."

"Prepare the chickens!" Ikena mocked in the mayor's stern, but old voice.

"Set the tables!" Sedric joined in and Ikena let out a giggle. It reminded her of when they were younger and used to mock the mayor and certain people in the village that they didn't like. Ikena always mocked the mayor's daughter who seemed to dislike her and had fallen completely in love with Sedric.

When the bath water drew colder Ikena thought it time to get out and Sedric disappeared to allow her to. She hopped out and stepped on to the sheep rug on the floor, allowing it to soak up the water from her feet. She put on her armour for the day and made sure she had her fans tied into their holsters around her thighs, before coming out of the bathroom. Sedric was dressed in his armour too, his trident ready and the two of them met the group on the deck.

"How was sailing through the night?" Ikena asked Aella by the helm. She had bags growing underneath her eyes and her face was sunken from exhaustion.

"It was rough, but we got through it and we'll do it again tonight."

It seemed like a good enough answer for Ikena who nodded and moved on to talk to Cato. Cato thought it best that the group practise their training, especially as they needed to be prepared for what lied ahead. The group did as instructed and lined up in two rows facing each other. Dax was opposite Ikena, his daggers tucked neatly into his back holsters.

"Now, I want you to fight each other, *without* using your *Forteys* today." Cato said, and upon command the group prepared themselves into a fighting stance.

Dax went on the attack first, he lunged at Ikena with a fist but Ikena was quick. She might not have had the hardest punch or kick, but she could definitely dodge one. She fell to the floor instantly and dodged his punch before sweeping in between his legs and coming up behind him. She went for a kick to the side but, to her surprise, Dax grabbed her leg and swung her around before letting go, causing Ikena to topple to the other side of the boat. The move caused the rest of the group to stop fighting and most of them winced as Ikena hit the ground hard. All eyes, even those of the crews, were firmly on her, wondering what she'd do next. Ikena wiped a trickle of blood from her lip and found her way to her feet. *So, you want to play dirty huh? I can do that.* She crossed over to him, dodging his left punch, then his right, then his kick which she jumped over when he tried to take her out at the ankles.

"Attack Ikena!" Cato demanded.

She dodged more of his punches before jabbing her fist out and smacking him in the jaw. His head jolted back at the force, but he was unharmed and retaliated with a side kick towards her. Ikena was ready, she felt alive. She dodged the kick and jumped high in the air before rotating her body and landing both feet on Dax's chest area and kicking off. The force knocked Dax to the ground and Ikena landed, impressively. Dax conceded and Ikena offered him her hand. He took it and as they both rose the crowd began to clap. Aella barked at the crew to keep working and Cato allowed the two of them to sit and watch whilst the other groups took their turn at fighting. Ikena watched as they worked hard, sweat dripping from their brows.

"You were quite impressive," Dax offered with a smile and nudged her shoulder.

"So were you." She managed before cheekily adding, "I'm sorry for showing you up."

Dax released a chuckle. It was currently Sedric against Flynn. Flynn, who was of a skinnier frame than Sedric, who had large protruding muscles, was no match for him and with one kick Flynn flew to the other side of the boat, just as Ikena had. He hit his head with a *thump* and caused a load of dirty laundry, which was balanced on a beam above him, to fall on top of his head. The crew couldn't stifle their laughter.

Kyra was next and it was her against Aella. Cato roared at them to begin and Aella came on the attack, kicking and punching but Kyra was actually blocking her attacks. Kyra was a Healer, not a fighter. She didn't look like she had any form of muscle on her body and yet she was holding up against Aella, a trained professional. She continued to block Aella's attacks before punching her in the face and sending her to the ground. The entire group cheered and applauded the sweet girl who had just defeated the very opposite of herself.

Kyra sat beside Ikena with a beaming smile. "Here, let me fix that," she said, turning to Ikena and hovering her hand above her broken-skinned lip. Ikena felt a slight tingle on her lip and after Kyra was done, she handed her a small pocket-sized mirror she had kept in leg boot. Ikena was shocked to see that the blood and cut was gone like she had never been hurt at all.

"That's some impressive stuff, Kyra!"

"Thanks, I'd really like to see how far I can test my magic, you know? Of course, I don't wish any harm but so far all I've been able to fix are cuts."

"Kyra, I have no doubt that if the time came your magic would succeed you. You're talented, truly. I am most thankful that you're here, not just as our Healer but as my friend."

Kyra's cheeks turned red and she stared at Dax who was practising using his daggers against Flynn's sword. He was winning effortlessly. "You know he likes you, don't you?" Ikena nudged her.

A smile crossed her face. "I know," she said sweetly and adjusted her glasses.

The group spent the rest of the day practising before they had dinner once again in the council room and headed off to bed shortly after. Ikena was kept awake by the snores of Sedric beside her and travelled to the deck of the boat to be in the cold evening's air. On her way, she heard a giggle from the corridor. She waited in the council room and slightly opened the door to see Kyra and Dax, holding hands and going into Kyra's bedroom. *Finally*, Ikena thought. Once she heard the door click shut, she allowed herself through the corridor and as she opened the door to the deck the chill swept down her throat. Aella was on the helm and various crew members were doing something on the boat, whether that was wiping down the decking or climbing the rigging.

"You should be sleeping," Aella disapproved as Ikena drew near.

"Sedric snores," Ikena replied grumpily. "Loudly." She let

herself relax on a stool and put her feet up on the side of the boat, noticing how the stars sparkled in the evening's appearance. "Beautiful," she whispered.

"I've always loved the stars," Aella began. "Look here." She pointed above at a group of stars. "You see that constellation of stars, what does it look like to you?"

Ikena looked up and noticed the group of bright stars. "It looks like a pan, or pot."

"Yes, that's the Little Dipper constellation and the star at the very top of the handle is the North Star. It's how I know that we're heading the right way, I can use maps but seeing as we're in the middle of the ocean with no sign of a navigation point, I have to rely on the stars."

"You're going to be a great Commander."

"I hope so," she said and with a warm smile returned to the helm.

Ikena returned to her quarters shortly after and tried to sleep. Ikena's mind drifted away. Away from the boat and to the darkness which drew her to it.

"Dalmask, your excellency. We know she's on a boat, on her way to find the key," a Sinturi spoke.

"How many days will it take for us to reach Aquarin?" the dark master spoke.

"Not many, one or two days. We'll ambush them." When the Sinturi spoke, the rest of the council snarled and slithered, needing a taste of Cloak souls. "We'll consume every last one of them, and the girl, my Lord. She'll be left for you."

Dalmask stood slowly, his palms facing upwards in a praying manner, he then outstretched his skinless hands on the table and whispered with his deep voice, "Prepare my horse."

Ikena woke in the middle of the night startled, causing Sedric to leap up and grab his trident.

"I'm… I'm sorry." Ikena struggled to breathe. They were coming. They would be at Aquarin. *He* would be at Aquarin. Were they ready to take on the dark master? After Sedric realised what was wrong he crawled back into bed and held Ikena close to his side, stroking her long, raven hair.

"Sssshhh," he said soothingly. "It was just a dream. You're safe." Ikena held on to each and every whisper, his soothing words sending her back into a deep sleep. She felt him kiss her on the back of her neck and mutter something under his breath, but she couldn't quite make out what it was before she fell asleep and awoke a few hours later to breakfast in bed. Sedric had ordered a meal of scrambled eggs and rye bread from the cook alongside fresh orange juice and all brought in on a wooden tray.

"You got this for me?" she questioned, wiping the sleep from her eyes.

"I did," Sedric said, pushing it towards her. "Now, I want you to eat every last bite."

Ikena didn't need convincing. She picked up the small knife and fork and swallowed the fluffy, creamy egg and savoured each piece on her tongue.

"Thank you." She finished the last mouthful and gulped at her orange juice.

Sedric took the tray from the bed and placed it on the side, before cuddling up next to her. Ikena looked up at his deep brown eyes and couldn't help but feel utterly in love.

"Ikena," he began. "When you left me at Lovrin it was the most scared I've ever felt in my entire life. It caught me completely by surprise, how much I needed to see your face again. I couldn't... I couldn't *not* see you again. On my journey to find you I found myself noticing things and turning to my side to tell you about it, how the sun shone so delicately on the petals, how the water by the lake was so fresh and I thought I'd never get used to muddy Endfell water again. When I remembered you weren't there, there was something in my heart that broke. I... I remembered our time in the forest at Endfell, our little games when we were young. I held on to that, knowing that if you loved me as much as I love you, then I'd find you. And sure enough, I did." His face was dangerously close to hers and as silly as it felt, Ikena felt the urge to say that she loved him too. He had said it. It's something that she had wanted to hear since she had first met Sedric.

"Sedric, I—"

She couldn't speak before their lips touched, a longing kiss that felt so natural to Ikena, so thrilling that it sent her stomach into knots. The warmth of his breath radiated through her body. His hand cradled her head, but it was enough. For so long she had wanted to give in to him, to confirm that she loved him. She was afraid, afraid that she would get her heart broken, that she was trouble. Look what happened to her father! Her mind screamed at her to stop, to push him away, to save him, but she was selfish. She wanted him. She drew back and gently touched her head on his, focussing on the gentle smile that had plastered across his face, his lips were wet. *If only Precious could see us now*, Ikena thought.

"Do you know how long I've wanted to do that?" A laugh escaped him.

"I've wanted it too." She managed; her cheeks were burning. "But you were always chasing after other girls."

"Do you know why I chased other girls? It's because I couldn't have you, so instead I tried to force myself to like someone else. It never seemed to work. Why did you push me away?"

This is what Ikena feared. She had pushed him away for years, every move he made on her she shut down quickly. Strictly expressing that they were friends and that's all they'd *ever* be. Her heart ached.

"I can't tell you." She wouldn't. She *couldn't*. She had a burden that was hers to bare and, for now, she was going against everything she had ever told herself. She was giving up a part of herself to him because she loved him. She trusted him. Ikena was relieved when a knock happened on the door, it was Dax.

"Cato wants to see us in the council room... now," he awkwardly said, tugging at his long hair.

"I'll let you get dressed." Sedric moved out of the room with Dax. He was radiating happiness.

Ikena couldn't shake the feeling she felt, the feeling of being in love, and as much as she loved it, it was also distracting her from the task at hand. She pushed the savoury feeling to the back of her mind and proceeded to change into her armour before trudging off to the council room. In the council room was Cato, Aella, Sedric, Dax, Flynn, and Kyra, who were all sat around the mahogany table, a seat empty at the head of the table for Ikena. They watched her walk and Cato began speaking when she had taken her seat.

"We're around one day away from our destination."

Kyra looked concerned. "I thought you said we were five days away. We've been on the boat for just three," she questioned aloud and Ikena was grateful that she had taken note of how many days they had been sailing for.

Aella groaned loudly, the bags under her eyes were as dark as she'd ever seen them, and she looked about as tired as Ikena's body felt. "My crew picked up the pace." She paused before yawning. "We're ahead of schedule and will arrive tomorrow at dusk."

Ikena processed this information and Flynn spoke about having a plan. Immediately all eyes were on Ikena and she felt pressed to speak. "We need to get under the water where there's an air pocket which holds oxygen so we can breathe. I say we lower the anchor slightly, allowing us to hang on to it before the crew drops it down to the bottom of the ocean so that it goes through the air pocket."

Cato seemed impressed with the idea of using the anchor and said that he'll stay on the boat in case of any trouble above water. Aella demanded that she come along, not wanting to miss out on the opportunity to say that she, Aella Stormbone, had seen the fallen village in person and Ikena knew better than to deny her that right.

"Now, Ikena. Do you know exactly where the key is?" Cato asked and Ikena tried to remember back to the nightmare she had at the palace. She remembered going to

273

the bottom of the water where a bright, white light shined the way to a shack at the back of the village. Inside that shack was a chest that glowed, it was in there.

"It's in a shack at the back of the village, encased in a chest. I must warn you that last night I had a nightmare where I saw the Sinturi council. They know that we're on the way to find the key, and they've dispatched Sinturis to come after us. In my dream... there were Sinturis in Aquarin. The dark master, Dalmask, was there too. We will have to fight him." Ikena allowed the group to process this information and nodded among themselves but grew silent. "There is no shame in backing out now."

"I'm with you," said Sedric.

"Ikena, none of us want to back out. *We're* with you," Kyra corrected, and it was decided.

"Thank you." Ikena managed.

"I suggest you practise your magic today, eat well tonight and get lots of rest because come tomorrow evening, you won't be resting." And with Cato's words, the group were dismissed and headed back to the deck, however Flynn seemed to run in the completely opposite direction, his face a mixture of emotions. Ikena noticed that Flynn's cheerful demeanour had changed so suddenly and decided that she needed to check on him. She hurried on after him, even following the sound of a door closing.

Reaching the door, she could hear the faintest sound of a whimper. Flynn was crying inside. *Should I go in?* She wondered but felt her fist knocking on the door. She pushed the door open. Flynn was sitting on the floor at the bottom of the bed, his head in his hands and tears streaming from his eyes. Ikena shut the door behind her and slowly crept over to where he sat.

"Flynn, what is it?" she asked, and hated seeing the boy, who looked so vulnerable in that moment, so sad. After a few sobs and sniffles Flynn mustered enough courage to reply.

"Ikena… I don't want to admit this but… I'm scared," he whimpered into her shoulder like a lost puppy.

Practising in class was helpful, but it makes it a lot easier knowing that the Sinturis back then were holograms. Although, the ones in the challenge weren't and Flynn didn't know that. Ikena had never told anyone because she didn't want to scare them but maybe she should have.

"Flynn, I have something to tell you. Back in the palace when we were doing Cato's challenge and the Sinturis spawned in that small cave underneath the ground—"

"You mean the *holograms*," he said sulkily with an eye roll.

"No Flynn, I don't. Look, I didn't tell you this before, or any of our friends, because I didn't want to scare you." He sat upright and his eyes had dried. "They were *real*. Somehow, they had spawned inside the palace. The King has extended the forcefield protecting the palace to the forest, so they won't be coming back there. But Flynn, you were amazing when you fought them with us. You are already more experienced than most in the palace." Flynn's eyes widened at the news and the crook of his mouth upturned into a small smile. "Why don't you freshen up and join us on deck for practise?" She offered and he nodded standing.

On the deck, Cato was barking orders at the group who were practising using their magic, making it into a physical thing and using their *Forteys*. Aella sent magic rippling through her knives and then practised throwing them in to the air and commanding them to go certain directions she wanted before returning back to her. Sedric practised with his trident and sent sparks of magic flying at the sea below. Kyra and Dax were practising fighting with magic and took it in turns to cast and block between them. Ikena joined the group and five minutes later so did Flynn. His eyes were still red and puffy but not as noticeable as they had been when she first walked into the room.

"Flynn!" she called him over. "Let's practise using our *Forteys* yeah?" He agreed and made his way over to her, his long sword out at the ready.

Ikena attacked first, swinging her left fan towards him but he blocked it with his sword. He then swung his sword at Ikena, which she luckily blocked with both fans and pushed the weapon off before dodging around him. To her delighted surprise, he shape-shifted into a ragged dog, eyes gleaming with his magic and leapt towards Ikena. She used her fans to block his blows but stumbled onto her back. The dog came leaping towards her, jumping into the air to land on top of her but she quickly brought her legs up and the dog landed on her feet, she kicked and sent it high into the sky. Flynn then turned from a dog, to a vulture and began attacking her from above, nipping at her hair and arms. She threw one of her fans at the bird, which lightly knocked it using the handle part and sent the bird toppling towards the ground. Flynn managed to turn back into his human-self but ended up in a ball on the

276

floor.

"That's perfect, Flynn!" Ikena exclaimed, impressed at how he had skilfully used his talent. "You used your talent well and, seeing as your magic consumes you when you shape-shift, it means you'd be able to defeat Sinturis when you shape-shift. I'd definitely recommend using it tomorrow." She knew she had said too much when the last word rang from her mouth and she felt nervous, unable to read the cold expression on Flynn's face. His expression went from a look of dread to a fierce look. "I will use it," he said, before working on his own at shapeshifting into different animals.

Ikena practised on her own too until it drew dark and the group were ushered into the council room where a glorious feast stood before them like it did every night. The group began to take their seats but Ikena couldn't help but notice that whilst they were tucking into the very best trimmings the palace cooks had to offer, the crew were outside in the cold, slaving away at keeping the boat running.

"What about the crew?" she wondered and wished she had mentioned it on the first day that they left for the key.

"They get the leftovers at a later time. They have to focus on running the boat." Aella said, holding a chicken drumstick and tearing into it carnivorously.

Ikena didn't like her answer and excused herself from the table, grabbing a roasted potato as she did and bit on it as she walked out to the deck. "Everyone! Join us for dinner in the council room!"

The crew looked between themselves before hollering with huge smiles and followed her as she led them to the feast. Her friends seemed shocked at first but, after realising Ikena had brought them in, started to load their plates up with food.

"You know. I don't like stuffing." Flynn said, noticing a crew member who was pondering over a tiny amount of stuffing that was left over. "Here, take mine." He said and scooped his stuffing balls off of his plate and onto the crew member's.

Ikena made a few plates up and gave them to the crew members who couldn't leave their stations, such as the bulky Cloak who would take the helm when Aella wasn't steering. Seeing the entire ship so happy was enough to make Ikena cry and that night, as her and Sedric laid in bed, she couldn't stop thinking of their happy faces and wondered why the King wouldn't want to feel as good as it felt to share. She was acquainted with Elion, and he didn't strike her as a horrible person but what did he offer the villages? They had glorious feasts, the best of wealth or of what money could buy. If he actually went to visit the regions in the kingdom, he'd change his mind for sure. Ikena pondered the thought.

TWENTY

I kena tossed and turned in the night as she slept, she was too anxious about the day's events that were going to play out. *Breathe.* She told herself as she felt her heartbeat begin to beat faster. *It was just another day as a Cloak.* She couldn't believe she even thought the words, as being a Cloak was definitely *not* another average day. After the morning light shone in through their cabin window and poured into the room, she felt restless and was careful not to wake Sedric as she got dressed in her armour and headed to the deck where the crew members bade her good morning. Aella was slumped over the helm, looking far more drained than usual, she must have commanded the crew through the night.

"How far are we?" she asked.

"We'll be there soon enough," she replied coldly.

"I'm a little nervous. I don't want anyone to die for me."

"For you?" The phrase seemed to disgust Aella and it struck a chord in her. A soured look plastered itself across her face and she spoke with harsh words, "None of us are doing this for you. We're doing it for the future of Nevera." Her words were like daggers to Ikena's heart, but she stood tall and took them like a leader. Aella was right. *It's not about you, Ikena.* She reminded herself and felt silly for saying what she had said.

As Aella made no attempt to make conversation with Ikena, she sat in a chair on the deck and tipped her head back, allowing the sunlight to fall directly on her face. The sea crashed around her but surprisingly the wave sound it made was calm and soothing and there was a distinct salty smell rising from below. A few hours passed and Flynn came out to the deck, yawning and stretching. He began doing some form of yoga with his legs tucked behind his body, just like she's seen dogs do when they stretch of a morning sometimes.

"Good morning!" Flynn said to Ikena in a cheerful tone. "What a beautiful day." He smiled and twirled in the sunlight. "You know what Ikena," he said. "I've got a good feeling about today." Ikena managed a giggle and was happy to see him in a better mood.

Dax and Kyra came on to the deck and shortly after so did Sedric, he seemed lost and was frantically looking around for Ikena. Once his eyes set on hers, he relaxed somewhat and couldn't help keep a smile from appearing at the sight of her.

Sedric made his way over to Ikena and gave her a good morning kiss, wrapping his big arms around her and kissing her on the cheek lovingly. Flynn made gawking noises from beside them. Ikena poked her tongue out at him. *Soon, the teasing will stop, and they'll get used to it*, she thought. Cato then came out through the door and gathered the group, including Aella, together.

"We're going to be practising drills again today," he said cheerfully, but Ikena could tell he was nervous about today's event just as much as she was.

They did as was instructed and practised using their magic and *Forteys* and Ikena and Dax were partnered with each other again. Cato wanted them to fight once more and he seemed to enjoy the light-hearted competition between the two of them. Last time Ikena had won, but it was a close call.

"Begin!" Cato yelled as the group watched on and Ikena and Dax began to charge at each other.

Dax attacked her with his daggers, bringing the sharp edge of one of them to her neck. Luckily, Ikena was ready with her fan blades and blocked the blow. She then swept behind him and landed a kick to his back. He scrambled to his feet and charged his daggers, throwing one towards Ikena. She used her charged fan to block and felt alive when she used her power, like she needed to use it or else she'd become weak. It was an itch that didn't seem to go away, and she knew that she would never want it to. Her magic called her, it called to be released and Ikena wanted to answer it. After an hour passed Dax yielded, a few cuts and bruises to his face which Kyra quickly healed. Ikena slumped on the deck, her back on the splintered wood of the side of the deck, and stared at the sky, taking in heaving breaths. The rest of the day went smoothly, some of the others practised fighting each other, and calling their magic or using their *Forteys* and by the time they had all taken their turn it had gotten dark, the moon being the only light that led them to their destination.

"We're around half-hour away!" Aella called to the group,

who scrambled to prepare themselves.

Ikena tucked her fans into the holsters at her thighs but re-tied them to make sure they were extra secure. Sedric stood by her, his trident majestically held beside him and as the time drew near the group had formed, suited and booted, ready to complete the assignment. The sky above them was dark and filled with stars, yet a cold wind streaked across their faces. Aella was at the helm, calling orders to her crew to slow the ship down, shutting the engine off and Ikena gave one last final pep talk to her friends.

"We've got this," she began. "I just wanted to say thank you for being here, what you're doing will save the kingdom. Don't be scared, you've all trained for this and I would personally trust you *all* with my life. I can assure you; you can trust me with yours." The group lifted their *Forteys* in the air and cheered, giving off a battle cry.

"Let's do this!" Flynn cried.

"We got this!" Dax roared.

"Remember, only I can touch the key," Ikena reminded, "For Nevera!"

Then her friends alongside the crew chanted, "For Nevera! For Nevera! For Nevera!"

It was time. The anchor was lowered a little so that the group could fit on, and Cato took over from Aella at the helm. All they had to do was shake the anchor chain when they wanted to be brought back up. Ikena began to climb over the side of the ship and hopped on to one side of the large, heavy anchor that hung daringly. Sedric climbed over next, hanging on to the other side of the anchor. Then, Kyra climbed over and wrapped her legs around the chain. Flynn was above her. Dax above him and finally Aella above Dax. All four of them wrapped themselves around the chain and held on tightly.

"Be safe!" Cato called, and Ikena felt the pang of sadness rush over her in that moment. It was exactly the same words her mother would call out to her before she ventured into the Endfell forest to hunt for the day's meat. Ikena wouldn't allow her emotions get the better of her and nodded towards Cato who yelled an order to the crew to lower the anchor. They did so by turning a big wooden contraption clockwise which took four crew members to do so.

Ikena watched as her eyeline caught sight of the crew, then the side of the ship, and as she looked down at the water and saw she was about to plunge in she yelled, "Take a deep breath!" They were submerged in the water.

The group had to hold on to the anchor tightly, otherwise they would float to the top of the sea. *Stay calm.* Ikena told herself. *Just stay calm.* She opened her eyes which immediately stung in the salty water around her. She looked below but could see nothing but the thick darkness of the ocean. Then, she used her magic, making it into a physical candle so that she could at least see when they were going to hit the ground, but it was too late. Just as she made the candle, the anchor crashed into the ground with a *thump*, sending the group tumbling off it and on to the dirty, wet, sandy floor where they laid sprawled out on. Ikena opened her mouth as she fell and realised she could breathe, they were inside the oxygen bubble. She heard her friends take deep breaths from behind her but then Ikena heard the cries of Sedric.

"Dax!" he shouted and as Ikena turned around she saw what he saw. As the anchor had crashed on the ground the group tumbled off it. Dax tumbled backwards and out of the oxygen bubble. He laid on his back on the wet floor with his mouth wide open, he was drowning. Sedric held his breath and went out to fetch him, dragging him by the legs back inside the bubble. The group scrambled around him and Kyra began to cry. She fell to her knees instantly.

"Dax? Dax please." Ikena pleaded, shaking his body but there was no response.

Sedric leapt on top of him and began pushing down on his chest hard before feeding him oxygen through the mouth. He was saving him and Ikena held a magic candle closer. One push. Two pushes. Three pushes. With each passing second it seemed that Dax would never wake. Ikena tried to stay calm for the group but already Flynn was freaking out, his arms flailing around him. He was having a panic attack and Kyra was weeping, desperately hoping that he would wake.

"Come on, buddy." Sedric said, being more forceful with his pushes, "Come on!" He breathed oxygen into his lungs again and continued to push.

"Kyra, can't you do something? Heal him!" Aella roared and began pacing up and down on the spot.

"I can't!" she blubbered. "I can heal wounds, not bring someone back from unconsciousness."

Aella and Kyra then started to get into an altercation of their own which wasn't helpful to the matter at hand, Aella snapped at Kyra to help but Kyra was powerless, it only made her weeping worsen. Meanwhile, Flynn had fallen to the ground and had started to rock back and forth uncontrollably, his knees drawn up close to his chest and he was humming something he found soothing. Ikena wanted to help him, to tell him to calm down but she couldn't go to him right now, she had to focus on Dax.

"Come on!" Sedric said, punching his chest now. He roared with each and every hit, willing him back to life but it seemed no use. Dax laid there, his eyes wide open, his body lifeless. *He's gone.* Ikena thought, sinking her head in shame. They hadn't even found the key yet and already one of their friends had been greeted by death. Flynn's humming got annoyingly loud and as Ikena was about to yell at him to be quiet Dax took a large breath and immediately sat up, so quick Ikena almost punched him from being so startled. He coughed out the water that had filled his lungs and struggled to breath for a moment until he was calm. He was okay. Kyra immediately wrapped her arms around him, nuzzling her face in to the bridge of his neck.

"I thought… I thought you were gone," she blubbered.

"I'd never leave you," Dax wheezed, breathlessly.

"We thought we lost you there." Sedric said, breathless himself over his hard work. "Can you stand?" Dax nodded and with Sedric's help he returned to his feet.

It was Flynn that Ikena was most worried about. He continued to rock back and forth, his fingers in his ears and his humming loud.

"Flynn," Ikena went over to him and crouched down, but as she laid a hand on his shoulder, he shook it back and began to yell. He was looking around frantically. "It's okay. Dax is okay."

Flynn looked from her to Dax who was standing, his

breath had returned to normal and Flynn took a deep breath himself before standing. He was an odd person and had a wild personality, someone who spoke his mind constantly, but he made the group whole. Ikena felt protective of him. The group looked around at their surroundings. Fish swam around the bubble and above it, but they always kept their distance from it, like they knew it was a pocket of air with no water. Even sharks avoided it, despite clearly seeing humans in their territory.

Up ahead, Ikena could see the makings of the village and the group took their steps up the stone path that was partially covered in furry, green moss. To the left of them was an old wooden sign that read, 'Aquarin' but the 'A' was slightly covered in the same moss that they were walking on. They deepened further into the village and saw chipped stone buildings all around them. *Houses.* Ikena knew immediately and they resembled that of the houses in Endfell. They reached a long building to the right which had the word 'MKT' written on the side in white paint, but they walked past it. It was the market.

"This is creepy!" Flynn couldn't help but remark, his hand placed firmly over the hilt of his sword.

One house had a dirt square with a wooden picket fence surrounding the patch and Ikena recognised it as a garden, her mother kept a similar looking one back at home, where they planted seeds to grow fruit and vegetables. They continued walking until they reached a white-stone dolphin fountain in the middle which seemed lost at the bottom of the deep blue sea. There were broken benches around it with moss that seemingly covered everywhere. Ikena peered round the statue and saw the shack from her nightmares, the one where the key was.

"The shack is up ahead. Be on guard." She took her fans from their holsters and held them at the ready.

The group followed closely behind her, struggling to keep up with Ikena's fast paced walk, but she couldn't slow down. It was like there was a force inside her, pulling her towards the key. It wanted to be found by her. She reached the shack door and carefully pushed it open with one of her fans. Inside stood a quiet room which resembled that of a fisherman's shop. Tools rattled on the side where they hung lost on the wall and there were large glass panels where dead fish would wait, ready for somebody to take it home and cook it. The group towered into the room behind her and Sedric kicked something as he did so. Ikena knelt to see what it was and with a great sadness she realised it was a children's toy. *How many lives were lost?* She thought to herself as she imagined her own family being swept underneath the sea, fighting the forceful waves with every last breath they had.

Through the shop was another door which was broken with half of it gone and Ikena stepped inside. Moss had covered most of the room and tiny little crabs could be seen scrambling to get away from the magical light that beamed out of their *Forteys*. The room had an old couch which had turned a black mouldy colour and a television laid soaked through. The glass cracked on the screen. The group explored the room when that pulling feeling inside Ikena demanded she turn around. She did so, and behind Kyra, hidden underneath a moss-covered towel, was the chest.

"The chest," Ikena said as she crouched beside it. The lock

287

had become unhinged and as she slowly lifted the lid she was blinded by the bright white glow of the key, just like she had seen in her dreams. Without looking in, she reached her hand inside and grabbed it. Upon being touched, the key sent a beam of magic through Ikena's body, her friends' bodies and out into the sea surrounding them. They were unharmed but they could feel that the demeanour had changed. Something was wrong. Ikena felt a great darkness overcome her and cold swept through the building, creating small icicles on the roof and frost on the windows.

"What's happening?" Dax called.

"The Sinturi!" She heard Aella call from the other room and stuffed the key into her thigh-high boot. They were surrounding the shack. Just as Ikena gathered her thoughts, one of them came in through the back door of the shack, behind her.

"Duck!" Sedric called to her and he lunged his trident out, narrowly missing Ikena's head. Ikena looked round for the other members of her group. She could see Sedric and Kyra, Aella was out the front with Dax but where was Flynn?

"Where's Flynn?" she asked, unable to calm the fear that struck through her. Sedric and Kyra both gave her blank looks, they didn't know either.

"Ikena!" She heard Flynn call from another room to their right and immediately ran to him. Flynn had his sword at the ready and was being cornered by a group of three Sinturis who dared closer and closer, taunting him with their hoarse voices. As Ikena burst through the door they turned their attention to her.

"The chosen one!" one of them said, with a husky voice

and dared closer.

"Stay back!" she roared, but it didn't falter them.

"I believe you have something for us," another one said. "Give us the key!"

"Sure! If you want to be disintegrated! But I'm afraid I can't let you have it." She charged her fans with magic and was ready to attack. Ikena glanced a look over at an unharmed Flynn who shook with fear.

"In that case. We know someone who will want to see you. Dalmask is right outside."

Without warning she leapt towards the Sinturis, arms outstretched and fan blades at the ready, hitting two of the dark beasts which roared as they disintegrated into nothingness. The last one roared and sent dark magic towering towards Ikena, who quickly blocked it with her own shield of magic. She was struggling to hold it when she saw an orange glowing sword pierce through the Sinturis body. The Sinturi disintegrated and behind it stood a breathless Flynn.

"It's okay, Flynn. You did it!" Ikena was by his side in an instant, pulling him up from the ground. "And you had the courage! Don't be so scared and use your abilities to your advantage." Her words received a nod of approval.

She led Flynn out the front of the shack where the rest of the group stood, casting magic at the Sinturi around them. Ikena did a quick headcount, Sedric was counted for, Dax was counted for, Flynn and Aella were in sights.

"Stop!" Kyra yelled from in the distance. All eyes were on her. Or more so, on *him*. Dalmask walked over with a knife to Kyra's neck, but not just any knife. A *Morthrealki* blade. One strike and Kyra would become a Sinturi.

"Kyra! No!" Dax charged for the dark master but Sedric charged for him and bundled him to floor before he could get close.

"Stupid boy!" the dark master taunted. "You'd come for me, knowing your little friend was in danger. *Pathetic!*" He glared around at the others, "Well, isn't *this* quite the gathering? I'm only going to ask once; give me the key and I will spare your pathetic friends life."

"Don't do it, Ikena!" Kyra warned but was jerked back by the dark master. Ikena focussed on his voice, it was so recognisable from long, long ago. And the medallion he wore, it couldn't be, but it was.

"Reveal yourself to me first!" Ikena shouted and with that the dark master chuckled.

"You haven't yet worked it out, flower?" he said, and he threw Kyra into the arms of another Sinturi standing nearby. All around them were hooded figures and skeleton-like hands but Ikena had to remember that these things were once human. "Very well." Dalmask spoke and slowly lifted his hood. Ikena took a step back. *No. It can't be.* Sedric gasped from beside her. It was. His face was sunken, similar to that of a skeleton but still human too. Dark mist covered his body and when he moved, the mist moved with it and he had a dark crown sit effortlessly atop his white hair. It was shaped like a black diadem and had black jewels lining it with a large silver one in the middle. It also had long sections protruding to high above the head that were shaped like daggers. *How dare he.*

"This is an illusion. You're not him." Ikena said, tears

forming in her eyes at seeing the person she had mourned for so many years.

"Oh flower. Yes, I am. To those of you who don't know, Ikena here is my daughter." There were cheers from crowd as the Sinturis called her name, chanting for her.

"What? Ikena, is this true?" Aella gasped, a shocked look on her face. On *all* their faces.

Ikena didn't know what to say. The dark master looked like him, sounded like him, but it couldn't be. The man who was her father died years ago.

"How?" Ikena managed, still focussing on Kyra who the other Sinturi was holding by her hair.

"Years ago, I crossed paths with a Sinturi who tried to consume my soul. You were there. *You* caused it."

"I… I didn't." She could hardly breathe. Ikena felt herself begin to shake and she couldn't stop it. She had carried around a burden all her life, a burden that *she* had caused her father's death. She was a stupid teenager at the time and was fascinated with the forest and animals that lived in it. The most beautiful butterfly she had ever seen fluttered over to her and bobbed on her head. She suddenly found herself chasing it, they were playing a version of tag and the butterfly was winning. She chased it away from her father to a branch and when she went to touch it, a skeleton hand reached out from the bushes.

"Hello," she said to the beast, unknowing of what it was. Back then, her parents, alongside the school she attended, had tried to keep the Sinturi a secret until children were sixteen. Thankfully, that changed after her father died, but if he had known, maybe things would have been different. "My name's

Ikena, what's yours?"

"Raigon, sweet one," the voice was dark, and husky, but there was something about it. Ikena wasn't scared.

"You scared away my butterfly."

"I'll fetch you a new one," Raigon uttered and from his hand protruded a beautiful butterfly, it was black and made of darkness, but the gesture was sweet. The butterfly pranced around Ikena and she laughed. She had made a new friend. She didn't have any friends and longed for one. That's when her father came. He saw the beast and roared at Ikena to stand back. Upon seeing her father, Raigon came into the light. He was a very tall figure, and his face was covered by the black hood. Mist swarmed around him, like it did for all the Sinturis. Ikena's father made the first move, he jabbed at Raigon with a wooden spear, but it passed right through his body, he was unable to kill it. The next thing Ikena saw was Raigon consuming her father. She saw his skin melt away from his body, his raven-coloured hair turned to white, and she heard him yell, "run!". For too long she had felt like she had caused her father's death. For too long she had carried around that burden and it made her afraid, it made her push away from Sedric. Her father betrayed her and her family, *he* killed himself. She was realising that now.

"What you didn't see is that I pleaded with the Sinturi. I begged for my life. The Sinturi struck me with a dagger of darkness and I soon became consumed with power. I became Dalmask, the Dauntless. Let me ask you this. Is it fair that some are gifted with power and deemed more special when non-magicals are seen as weak?"

Ikena refused to answer the question. It wasn't fair. She

felt the same way he had, and it sickened her. "You don't deserve to wear that medallion and pretend like you're my father. *We mourned you!* Asher and Aliza have grown up not knowing who you are. And what of mother, did you even love her?"

"Ikena, *of course I did.* I still do. I did this to save my life and I have become glorious for it. If we were to create a world of Sinturis together, the world would be at peace. Non-magicals would *thank me.*"

"*Thank you*? You're *killing* them! Turning them in to despicable beings who must consume others to stay powerful. What happens when there are no Cloaks or humans left to consume? What happens when you simply run out?" Ikena asked, she couldn't believe what she was hearing.

"That is why we need the key, Ikena. It is the last step. If a Sinturi opens the box, the power manifests on us. It will mean we will forever be immortal and won't ever have to consume a soul again. A world of *peace.*"

"Ikena, we need to go," Sedric whispered by her side.

"Ikena, you are my blood. My flesh. My darkness lives inside you. I was born to be a Sinturi, and so were you. We can rule together, we can be *Gods* together," he spoke with such authority, almost like the King's double. The family loving man Ikena had cherished was gone. Something else was in his place. "And if you don't give me the key, your friend will die." He signalled to the Sinturi who had Kyra and he took out a *Morthrealki* blade of his own to Kyra's throat. She let out a cry.

"Don't you dare!" Dax said, his fists clenched in balls next to him.

"Let's all just *calm down*," the dark master chuckled with a low, menacing tone. He paced up and down, his cloak swaying behind him, mist consuming him as he walked.

Kyra wouldn't want Ikena to do this, to give up the key but she had to. She couldn't let Kyra die. She took out the glowing key from her boot.

"Ikena, no!" Sedric grabbed her arm but she shook it off.

"It's okay. I promise. Sedric... I love you." She gave a pitiful smile and stepped towards the dark master, crossing the short space towards him. She looked at Kyra and hung her head, Kyra didn't want her to do this. Everyone would hate her, but she couldn't do it. Ikena reached into her leg boot and pulled out the glowing key. She slowly stretched her arm out, to give up, to give in, to let this beast take over the world, when something called to her. The glowing key began to shake in her hands and glowed an even brighter brightness than though imaginable.

"What's happening?" Dalmask scowled.

Then, Ikena's hand began to glow. Then her arms, her neck, her torso before there was a persistent glowing that hovered around her, like she was pure starlight. The Sinturis recoiled at the light. Her magic called to be let out, to be released. If anything, it served as a perfect distraction.

"Now!" Ikena yelled, hoping someone on her team would be ready to attack. She snatched the key away from Dalmask and kicked him with force, sending him cowering on the floor for a brief moment.

Behind her, Flynn had turned in to a bear and charged at the Sinturis around Kyra. The Sinturi who held Kyra dropped her to the floor and tried to run, but Flynn had caught up to him, ripping through his body until it disintegrated into nothingness. The distraction allowed Aella and Dax to attack the others around them and began to push their way through.

"Let's go!" Ikena yelled, fitting the key securely in her boot again. The dark master rose and cast his magic at Ikena, but she blocked it using her fans.

"My blood is yours!" he roared but Ikena ignored it. She grabbed Kyra and helped her to where Aella and Dax were. Sedric followed close behind and Flynn continued to tear through his prey, ripping one clean in half where it fizzled into nothing. There was a path beginning to form and they swiftly made their way through, running to the front of the village but on the other side of the dolphin statue was another pack of Sinturi. They were surrounded by the darkness that swarmed at them in every direction.

Sedric jabbed his trident whilst Dax was in the middle of it all, using his daggers to pierce his marks, their misty bodies disappearing with each touch. Ikena seized the moment and pushed Kyra and Aella through the small gap that had formed before whistling for Flynn who was still back at the shack. Upon her call the great bear came charging towards her before turning back into the Flynn she knew. He had used a lot of energy as a bear and struggled to walk. Ikena hoisted his arm around her shoulder and pulled him ahead with her to the anchor, but the pack of Sinturis were nearing close, there were at least a hundred of them. The anchor was firm in the ground, all they needed was for Cato to hoist it up.

"Get behind me!" Ikena yelled to the boys as Aella, Kyra and Flynn began to climb the anchor. The boys did so and ran towards Ikena, the pack of Sinturi chasing after them, cackling with dark battle cries as they did so.

"Aella, send Cato the signal!" Ikena shouted and she could hear the rattle of the anchor chain behind her.

"We're not leaving without you!" Sedric called but Ikena didn't expect them to, she had a plan.

The anchor started to rise as the Sinturi pack were just moments away and, in that moment, Ikena closed her eyes and relaxed, allowing her breath to become shallow as she slowly breathed in and out. *Focus*. She told herself and felt the magic rise up inside her, crying to be let out. She quietened the voices screaming from behind her as the anchor lifted from the ground and then raised both her fans to the top-left of her body before sharply swinging them down to end in her bottom-right corner of her body. It was enough. The Sinturis who were moments before her, fell to the ground, they cowered as the magic cut into them with such force, their bodies sliced in half before they disintegrated.

"Ikena!" Sedric called, distracting Ikena from the ashy sight before her.

She turned to see him high in the air, his arm outstretched towards her. She only had one chance to jump, which she did so with both feet, her arm outstretched towards his, her hand nearing his. Their fingers touched, before she felt herself slipping away, but he reached out further and grabbed her hand, swinging her as the anchor proceeded to be pulled up.

"Hold your breath!" Aella called before being taken out of the oxygen bubble.

Ikena sucked in a deep breath, holding on to Sedric's hand for dear life, but she could feel her hand slipping. His eyes widened as he could feel it too and with one drop, Ikena would plummet to the ground where the rest of the Sinturi would devour her. *Just hold on.*

Her mind raged but it was no use, in a second her hand slipped from Sedric's and she began to fall. Her eyes met his, and it seemed everything suddenly went in slow-motion. She was glad that the last thing she would see would be Sedric's face, his brown eyes gleaming at hers. She felt something kick into her side and realised it was Sedric's foot. He had swung his leg towards her, kicking her in the stomach but it was enough for her to hold on to it. She struggled for oxygen. They were so close to the top and Ikena could see the moon beaming down at the water. She saw Aella get lifted out of the water, then Kyra and Flynn, then Dax and Sedric, who didn't take his eyes off her. She took a deep breath and wheezed as she struggled for air, not to mention her side ached from Sedric's forceful kick.

Cato was at the side of the boat helping to pull each person onto the deck but Ikena couldn't think about that, she was firmly gripping Sedric's steel booted leg. Once everyone else had climbed to safety, Sedric leaned down and held out his hand for the second time, Ikena pushed herself up and grabbed it allowing him to hoist her up to the other side of the anchor where she could then climb up the chain to the deck. Aella pulled her onto the deck but she toppled over with a thump on the hard-wooden floor. Sedric was pulled over shortly after and immediately he scrambled towards Ikena, holding her so tightly. Ikena noticed that he was shaken, a strong, muscular man who seemed like he wasn't scared of anything was scared of losing her and it shook him to the core.

"Don't you ever scare me like that again." he scooped her up in his arms and leaned his forehead on hers.

Her friends were spluttering on the floor, struggling for their own breath and calmness. Cato crouched down beside Ikena, helping her stand.

"Did you get the key?" he asked, his eyes trained upon hers.

For a moment Ikena forgot all about the key and was thankful that her friends were safe. She gave a quizzical look before remembering where she had put it and reached into her thigh-high steel boot to take out the key which still glowed its bright white light. She held it tightly in her hands and gave a long, thankful sigh. They had done it.

TWENTY-ONE

T he key that glowed between Ikena's hands was the key to saving the world, the key that unlocked the box that held power so great that it would *destroy* all darkness in the Kingdom of Nevera. Imagine, a world of peace where little children could play out at night or could hunt for the days food without being scared of running into the forest alone because there would be no darkness to hurt them.

Ikena found her way to her feet and held the key up to the sky. "We've done it!" she chanted and was welcomed with applause and hollers from the crew. Her friends were roaring and clapping. "We've…" But as she spoke the creaks of the boat got louder and louder. There was a shuddering beneath her feet, a vibration that became loud clanking noises. It was coming from underneath the boat.

"What is that?" Kyra called over the chants, noticing it too.

"Quiet!" Aella roared, who immediately shut the crew up.

Crack. The sound was intense now. Suddenly, Ikena found her body weight begin to shift to her left, and then to her right. The boat was rocking. The rocking became more aggressive with each second, and a few members of the crew stumbled on their feet. Ikena felt herself drag with gravity to one side of the boat, hitting the side beam hard in her rib. Then, gravity took her to the other side, luckily, she used her hands in front of her to stop the blow. She quickly tucked the key into her boot and drew out her glowing fans.

"What's happening?" Sedric yelled but he was met with silence as Ikena didn't have the answer. The boat continued to rock until it was the entire crew who were dragged to one side of the boat with a thump, and then swiftly taken to the other. If they continued like this, the boat would topple over, surely. As Ikena sped into the side of the beam again, unwillingly, she saw it. There was something big moving in the waters below, its body weaning around the ship with snake-like scaly skin. *You have got to be kidding me.*

"Okratica!" a crew member yelled, pointing down at the thing Ikena saw.

"Everyone get to the middle of the ship!" Ikena called. "Stay away from the edges!" She feared the beast might knock the crew members underwater, but it seemed it had other ideas. Behind Ikena the moonlight had suddenly disappeared, leaving them with dim light that only came from the few lanterns on the ship. She turned immediately and saw that the monster had lifted itself up so that it was double the height of the boat and was glaring at the members below. It was gigantic, its octopus legs wriggling in the air, its tail rocking the waves beneath the boat and the beast showed its rows of razor-sharp teeth. The monster didn't look like the colour of the picture Cato had showed her in the book, instead its body was jet black and a dark mist surrounded it which looked almost like small sand pieces which were drawn to it.

"It has become a Sinturi," Cato whispered in pure shock and disbelief. Alarm rippled through Ikena's body.

Ikena's father was smart. He knew she'd find the key, prepared for it even and so he set a trap. He must have hunted the Okratica before plunging darkness into it, causing it to become a weapon of mass destruction with only one goal in mind. To *kill*.

The beast roared a noise so high-pitched that the crew had to cover their ears with their hands, sending thick saliva onto the boat which covered one crew member. He screamed that it burned before the very skin on his body began to slowly melt, leaving nothing but a pile of ash behind.

"What do we do?" Ikena asked as the beast swung its tentacle legs at the crew. It was Aella who spoke next.

"It's weakest at its heart. Just don't—" Before she could finish her sentence Dax had crossed the deck, his daggers at the ready, and with one swift motion cut a tentacle leg sending the slimy thing to the ground of the deck. The beast cried out in pain with another piercing sound but Ikena couldn't help but be impressed with Dax's quick thinking.

"No!" Aella called, a worried look on her face.

Just then, the beasts body began to bubble and, in the space where its leg was, grew two more legs with razor sharp pincers on the end and sharp thorns around it. Dax couldn't help but hang his head in realisation at what he had done. He didn't have much time to think as the Okratica swung its leg at Dax, hitting him and sending him flying to the other side of the boat where Kyra helped lift him up. His body had caught on one of the razors and he was gushing blood from his side.

"I need time to fix this!" Kyra called as she began using her magic to heal Dax's wound.

The Okratica then sunk back beneath the waves and appeared on the other side of the boat, causing it to rock once more. The crew around them tried to swing ropes at it, hoping to stop its legs from causing any more damage, but in doing so they just ripped off more legs and by the time Ikena had stopped thinking the beast had twelve legs with sharp pincers and thorns on each one.

It shrieked and swung at the crew members, using one of its pinchers to lift a young boy up by his boot, holding him high into the air before dropping him in to its mouth with a satisfying crunch, destroying the poor Cloaks with its razor-sharp teeth. *It's weakest at its heart.* Ikena remembered Aella's words and a quick look behind her told her that Kyra seemed to have patched up Dax well enough that the both of them were now standing, *Forteys* out at the ready.

She wanted to get to high ground, maybe then she could attack it with magic from above and noticed that the tallest part of the ship was the mast. Upon instinct she leapt to it, using nearby rope to hoist herself up the pole and began the climb. As she climbed, she noticed Sedric had repeated the same beneath her, not wanting her to face the beast alone and Ikena was grateful for it. She saw Cato cast his magic at the beast, sending it toppling away from the boat for a moment, but not before long it leaned back in, causing the boat to shake and Ikena to lose her footing.

She fell, she had let go of the rope in her hand and was left clinging on to the pole for dear life, her foot on Sedric's shoulder just to keep her stable as he reached up with one hand to grab and hold her steady. She swung her fan into the beam and used it to hoist herself up, before proceeding to climb with her fans as Sedric used rope below her. *Now he's angry.* Ikena thought.

From below, Kyra moved at a pace across the decking with her crossbow a glow. She sent a flurry of magical arrows soaring for the beast's eyes which pierced them, and blue blood trickled down its slithering body and on to the decking. Similar to its saliva, the blood burned holes into the deck and water began to seep on to the wooden floors. Cato bounced over and worked on preparing the holes as the beast swung in the air. It was now blind but that only made it worse. It swung its pincers towards her so quick that Ikena thought it was the end for her friend.

"No!" she yelled from above, but Flynn, who had shape-shifted into a lion, jumped in front of Kyra and bit the pincher with his teeth, shaking his head side by side and pulling at it. At the same time, Dax had leapt towards her and pulled her on to the ground.

Ikena focussed on climbing and neared the top of the helm where she hung on to the ship's flag that bore the Cloak symbol, the same one embossed into their armour. Sedric had also reached the top and jabbed his trident at the beast, sending magic sparks flying towards it which seemed to stun it for a few short moments. In those moments Ikena recharged Sedric's trident and worked on a plan. *Think, Ikena. Think.* Then it came to her. If she swung at the beast and performed her finishing move whilst moving towards it, aiming at its heart, then she should be able to kill it. Its skin looked too

303

hard to be penetrated by any blade, only magic could bring it down.

"Sedric," she called to him. "I need you to get the beast to the other side of the ship."

"Why?" he questioned but she didn't have enough time to explain.

"Just do it! Trust me!" He stared at her coldly for a few moments before he nodded and used his rope to slide down the mast. Ikena saw him run towards the beast, using his trident to grab its attention.

"Come and get me!" he called to it, hitting it again before moving to the other side of the boat.

The beast once again roared its piercing sound and head dived into the ocean. Ikena almost lost her footing but managed to hold on to the beam she had climbed and watched as the beast came up to the side of the boat on the other side. Ikena began to cut the flag in to long pieces of fabric, tying them together to create a makeshift fabric rope. The Okratica's tentacles were outstretched wide and just as Ikena was about to seize her moment and jump, a cannon went off from below her. It was Aella and a few of her crew who had begun flying cannon balls at it. They struck the beast but, as Ikena had already worked out, it seemed only magic could kill it.

"It's a Sinturi!" she called down to Aella, "You have to use *magic*!"

The beast roared its high-pitched squeal again, so loud that it knocked Kyra out. Their only Healer was gone. Dax was standing next to her and stopped her head from hitting the deck as she fainted. He grabbed her legs and carried her to the door where the bedrooms were, shifting her inside and shutting the door so that she was out of harm's way, before returning with his daggers aglow. He was angry. The beast dived back into the water before coming up at the front of the boat, leaning its slithery long body on the edge so that the back of the boat began to tip forward.

"Everyone hold on!" Ikena screamed, holding onto the fabric rope and beam herself.

She saw Sedric and Cato who were held on to the anchor's knob. Aella and Flynn who were holding on to another beam of the boat and Dax who was holding on to the knob of the cabin door to the bedrooms. As the boat tipped, the door Dax was holding on to swung open and Kyra came tumbling out, gravity taking her knocked-out body and sliding it across the floor towards the beast. Dax let go of the knob, grabbing Kyra before cracking into the mast beam Ikena was holding onto from above.

There were a few crew members who were unable to hold on and the beast swallowed them savagely.

"No!" Ikena cried, but they were already gone. The Okratica wouldn't stop until it had the key. The key Ikena had in her boot. The beast's slimed legs were still flailing in the air, attacking members before it raised them to fling its pincers at Ikena. She quickly ducked behind the beam, narrowly missing being hit by seconds. It was time to put her plan into action. She checked the key was still in her boot, which it was, and grabbed on to the fabric rope with both hands, allowing her body to slide down it and use the momentum to swing herself backwards and then straight towards the beast. She let go. She only had a few split seconds to cast perfectly. Ikena allowed her magic to rise, consuming her veins. She raised her fans as she continued to fly towards it, bringing them both to the top left of her body and in one, quick motion she brought them down to her right-side.

She felt the magic leave her body as a beam, but instead of dropping to the ground like she expected, she was hovering in the air. The strength of her magic keeping her afloat as it attacked the beast, tearing through it bit by bit. The Okratica cried, but Ikena knew she needed to hit it again. She raised her hands, palms out towards it, and sent rays of golden magic towards the beast, using what little strength she had left.

From below, she could see that Cato had joined in, sending beams of his own magic towards the beast. Aella joined in too, then Flynn, Dax and Kyra who had awoken in Dax's arms. Sedric jabbed his trident repeatedly, sending constant sparks of magic at it and the beast roared, cowering before them. Ikena was focussed on destroying the beast and found her teeth clenched and her voice roaring as she summoned every part of her magic that screamed to be let free. She allowed it, like a weight was lifted off her shoulders with every second that she continued. The mist around the beast began to lessen, and slowly pieces of the dark being began to disintegrate into thin air.

Hold on. Ikena told herself as she struggled, her powers weakening when she tired, the group had done it. She watched the entire beast disintegrate before releasing her magic and immediately falling to the ground with a *thump*. It was her head on the decking that made the sound. Ikena lay there, faintly seeing Sedric's and her friends faces above hers before blacking out into darkness. She heard Sedric call her name, but she couldn't respond. Around her the waters had calmed and the beast was gone, but so was the most-part of the crew. Although they had won, they had suffered a great loss of lives, ones Ikena couldn't bring back.

Ikena awoke to a different sight and immediately her headache grew in her brain, forcing her to fall back on the plush bed, with silk sheets beneath her. She had the most terrible dream about a sea monster, and a key and all her friends were there, but as she lay there, she found herself remembering more and more of the assignment. *It wasn't a dream.* What was going on? She immediately began to panic before realising that Sedric was by the foot of the bed, his arms crossed beneath his head over her feet. When he heard Ikena wake he had immediately lifted his head and Ikena had seen that he had been crying, tears were streaming down his sunken face.

"I thought I lost you," he said with a whimper as he took Ikena in his strong arms.

She savoured the scent of his masculinity and couldn't help but release a small giggle.

"You're squashing me!" she bellowed and Sedric allowed her space to sit up. "What happened? Where's the key? Is everyone safe?" She had so many questions and so little time.

"Ssshhhh," Sedric said as he kissed her scabbed hands. "It's all okay. We're all safe. Ikena what's the last thing you remember?"

Ikena didn't quite know how to answer that question. She remembered retrieving the key and fighting the Sinturi before boarding the boat and having to face down the Okratica, the sea monster. She was on the mast, high up but that was all she could recall.

"You were hovering in the air," Sedric said. "Glowing a bright golden light all around you. Your magic consuming you and then…"

"And then what?" she pressed.

"And then you had wings. They weren't real, but see-through golden wings stretched from either side of your back."

Ikena almost told Sedric to shut up and stop messing with her, but by the look on his face and the dried tears on his skin, she knew he wasn't lying. The animal connected to her *Forteys* was an eagle… could she have used enough power to bring it out like some say the King had in the Great War?

"Did I kill the beast?" she whispered, so quietly she thought Sedric might not have heard her.

"Yes, Ikena. You did it."

"Where's the key?" She had noticed that she had been changed into the familiar golden pyjamas that all the Cloak women wore.

"Cato delivered it to the King. He has refused to do anything until you're awake. Ikena the kingdom is rejoicing. Word has spread around about what you did and how you saved everyone. You really are the *chosen one*."

This was all a little too much for Ikena to bear, "How long have I been asleep?".

"Seven days." It had been an entire week.

Ikena immediately got up from her bed but felt the dizziness kick in and fell to the floor. She was incredibly

308

weak and unable to stand, unsure of this awful sensation that overwhelmed her. Sedric ran to her side and helped lift her to her feet. She struggled to place her feet straight and instead relied heavily on him for aid. Every part of her ached and she refused to look in any mirrors.

"Take me to the King," she demanded. Sedric tried to interject, but there was no point. She'd crawl there if she had to. He wrapped an arm around her waist and allowed her to grab on to him as they made their way through the room which led to the Elion's chamber. Ikena realised that she had been sleeping in the King's bed. The King, alongside the familiar council members and Cato and her friends were gathered around the circular table. They stood when Ikena had come out with Sedric and he helped her make her way to any empty chair on the side.

"I need an update," she affirmed, bringing her chair in closer to the table. Her head was swarming and something pulsed.

"Ikena, you're awake," the King welcomed, his handsome features glistening in the light.

"Yes, I am. Now, I need an update on what happened from the moment I supposedly… hovered, to right now."

Cato spoke for the King, "Ikena, on the ship you used your power, your true power, to save us all. You used so much so that you immediately fell to the ground and hit your head. We took you back to your bed, but you didn't wake, you must have been so drained." He paused to let that sink in, but it isn't what Ikena wanted to hear. She wanted to know exactly the whereabouts of the key and if it was being guarded.

"Aella sailed us back to the palace, which was tough

because most of the crew had…" *Been eaten.* Ikena thought but she refused to say it aloud. "Any who, we got back. We took you to the King, along with the Key—"

"Where is it?"

"It's safe Ikena."

"*No*, I want to see it." Her words were stiff as if she felt a great betrayal from it being taken from her.

The King clicked his fingers, and a Cloak came in, Ikena recognised Osirus, who was holding the key in an enchanted glass case. Of course, it's the King's doing to put it in some fancy case where it could be stolen at any moment.

"It is being guarded by a group of Cloaks at all times. I assure you; no one will steal it." But she wasn't afraid of the Cloaks from stealing it. She was afraid of the King. He seemed to enjoy greed, given that he wouldn't share in his wealth with the surrounding villages, and she knew what greed can do to a person.

"So, what's the plan?" she spoke, looking at each person in the council whose mouths escaped soft giggles. She didn't know what was so funny.

"Ikena, you need rest before anything else. First, I need you to tell us everything you know about your father."

Ikena dreaded the conversation but she couldn't pretend anymore. The person she had seen was her father and he had wanted her to join him.

"There isn't much to tell. He said that if the box was opened by a Sinturi, then it would give them the power of immortality. They would no longer have to consume souls for power and could focus on creating their world. If they get that key, we won't be able to stop them."

"We won't let that happen. We have the key, so now we need the box. We just have to figure out a way to get it," the King spoke graciously.

Ikena took in a deep breath and tried her best to speak confidently, "Elion, I need to get my family out of Endfell. Dalmask will be after them, if he hasn't gone there already."

The King nodded and dismissed the group to allow him time to think, but Ikena was certain he'd allow her to bring her family into the palace, or at least in to one of the surrounding villages. Ikena realised she was starving and thankfully it was time for dinner. With Sedric's help, she slowly made her way to the dining hall, alongside her friends.

As they entered, Cloaks stared at Ikena before one began to clap. There were whispers and then one clap became two, two claps became four until the entire hall were clapping for the group. They cheered, a few cried and it reminded Ikena of the market where she was bombarded by folk who wanted to see the chosen one. A tear fell from Ikena's eye, although she tried not to let it show. It was beautiful. People moved out of the way for the group and continued to clap until they had sat at their regular table, ready to have the best feast of their lives. Ikena felt different, like she had a clearer view of everything. It was as if a great piece of her puzzle had been unravelled. She knew who Dalmask was, finally *and* they had the key.

They would save Nevera, she was certain of it.

And they would do it together.

CLOAKED SHADOWS

BONUS MATERIAL

Dear Ikena,

We've heard the news of what you did on Ocean Atlantia, is it true that you battled the Okratica? I've only heard stories of that beast, make-believe, I would have never in my wildest imaginations thought that it was real! There are whispers that you transformed into an eagle, although I highly doubt that, and some are now calling you Goddess, I hope you thoroughly enjoy blessing those around you and receiving the utmost attention.

We have received a mass amount of fruit, vegetables, and medication all kindly gifted from the Cloaks, what did you have to do or say to get us this? You'll be pleased to know that we have kept the good stuff, all the fatty parts of the meat and the absolute best vegetables, although I do share within the town. The mayor, of all people, comes to my door often now and peers his nose in, wondering what I can offer him. The cheek! Like he doesn't already have enough of it all in his polished home, and don't get me started on his daughter. She is something else! Always tries to steal from my garden, which you'll be happy to know is blossoming. I think I've learnt a thing or two from you, my dear, because the last time she came I told her that I'd offer her father soup laced with poison, not that I have any of that lying around but she hasn't been back since.

Asher and Aliza ask about you every day, and Asher has even started calling himself Ikena's soldier, he's one of your most loyal followers. We do not need to hunt anymore, but I do take the twins out to the forest for fresh air and to practise what you taught them, I wouldn't want them to forget a single thing. Aliza has started styling her hair like yours, in a frizzy mess. She likes to take my brush and coarse the hair through it in a way so that it sits atop her head like a bird's nest! In fact, I've seen a few children do the same.

Yes, I have been wondering about that kiss of yours. I remember a young boy who would knock on my front door and ever so politely ask if Ikena could come to play. I remember him as the boy who offered us his own meat, when he and his grandma had none, just to keep us, and you, well-fed and protected. I hope you always keep him in your life, Ikena. He loves you more than anything in the world, I can see it a mile off.

Now, I do have to be the bearer of bad news... Sedric's grandma passed away in the night. I was with her when it happened, she kept calling out Sedric's name. I told her that he's safe, he's with Ikena and the last words on her lips were 'Ikena, I always liked that little girl'. It brought tears to my eyes, but she went with a smile. She was listening to her radio and exclaimed that she liked this song. I sang it to her as she slept, little did I know that she was passing. I do not know what is happening to Sedric's house, some are pushing me to sell it, the mayor being one of them, but I have refused. His grandma has given the house to Sedric, along with all that's in it, I know you won't be able to visit but maybe they'll allow him? We held a funeral for her and buried her next to Mr. and Mrs. Plumith in the graveyard. I take colourful flowers there every day and sit and talk to them. Sometimes we pray for yours and Sedric's safety, but mostly we talk of how you were when you were little. I know you will have to bring this news to Sedric, I ask that you do it gently. He may seem tough on the outside, but I fear he is not.

Ikena, I miss you greatly. We all do, but I keep my head high and when someone asks me who I am, I say Ikena Ralliday's mother. Your father would be proud of you, he is watching over you from above.

Please write to me again soon.

Pleasantly-humanly signed,
Margaret Ralliday.

ACKNOWLEDGEMENTS

I finally get to write an acknowledgement section because, hooray, I finished writing an actual book! This process has been truly wild in the best possible way. I wrote this book as a way to help keep myself sane during the coronavirus (COVID-19) pandemic that caused havoc all over the world, and ease anxiety symptoms that were creeping up with the uncertainty that the virus brought. Without writing this book, I truly don't know how I would have coped.

I am so blessed to have a fantastic support group around me. I'd especially like to thank my family and friends for helping spur me on and always finding great interest in my writing. I'd like to thank my brother, Gareth, who spent hours of his time editing my work sentence by sentence. I can't wait to see one of his books on the bookshelves in the years to come.

I'd also like to give special thanks to my wonderful boyfriend, Jordan, who has supported me with wisdom, love and has been a fantastic friend to confide in when I was ever stuck on a plot or needing a cuddle and a cup of tea after hours and hours of writing.

I am beyond grateful for my fantastic beta reading group who read the entire book and provided exceptional feedback throughout this process: Gioia Cok, Abreanne Joy Fernandez,

Kaylie Tester, Lily Lawson, Anja Hendrikse Liu, Brenda Radchik, and Danielle Greaves – Danielle also designed Nevera's map which looks absolutely fantastic!

I want to give a huge shout out to those who follow me on social media and have been genuinely excited for the launch of my book. Your comments, messages, love and support mean the absolute world to me. THANK YOU!

Finally, I would like to thank YOU, the reader. I am entirely thankful, and I appreciate you more than you will ever know. I hope you enjoyed the story and are excited for the next series release – coming soon!

ABOUT THE AUTHOR

Melissa Hawkes is a British author who at the age of eight found herself in foster care. It was at this age that she explored creative writing, at first through song writing, before she fell utterly in love with books. When Melissa isn't writing, she's working as a full-time marketing lead, reading masses of books and being creative through music and art.

WWW.MELISSAHAWKES.COM

INSTAGRAM: @MELISSAHAWKESAUTHOR

TWITTER: @MELHAWKESAUTHOR

FACEBOOK: /MELISSAHAWKESAUTHOR